Lee left her without looking back.

Rachel slumped in her chair. She lifted her hand to her cheek where his callused fingertips had gently stroked her skin. The longing she'd suppressed all this time welled up strong again.

"Hold me, Lee," she whispered after he was gone, uttering the words she wished she could have spoken to him. Instead she'd said, "Please don't, Lee," keeping the barrier up between them.

For just a moment Rachel allowed herself to imagine Lee's muscular arms closing around her tightly, enveloping her in his flinty strength, his rugged maleness.

But the fantasy couldn't ease the aching need inside her.

A need that Lee alone had brought to life. Twenty years ago—and today.

The need to love and be loved by a man.

Dear Reader,

Welcome to Silhouette Special Edition...welcome to romance. Spring is here, and thoughts turn to love...so put a spring in your step for these wonderful stories this month.

We start off with our THAT SPECIAL WOMAN! title for April, *Where Dreams Have Been...* by Penny Richards. In this story, the whereabouts of a woman's lost son are somehow connected to an enigmatic man. Now she's about to find out how his dreams can help them find her missing son—and heal his own troubled past.

Also this month is *A Self-Made Man* by Carole Halston, a tale of past unrequited love that's about to change. Making the journey from the wrong side of the tracks to self-made man, this hero is determined to sweep the only woman he's ever truly loved off her feet.

To the West next for Pamela Toth's *Rocky Mountain Rancher*. He's a mysterious loner with a past...and he wants his ranch back from the plucky woman who's now running it. But complicating matters are his growing feelings of love for this tough but tender woman who has won his heart. And no visit to the West would be complete without a stop in Big Sky country, in Marianne Shock's *What Price Glory*. Paige Meredith has lived with ambition and without love for too long. Now rugged rancher Ross Tanner is about to change all that.

Don't miss Patt Bucheister's *Instant Family*, a moving story of finding love—and long-lost family—when one least expects it. Finally, debuting this month is new author Amy Frazier, with a story about a woman's return to the home she left, hoping to find the lost child she desperately seeks. And waiting there is the man who has loved her from afar all these years—and who knows the truth behind *The Secret Baby*. Don't miss it!

I hope you enjoy these books, and all the stories to come!

Sincerely,

Tara Gavin

Senior Editor

CAROLE HALSTON

A SELF-MADE MAN

Silhouette®

SPECIAL EDITION®

Published by Silhouette Books
America's Publisher of Contemporary Romance

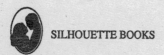

SILHOUETTE BOOKS

ISBN 0-373-09950-9

A SELF-MADE MAN

Books by Carole Halston

CAROLE HALSTON

is a Louisiana native residing in a rural area north of New Orleans. She enjoys traveling with her husband to research less familiar locations for settings but is always happy to return home to her own unique region, a rich source in itself for romantic stories about warm, wonderful people.

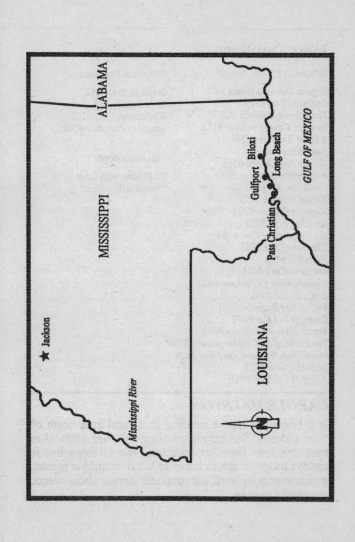

Prologue

It wasn't one of Nell Tate's best days as a reporter. Her assignment was to cover two unrelated happenings in the local real estate scene for her newspaper, the *Mississippi Gulf Coast Gazette*. She got off to a bad start on both interviews and left them feeling that she'd put her foot in her mouth.

Her first appointment was with a big developer named Lee Zachary. She was scheduled to meet him at the building site of Plantation Village, an upscale residential development for retired people. His architect for the project, James Livingston, and his general contractor, Carl Beatty, were both supposed to be on hand. Nell, a newcomer to the Gulf Coast, didn't know who was who when she arrived and approached the three men. They were all about the same age, fortyish.

She proffered her hand first to a distinguished man wearing a suit. "Hello, I'm Nell Tate from the *Gazette*."

"A pleasure to make your acquaintance, Ms. Tate," he replied in a courtly southern drawl. "James Livingston."

Flustered, Nell turned next to a burly man in dress slacks and a sport coat, with no tie. He enclosed her hand gently in his big beefy hand. "Carl Beatty. Pleased to meet you, ma'am."

Her cheeks crimson now, Nell smiled brightly up into the hard, rugged face of Lee Zachary, the developer, whom she'd typecast on first sight as the contractor. Tall and powerfully built, he wore jeans and boots and a long-sleeved shirt open at the throat. His dark brown hair had been cut in a barbershop, not a salon, and Nell didn't get a whiff of cologne or shaving lotion. His was the kind of tough, all-male good looks that most of the women in the world found irresistible, even the happily married ones like herself who wouldn't trade their couch-potato husbands.

Nell immediately classified the developer as a self-made man, his ride to success probably not having been easy. The next fifteen minutes strengthened the impression. Zachary was all business as he answered her questions in his deep, masculine voice, his manner almost brusque. And yet Nell found herself liking his directness, liking the absence of any hint of "good ole boy" male condescension.

She was feeling good about the interview toward the end when she asked, "Will a Gulf Coast real estate agency be acting as your exclusive listing agent, Mr. Zachary?"

"Yes," he replied. "But I haven't picked the agency yet."

"Shall I mention that fact in the article?"

He shrugged broad shoulders. "Sure."

James Livingston spoke up. "I'd think twice, Lee. You'll have every Tom, Dick, and Harry real estate broker on the coast pestering you."

Nell couldn't let that sexist remark pass without comment. "I expect the Janes and Alices and Susans who are brokers will be just as interested," she said sweetly. "My next stop is a new all-female real estate agency in Gulf-port—Magnolia Realty. Maybe Mr. Zachary will give them a shot."

"Is that the agency that Blaine Cavanaugh's widow is opening up with a couple of other go-getter agents?" Livingston asked curiously. Before she could answer, he added for the benefit of the other two men, "Rachel Preston. Her folks owned a pharmacy in Gulfport for years. They just sold it about a year ago."

"It must be the same agency," Nell replied to his question. "One of the three women partners is Rachel Cavanaugh. She's the licensed broker."

"Did you plan to take a picture for your article, Ms. Tate?" Lee Zachary inquired harshly. His fierce expression matched his voice.

It took Nell a moment to activate her vocal cords and break the strained silence. The architect and the contractor were gaping with surprise, just as she was. "Er, yes, I did."

She had them pose near a large sign on the property. Livingston and Beatty managed self-conscious smirks, but Lee Zachary gazed soberly at the camera. Nell wondered if he was seeing it or her. She sensed that he was distracted, his thoughts elsewhere.

What had happened to put him in a bad mood all of a sudden? Had the mention of Rachel Cavanaugh touched a raw nerve?

Nell didn't waste a lot of time on pointless speculation as she made her departure and drove to Gulfport for her second appointment. She was a journalist, not a novelist.

Magnolia Realty was located on a quiet, tree-shaded side street a couple of blocks from the beach. The building was an older cottage with a cozy front porch. It had been freshly painted in the colors of a magnolia blossom, creamy white with the trim done in a rich, dark green. The sign out front was artistic and eye-catching—black letters on a pale yellow background. The logo was a stylized magnolia flower.

Nice, Nell approved and went inside to meet the three women, all of them million-dollar agents. Once again, she got off to a bad start.

A thin, sharp-featured, red-haired woman in her mid-forties opened the door. Shrewdness and intelligence gleamed in her narrowed green eyes, and she radiated nervous energy. After a glance at the other two women in the background, Nell was reasonably certain that she was introducing herself to Rachel Cavanaugh, the partner who was bright enough and ambitious enough to take courses in her spare time and pass a rigorous exam for her broker's license while managing to be a top-selling agent.

Nell extended her hand, smiling. "Ms. Cavanaugh, I'm Nell Tate with the *Gazette.*"

"Wrong person, Nell. I'm Mary Lynn Porter."

"I beg your pardon."

"No apology necessary," Mary Lynn assured her. "It's no insult being mistaken for Rachel, believe me."

The other two women had stepped closer. Nell proffered her hand uncertainly to the older one, who seemed the next most likely. In her late fifties perhaps, she was small boned and plump with salt-and-pepper hair. Reading glasses hung from a jeweled chain around her neck.

"Hello, Nell," she said graciously, clasping Nell's hand in a ladylike handshake. "I'm Alice Kirkland."

"Hi, Alice." Her embarrassment probably showing, Nell shook hands last with Rachel Cavanaugh, a slender, blue-eyed blond woman, who could have modeled her beige suit and taupe silk blouse at a charity luncheon fashion show. She couldn't have been past her mid-thirties.

It was soon apparent that Rachel was the key partner, held in high esteem by Mary Lynn and Alice. They gave her full credit for the tasteful decoration of the office interior, also for the exterior color scheme. She'd worked with the commercial artist who'd designed the striking sign and logo.

Nell spent a longer time on this second assignment of the day. By the time she'd finished her interview, she'd shared personal information about herself and pulled out snapshots of her children. She'd learned personal information, too—that Alice Kirkland was a proud grandmother, that Mary Lynn Porter was putting twin daughters through college, that Rachel Cavanaugh was rearing a teenage daughter. There were no husbands in the picture. This wasn't one of those small businesses backed by spouses for tax write-off purposes. These women were serious professionals earning a living.

"Good luck. I'll send you any business I can," Nell promised sincerely as she flipped her notebook closed. Tucking it into her bag, she was thinking about returning to the office and writing up both stories. "I can give you a scoop," she said impulsively, with the best of intentions. "It'll be public knowledge in a few days, anyway, when the *Gazette* hits the stands."

Mary Lynn and Alice both pounced on the news that Lee Zachary hadn't chosen a Realtor yet. Through the grapevine, they'd heard about his latest venture, a retirement community.

Rachel Cavanaugh was noticeably quiet. Glancing at her, Nell noted the faraway, sad expression on her face and could have kicked herself for bringing up Lee Zachary's name. She hadn't meant to be unkind. There was obviously some old history between him and Rachel that had left them both with painful memories.

Nell cut the discussion short with the cheerful request that the three partners come outside and pose for a picture beside their sign. "Okay, smile at the camera!" she coached. Through the lens, she could see that Rachel's smile was forced.

The small episode put a damper on the whole interview.

Back at the office, Nell labored the entire afternoon, writing up the two features. The least she could do was make them good and give Lee Zachary and Rachel Cavanaugh some great free advertising.

Her editor was complimentary. The two stories were run on the same page.

Chapter One

"What a nice picture of the three of us!" Alice exclaimed. "Especially of you, Rachel. And our sign shows up beautifully."

"Doesn't it, though?" Rachel agreed. "I'd like to get an enlargement to frame and hang in the reception area."

The two women were in Alice's office, the *Mississippi Gulf Coast Gazette* spread out on Alice's desk. Rachel stood behind her partner, looking over her shoulder. Cindy Stoker, the agency's secretary, who'd been out ill the day the reporter had interviewed them, hadn't arrived yet. Nor had Mary Lynn, who had an early appointment at a prospective client's house to make a listing presentation.

"This is wonderful free advertising, isn't it?" Alice began to read the article aloud.

Rachel wasn't listening. Her gaze had drifted to the other photograph on the same page of the newspaper and was fixed on Lee Zachary. She found her reactions to his picture very disturbing. They were absurdly similar to her reactions to the brash teenage boy back in her high school days, when she'd felt a flush of pleasure and a thrill of danger at the sight of him. It had been so many years since she'd seen him, and yet the memories came rushing back easily.

At seventeen, Lee had been old for his age and rough around the edges. Only fourteen, and naive and sheltered, Rachel had been a little frightened by her attraction to him. Always the obedient daughter, she'd been secretly relieved that her parents hadn't approved of Lee as a boyfriend for her and hadn't let her date him. It was ironic that they'd approved so highly of Blaine Cavanaugh a few years later. And Rachel hadn't felt at all threatened by her attraction to him. So much for her instincts about men.

She was glad that Lee had done well for himself. His background hadn't given him any boost. He'd lived in a poor section of Biloxi. His father had deserted the family, and his mother had worked in a seafood-processing plant, supporting herself and three children. Lee had apparently had to earn his own spending money. He and Rachel had met when her father hired him to work part-time as a stock boy at the pharmacy.

Of course, that employment hadn't lasted. Lee had quit in anger when he'd asked Rachel out and been turned down. Her father had been sorry to lose him, she remembered. Lee had been a hard worker and honest and dependable.

"Isn't that a nice article?" Alice had finished reading the story. "My *word!* What was that noise?" she gasped. A loud crashing sound had come from the street outside.

"It must be a car wreck!" Alarmed, Rachel was already on her way to the door to see what had happened. *Please don't let anyone be hurt,* she prayed.

There had indeed been an automobile collision immediately in front of the Magnolia Realty office. But, thank heaven, it appeared to have been only a fender bender, Rachel observed from the porch with relief. The narrow tree-shaded street intersected Highway 190, the busy, scenic route along the beach. The driver of a new, sporty little red car had been headed toward the four-lane highway, while the driver of the other larger car, a luxury sedan, was headed away from the beach.

A young man had gotten out of the red car and was inspecting the damage. From his body language, he was understandably very upset. His car had taken the brunt of the impact. Hurrying down the steps, Rachel called out to him anxiously, "Are you all right?"

"Yeah, I'm all right," he burst out angrily. "But look at my damn car!"

Rachel realized, hearing his voice, that he was a teenager. "Your car can be repaired," she reassured him, making allowances for his language. An elderly woman had emerged from the sedan, also seemingly unscathed. Before Rachel could make a concerned inquiry, she began to lecture the boy shrilly.

"You could have killed us both! Don't you know you shouldn't drive like a maniac down side streets like this one? I'm going to see to it that they take away your license!"

"Lady, you swerved right out in front of me!" he shouted at her indignantly. "If you can't keep that big tank on your side of the street, you should park it!" He cursed aloud in frustrated disbelief.

"Watch your language!" Rachel ordered sternly. She had come up beside him. A tall, well-built youth dressed expensively in casual designer's clothes, he towered over her.

"My dad just bought me this car for my birthday! It's brand-new! And this crazy old lady runs into me!"

"I'm sure your father would want you to show some manners. Being rude isn't going to undo the damage to your car."

They were joined by Alice, who'd stayed behind to call the police. Soon a police car pulled up. The officer took down names.

"I'm Mrs. Herman Graham," the elderly woman said, introducing herself haughtily.

"Mark Zachary," the teenager muttered sullenly.

Rachel didn't need to ask him if his father was Lee Zachary. She could see the physical resemblance now. Probably the reason it hadn't registered before was that she'd typecast him as a rich man's rude, spoiled son.

But then, Lee *was* a rich man now, according to the newspaper article. He could afford to give his son all the material advantages. It was too bad that he hadn't taught him better manners, Rachel reflected.

The accident had been more Mrs. Graham's fault than his. She'd swerved to avoid hitting a squirrel scampering across the street. But by Mark's own admission, he'd been exceeding the speed limit. He wasn't entirely blameless and would have to face the consequences, perhaps a speeding ticket and a higher insurance premium for his automobile coverage.

The incident had been unfortunate, but not tragic, Rachel mused. From Mark's behavior and attitude, it seemed likely he wouldn't benefit from the experience and become a safer driver. In his mind Mrs. Graham was entirely to blame.

It was revealing that he didn't seem to be worried about parental censure, as would have been the case with most teenagers. Rachel wouldn't be surprised to learn that this wasn't his first fender bender.

After she'd been excused by the officer, she went back inside and tried to settle down and get to work. But she had trouble concentrating. How old was Mark? she wondered. He'd been on his way to school, a private boys' high school, so he couldn't be older than seventeen or eighteen. When he was born, Lee would have been only nineteen or twenty. He was thirty-seven now. That was easy to figure out, since Rachel was thirty-four and he was three years older than she.

If her arithmetic was right, Rachel had seen Lee and
Mark's mother together once when the latter was pregnant
with Mark. The long-forgotten memory came back with
astonishing clarity. Rachel had been standing in line at a
movie with her date. Lee and a girl his age wearing a mater-
nity outfit had emerged. She'd been loudly criticizing the
movie they'd seen, using crude language. Lee had seen Rachel and given her and her date a hard look. She had braced
herself for an unpleasant encounter, but he hadn't spoken
to her.

That's what would have happened to me, she'd thought,
covertly watching him escort the pregnant girl away, his arm
around her shoulder. *He would have gotten me in trouble
and had to marry me.* The prospect had held a forbidden
thrill.

She'd assumed—and still assumed—that the pregnant girl
was his wife. Had they stayed married? Did Mark have
younger brothers and sisters? These were questions that
shouldn't occupy her thoughts and interfere with her work.
The answers had no bearing on her at all.

Her path hadn't crossed Lee's during the past eighteen or
so years, although they were both involved in the world of
real estate, and there was no reason to expect that it would
in the future. Or at least that was Rachel's view. Something
told her it wouldn't be a good idea.

Mary Lynn arrived at ten o'clock with the good news that
she'd gotten the listing from the home owner she'd met with
that morning. Once that excitement had died down, Alice
filled her in on the automobile accident.

"Zachary's son was in a wreck on our street?" Mary
Lynn demanded, plopping down into a chair in the kitchen,
where they'd gathered for a coffee break. "Did anyone call
him?"

"Why, no," Alice admitted. "I called the police. At that
time we didn't know who the drivers of the two cars were."

"The *perfect opportunity* to meet a big developer who's in need of a good real-estate agency, and you didn't call him? Oh, well. We can still phone Zachary and inquire about his son. Use the conversation as a lead-in and ask for an appointment to pitch Magnolia Realty. One of you should do it, since you were both at the scene of the accident." She sipped from her mug, looking at them questioningly over the edge.

"Not me," Rachel said.

"Why not?" Alice asked curiously. "Don't you think it's a good idea?"

"If the developer were anybody else, I would think it was a good idea. But it just so happens that I know Lee Zachary. Or I once knew him," she added.

Surprised, Alice and Mary Lynn exclaimed in unison, "You *know* Lee Zachary?"

"When we were both teenagers he worked briefly for my father at the pharmacy. He quit in a huff when my parents refused to allow me to date him."

They both waited expectantly for more. "That's it?" Mary Lynn demanded after a moment. "That's the full story?"

"That's a summary of the full story." It seemed rather trivial in the telling, Rachel realized.

"Why didn't your parents approve of him?" Alice asked.

"He was several years older and too streetwise. I was only allowed to double-date at that time. And the boys I dated were my age, usually the sons of people my parents knew. Lee made his own interpretation. He accused my parents—and me—of being snobs."

"Don't you suppose that's all water under the bridge for him now?" Mary Lynn suggested reasonably.

"It probably is," Rachel concurred, feeling rather foolish. "He may not even remember me. If you both think that I should contact him on behalf of Magnolia Realty, then I will. As long as you know in advance than I may not get to first base."

Her partners were of the opinion that she was their best bet.

"However, you should be forewarned that Zachary's single," Mary Lynn said. "I got the scoop on him. He's been divorced for years and has custody of this son who crashed his car today. They live in a condo on the beach in Biloxi." She mentioned the expensive condo complex by name.

Alice drew the obvious conclusion. "Zachary may remember you as well as you remember him, Rachel. He might be interested in dating you now."

Mary Lynn grimaced at that possible complication. "Let's hope that he's no longer attracted to blondes. Or has learned to handle rejection with a little more grace."

Rachel's business partners knew what had happened with Blaine and accepted her rule that she didn't date. They'd both been deeply disappointed in marriage themselves and had no intentions of ever remarrying either. Aside from that, it wouldn't be a wise policy to date a client or potential client.

"Just because Lee's single doesn't mean he's free," Rachel pointed out. "More than likely he's involved in a relationship. But perhaps I should stay in the background and let one of you approach him."

She really should be stating the suggestion more strongly. It bothered her that she had such mixed feelings about talking to Lee on the phone and possibly meeting with him, if he agreed to an appointment.

"You wouldn't stay in the background for long. Either you pose a problem to Zachary or you don't. We might as well find out." Mary Lynn got up to refill her coffee mug.

"Yes, you're the logical person to contact him." Alice went over to the sink to rinse her porcelain cup and saucer.

"I'm so proud of myself. I didn't stop at the bakery this morning for a muffin."

Apparently it was settled. Rachel would call Lee Zachary and try to sell him on giving Magnolia Realty his exclusive listing for the Plantation Village development.

Too shaken and upset to go to school, Mark drove instead to L.J.'s Body Shop. The owner, L.J. Leonard, was an old school buddy of his dad's, but Mark had always called him Uncle L.J.

He poured out the story of what had happened, his account liberally sprinkled with profanity. It was okay to let go and cuss in the company of men. He'd cleaned up his language as much as he could, given the circumstances, at the scene of the accident.

"We'll make her like new." The body-shop owner, dressed in disreputable old jeans and a T-shirt, slapped Mark on the back.

"It honestly wasn't my fault, Uncle L.J. Even though I was going a little faster than the speed limit, I couldn't have stopped in time. She plowed right into me."

"I think the cop must have seen that for himself, since he didn't give you a speeding ticket. These things happen. Hell, they keep me in business." He guffawed heartily, poking Mark in the shoulder with his fist. "You've been lucky, boy. This is your first accident."

"I'm a good driver, just like my dad. He's never had an accident."

"Oh, I see. This spoils your good record. That's why you're so down in the mouth. Come on inside. We'll give that no-good father of yours a call and tell him to get his butt over here. I haven't seen his ugly mug for a couple of weeks."

"He's real busy."

"He'll be over in a shot to make sure you're all right. You're the apple of his eye, Mark Boy."

Using the phone in L.J.'s cluttered office, they reached Lee on his car phone. He was there in fifteen minutes, a somber expression on his face.

"You okay?" he asked his son.

"I'm fine, Dad. It's just my car that got messed up."

Perched on the corner of L.J.'s battered desk, Mark recounted the details of the accident again. Lee listened, all the while reassuring himself that his son was uninjured. That was what really mattered.

"There wasn't anything I could have done to avoid her hitting me, Dad."

Lee nodded in sympathy. "That's the scary part about driving on the highway. You can only operate your own vehicle safely."

"From now on, I'll definitely be more careful."

"Take a load off your feet, old buddy," L.J. urged Lee. Taking his own advice, he sat down in the swivel chair behind his desk. "I was just reading this article about you in the local rag. Seen it yet?"

"No." Lee took a step closer as the other man turned the newspaper around so that both Mark and Lee could peruse the article.

"Hey, Dad! That's where I had my accident—right outside that same real-estate agency." Mark jabbed a finger, indicating a picture on the same page of the newspaper. "Two of those women came out." He pointed. "That one bawled me out for cussing."

Lee frowned, feeling a jolt of recognition as he gazed down at the lovely blond woman. Rachel Preston. "Were you using bad language?"

"Not really bad. I guess I was kind of rude." Mark bent closer. "Her last name is Cavanaugh. Jeez, I hope she's not Stephanie Cavanaugh's mom."

"A new girlfriend?" L.J. asked with a teasing grin. "And here you are with no wheels."

Mark grinned sheepishly. "I just met her at the mall the other day. Boy, is she pretty. I was planning to ask her out this weekend."

"I'll give you a ride to school," Lee said brusquely, interrupting the conversation. He didn't like one little bit the idea of history repeating itself. It would be salt in an old wound if Stephanie Cavanaugh turned out to be Rachel Preston's daughter and Mark asked her out and got turned down.

Lee's son was good enough to date any girl on the Gulf Coast.

"Who was the high school boy driving the little red car?" Stephanie inquired of her mother with interest.

She and Rachel were on their way to Biloxi to have dinner at a seafood restaurant. Rachel had been telling Stephanie about the accident outside Magnolia Realty that morning.

"I doubt you know him. His name is Mark Zachary."

"Mark *Zachary?*" Stephanie repeated. "I *do* know him. I met him at the mall. He's *cute.*"

"Yes, he's a very handsome boy," Rachel had to admit, visualizing Mark. *So was his father at about that age,* she thought, the image of Mark fading into an image of Lee at seventeen.

"Candy is sure that he likes me and is going to ask me out on a date." Candy Wakefield was Stephanie's best friend.

"He's much too old for you to date, darling," Rachel said firmly, wanting to nip any such notions in the bud. "So don't encourage him to ask you out." Had she been guilty of encouraging Lee? She'd have to say yes. Like her daughter, Rachel had been an innocent coquette, batting her big blue eyes, too, and smiling prettily.

"Daddy was five years older than you. You started dating him when you were just out of high school, and he had finished college and was in law school."

"But I would have been too young to date your father when I was your age and a sophomore, even if he'd been only three years older." Just as Rachel had been too young to date Lee.

"Oh, *Mom*. You're so *strict*." Stephanie pouted.

"If I am, it's because I don't want any harm to come to you. Let's talk about something else. How did your English teacher like the poem you wrote?"

"She *loved* it. I had to read it aloud to the class. Afterward, at lunch, Heather Smith and Megan Trent were making real insulting comments. They *hate* me. Candy says they're just jealous."

"Candy's probably right. Just try to ignore them when they're acting ugly. Don't sink to their level."

It was advice her own mother had given her. Ironically, Stephanie's enemies were daughters of two of Rachel's old classmates who'd disliked *her*. To this day, when she encountered Rita Smith and Kay Trent, she could sense that it was an effort for them to be sociable.

At the restaurant, Rachel and Stephanie were sitting at a table with their menus open in front of them when Stephanie suddenly said in a loud stage whisper, "*Mom!* Look who's just come in!"

Rachel glanced up and did a double take. Lee Zachary and his son were being greeted by the hostess.

"Isn't he *cute?* Oh, I wonder if he'll see me."

At that moment Lee looked across the restaurant straight into Rachel's eyes. Embarrassed that he'd caught her staring at him, she nodded and smiled her professional real-estate-agent smile. He didn't nod or smile in return. His gaze flicked from her to Stephanie.

Evidently he hadn't recognized her. Feeling rebuffed, Rachel pretended to study her menu.

"He *has* seen me, Mom!" Stephanie divulged in a panicky murmur. "They're coming to our table!"

It was absurd how closely Rachel's reaction matched her daughter's. "The man with Mark is his father," she explained in a calm undertone. "He worked for Grandpa Preston at the pharmacy years ago when he was about Mark's age."

"You didn't tell me you knew Mark's father."

"It didn't seem important," she lied.

Lee was leading the way, Rachel saw, with Mark trailing behind, looking slightly uncomfortable.

"Hello, Lee." She greeted him when he was two long strides away from their table. "I didn't think you recognized me." It was such an involuntary pleasure to gaze up into his rugged, attractive face, even though his expression was hardly friendly.

"Hello, Rachel. It's been a long time." His voice had deepened with maturity. It held none of the brashness it had had when he was seventeen, nor did it hold any warmth.

"This is quite a coincidence. Tomorrow I was going to call and inquire about Mark. He had his accident today in front of my real-estate agency."

"So he told me. Now you won't have to call and inquire. He's fine."

"Hi, Mrs. Cavanaugh." Mark had come up beside his dad. "Hi, Stephanie."

Stephanie was blushing a pretty pink. "Hi, Mark."

"Lee, this is my daughter, Stephanie." Rachel made the unnecessary introduction.

"I'm pleased to meet you, Mr. Zachary." Her daughter smiled at him as she responded with social correctness.

"Hi, Stephanie. You look exactly like your mother did when she was your age," he said brusquely.

"That's what everyone says."

The observation was usually made as a compliment, but coming from him, it didn't sound that way.

"Mark certainly resembles *you*," Rachel said, fighting the sensation of being assaulted by Lee's masculinity. He was dressed tonight in slacks and a long-sleeved knit shirt that molded his powerful chest and shoulders.

Lee looked at his son with pride and then glanced pointedly at Stephanie. "Yes, but I hadn't realized that he might be a chip off the old block when it came to dating girls." His curt tone made it plain that he wasn't pleased at all that his son was attracted to her daughter. "Mark, I see our table's ready. You two enjoy your dinner."

Before she could get out a reply, he was striding away toward the far side of the restaurant, with Mark following.

"Mom, Mr. Zachary wasn't very friendly. What did he mean?"

"No, he wasn't very friendly, was he?" Rachel ignored her daughter's puzzled question. There didn't seem to be any point in explaining why Mark's father objected to a teenage romance between Stephanie and Mark just as strongly as she did.

Tonight's chance meeting had cleared up any doubt about whether he remembered her. Obviously he did, and his memories still rankled.

Rachel and her real-estate partners didn't have a prayer of getting the exclusive listing for his residential development for retired people. Tomorrow she could report that news back to Mary Lynn and Alice.

Knowing them, they wouldn't be satisfied unless she at least went through the motions, though. Before she left the restaurant, Rachel would detour by Lee's table, hand him her business card and request an appointment.

She was prepared for him to tell her point-blank that she could keep her card. Maybe giving her the cold shoulder in a business context would salve his wounded male pride. Rachel sincerely hoped so. She'd never intended to hurt Lee's feelings.

* * *

"When we were looking at the picture of Stephanie's mom in the newspaper today at Uncle L.J.'s shop, you didn't mention that you knew her, Dad."

"At the time we weren't certain that she was Stephanie's mother," Lee said, sidestepping the issue.

"Isn't Stephanie pretty?" Mark sneaked a glance across the restaurant, his expression love struck.

"There are lots of pretty girls in the world," Lee said cynically. "Find yourself another little blonde with big blue eyes."

"Why are you so against me dating her?"

"Because I would definitely have a problem with your asking her out and getting turned down."

"I don't think she'll turn me down," Mark replied with young male confidence. "I'm not bragging, Dad, but I haven't been turned down for too many dates. Guys have an instinct about these things. I think Stephanie likes me, too."

"At her age she has to have her mother's permission to date you. You could have a big strike against you with Stephanie's mother—you're my son. I wasn't good enough to date her when I was your age, and that attitude could carry over to you."

"You tried to date Mrs. Cavanaugh, and she wouldn't go out with you?"

"I asked her out, and she said no, just as nice as you please. That male instinct you were talking about had completely let me down. I was sure she liked me. She'd acted friendly and had flirted with me, just like Stephanie flirted with you tonight. Not only that, but her parents were nice as pie toward me. I worked for them at their place of business. They turned out to be snobs, and so did she. I'd place money on it that Mrs. Cavanaugh is still a snob."

"She and her parents didn't think you were good enough to date her because you were poor?"

"Because I was poor and lived on the wrong side of the tracks." Lee was bluntly matter-of-fact.

"Did you take your own advice, Dad? Find yourself another girl just as pretty?"

"I found myself another girl," Lee replied. "But no girl looked as pretty for a while." A long while. Lee hadn't been very resilient when he was seventeen. He'd fallen hard for Rachel Preston. She'd touched some tender spot in his heart that he'd guarded well ever since.

Lee hated like hell to think of Mark's being hurt the same way by any girl, but it would be a bitter pill to swallow if the girl was Stephanie Cavanaugh.

Mark had flipped opened his menu. "So what are you going to order?"

"The stuffed flounder, I guess." Lee had lost his appetite. He wished they'd picked another restaurant. He'd deliberately sat with his back to Rachel's table, but he couldn't block out the awareness that she and her daughter were in the same room.

She was so damned lovely, so classy. Looking at her tonight, Lee had felt a completely involuntary pleasure. It angered him that the grown-up Rachel appealed to him more than any woman had appealed to him in a long time.

The effort to discourage Mark's interest in Stephanie obviously hadn't been successful. He had stationed himself so that he could watch her, and he glanced often in her direction throughout the meal as he devoured his food.

"The waitress is bringing them their check," he reported. "Maybe we could hurry up and get ours, Dad, and walk out at the same time."

"Finish your dinner," Lee ordered, hitching his chair around so that he could see the restaurant door. When Rachel made her exit, he wouldn't have to crane his neck to get a glimpse of her.

"Dad, Mrs. Cavanaugh is heading this way," Mark warned a few minutes later. Lee was downing the last swallow of his beer and choked on it. "Darn, Stephanie's not coming with her."

Stephanie had been sent to wait for her mother at the door, Lee surmised grimly as the pretty blond teenager crossed his line of vision, a sulky pout on her lips.

"Excuse me for interrupting your dinner." Rachel had reached their table. Lee got a faint whiff of her perfume, an elegant scent. "I wanted to give you my business card, Lee, and ask you for an appointment. I'm part owner of Magnolia Realty." She offered the card to him. "There was an article about my partners and me in today's *Gazette* on the same page as the article about your new development, Plantation Village."

He took her card and pretended to study it, while he recovered from his sheer surprise. "I saw the article about your agency."

"At your convenience I'd like to sit down with you at your office or mine and try to sell you on choosing us as your Realtors."

She wasn't exactly making a hard sell on getting an appointment with him. Lee could sense that she was expecting him to turn her down. Still, she'd come over.

"I'll tell you what I've been telling the other Realtors who've been dogging me," he said. "You can track me down, and I'll listen to what you have to say."

"Track you down?" she questioned hesitantly.

Lee shrugged. "The most likely place to find me is the construction site of Plantation Village."

"Then I'll come by next week. Good night." She included Mark in her polite, smiling farewell.

Lee watched her thread her way gracefully among the tables of diners, stopping a couple of times to speak to acquaintances. There wasn't a snowball's chance in hell that he was going to pick Rachel Preston as his Realtor. So why hadn't he been up-front about it?

Easy question with a galling answer: because he wanted to see her again. And his pride wouldn't ever let him take the initiative.

Lee wouldn't string her along, though. He wasn't that type of guy. Sure, it pleased something in his gut to think of her seeking him out, of her *wanting* something from him. But if she did follow up, he would play straight with her. Tonight he'd been taken off guard.

Rachel could feel Lee's gaze following her. He awoke an adolescent self-consciousness in her. It had been years since she'd been so aware of being a woman.

Was he getting his revenge by giving her phony encouragement to pursue his business—the way she'd given him false encouragement when they were teenagers? She'd flirted with him, knowing she wouldn't be allowed to date him.

No, surely Lee wasn't that petty, Rachel told herself. Surely he made some allowances for her past behavior. She'd been very young and not intentionally cruel. And it wasn't as though he'd been in love with her. Theirs had been a superficial teenage attraction, like the one between his son and her daughter, which neither Rachel nor Lee condoned—though for different reasons, she guessed.

Lee's objection probably had to do with pride, while Rachel's was the same as that expressed by her parents when she was fourteen: Mark was too old for Stephanie to date. And possibly too wild and irresponsible. He hadn't made a good impression on Rachel today. She doubted that she would have wanted a seventeen-year-old daughter of hers to date him.

It was clear that Stephanie hadn't given up on the idea, though. Outside the restaurant, she complained, "Mom, that wasn't fair. Why couldn't I have gone over and talked to Mark, while you were talking to Mr. Zachary?"

"I was only a minute, and, as I explained, my sole purpose was to discuss real estate. Mr. Zachary is a big developer. He could become a major client of Magnolia Realty."

She changed the subject to get her daughter's mind off her grievance, asking, "Are you and Candy going shopping tomorrow?"

"Tomorrow afternoon we are. Mrs. Wakefield's going to drop us off at the mall. I told her you would pick us up. Candy's going to spend the night with me."

"Maybe the three of us will take in a movie. Or rent a video."

The suggestion was met with enthusiasm, and Stephanie chattered on about sales at the mall, Mark Zachary having been forgotten, at least for the moment.

It occurred to Rachel that Stephanie took it completely for granted that her mother didn't have social plans of her own on a Saturday night. Aside from attending real-estate functions and occasionally getting together with Mary Lynn or Alice or other women friends when Stephanie was going out, Rachel had no social life to speak of.

After Blaine's death, couples who had been their friends had made an effort to include Rachel in dinner parties and holiday events, but it hadn't worked. It seldom did work out to include a single person in a group of married people. She'd spurned well-intentioned matchmaking and gradually had been left out.

Becoming a wife again was unthinkable for her. She'd lost the capability of ever being able to link her life, her identity, her very soul with a man's, as she'd done during her marriage to Blaine. Any time she had doubts, all she had to do was let herself remember the nightmare of walking into his law office and finding him partially naked and dead of a gunshot wound. His young, voluptuous receptionist, too hysterical to get dressed before Rachel arrived, had been wearing nothing but black lace underwear.

Along with her grief and devastating sense of loss, Rachel had also been hit by the agony of his betrayal. She'd loved Blaine devotedly, trusted him implicitly.

During the time that it took for her and the receptionist to dress him before the police arrived, Rachel's love had turned into contempt, her trust into bitterness. Yet, for Stephanie's sake, she'd had to lie for Blaine. She'd had to protect his memory in death. At his funeral and afterward, she'd played the role of the grief-stricken widow.

It hadn't been easy to pay lip service to his innocence in face of rumors that were close to the truth. Nor had it been easy to continue to live in the same house, sleep in the same bedroom and preserve the illusion for Stephanie that she and her daddy and mommy had been the ideal family.

Rachel had done some redecorating and bought new furniture as she could afford to do so during the past nine years, deliberately changing the house. But one change Stephanie wouldn't allow. She refused to let her mother remove any of the photographs of her beloved daddy out on display, including a nine-by-twelve wedding portrait of Rachel and Blaine that hung on the wall of the family room.

Rachel had schooled herself not to look at it. But tonight it drew her gaze as she entered the room. All the old humiliation and hurt welled up. Fortunately, Stephanie noticed nothing amiss, intent on turning on the television set and checking the program listings.

What was stirring up these painful pointless emotions? Rachel asked herself as she sat down with a stack of unopened mail. As though her subconscious mind were providing an answer, she had a mental flash of herself standing at Lee Zachary's table in the restaurant and him remaining seated. Blaine would have been on his feet instantly. He'd always acted like a perfect gentleman. Rachel had been so proud of his manners, so proud of him.

But his manners and intelligence and charm hadn't kept him faithful to her. There'd been other women besides the receptionist. Going through his things, Rachel had discovered evidence. How could she have been so *blind,* so *stupid?*

The worst anger was what she felt toward herself because she'd been duped. Manners or no manners, she wouldn't be taken in by a man again.

"Here's a postcard from Grandma and Grandpa Preston," she said to Stephanie. "They're in Phoenix, Arizona." She read the card aloud and then her thoughts drifted again.

When her pharmacist father, Elliot Preston, had retired six months ago, he and her mother, Rose, had bought a luxurious motor home and begun traveling around the United States. Rachel knew that her mother was probably missing her bridge games and her church and civic committee meetings, but Rose would never let on to her husband. This retirement travel was his dream, something he'd talked about and planned for years, so she was being a sport about it.

Her parents had a good, solid marriage. They hadn't given up hope that Rachel would find a nice man and remarry. For all their support and understanding, they didn't comprehend that Blaine had killed her confidence in her instincts about men.

The next time her parents telephoned, she would mention that she'd run into Lee Zachary, Rachel reflected. They would remember him and be happy for his success. There hadn't been any intention on their part to deal harshly with him.

They'd just been protecting her, using their best judgment. That was all parents could do—use their best judgment and try to cushion their children from harm.

Blaine had fooled Rose and Elliot, indicating that their instincts about human nature hadn't been any more infallible than Rachel's. Maybe it would have been okay for her to date Lee Zachary. Maybe he would have treated her like a princess.

Maybe he wouldn't have.

It was senseless speculation and had no bearing on Rachel's duty as a mother. She couldn't gamble on giving Mark Zachary the benefit of the doubt on the chance that she might be wrong about him, any more than her parents had dared to gamble on Lee's being a diamond in the rough.

"I'll drive, Dad," Mark offered in the parking lot of the restaurant. "Unless you're worried that I'll wreck your car."

Lee tossed his son the keys, giving him the vote of confidence he was asking for. "You're still a good driver," he stated.

When they'd gotten into the car, a top-of-the-line sedan by an American auto maker, Mark glanced over as he fitted the key into the ignition. "Thanks, Dad, for...well, for not being bent all out of shape about my accident. And for believing that it wasn't really my fault."

"If it had been due to your carelessness, you would have been man enough to own up to it. You've never lied to me, even when you were at fault and got yourself in hot water."

"I just wanted you to know I feel kind of lucky." Mark started up the car.

"I feel damned lucky. And damned proud," Lee said gruffly, genuinely touched.

It was one of those infrequent and precious instances when father and son verbalized some of the feelings that formed the basis of their close relationship.

Lee absolutely trusted his son to be truthful with him. Mark was a fine kid in every way, even if Lee was biased. He didn't smoke or do drugs. He made the honor roll at school. He was headed for college. He had good looks and personality. So he was a little cocky and full of himself sometime. What seventeen-year-old boy wasn't?

He wasn't a chip off the old block, and Lee was proud of the fact. Mark would grow up to be a different man—a better man—than he was because he'd had more opportunity.

It wasn't necessary for him to be as tough as nails to survive.

When his bachelor days were numbered, Mark would marry a woman who was nuts about him and would make her a good husband. He wouldn't follow in Lee's footsteps and get tricked into a shotgun wedding by someone like Mark's mother, who hadn't had any morals to speak of.

Lee's biggest satisfaction in life was his kid. Mark made all the hard work, all the striving to get somewhere and be somebody worthwhile.

"You can use my car while yours is out of commission," he offered during the course of conversation on their way home. "Roy Payne will lend me a car to drive." Payne was the owner of a local car dealership, and Lee was a valued customer.

"I can catch rides with my buddies for a few days," Mark replied. "I won't be stuck without a car. Carl is picking me up in the morning. We're going to the country club to play golf, and then tomorrow afternoon we'll probably bum around and go over to the mall."

"To do some girl shopping?" Lee asked dryly.

His son grinned. "That's where I met Stephanie Cavanaugh—in the food court of the mall," he confided with a guilty glance that Lee didn't have any trouble reading.

"And you're going looking for her tomorrow afternoon."

"She's pretty, Dad. I really like her."

"I take it she wasn't shopping with her mother when you met her."

"No, she was with a girlfriend."

Lee shook his head in frustration. "You commented on the fact that Mrs. Cavanaugh didn't bring Stephanie with her over to our table tonight."

"Yeah, but Stephanie waved to me while she was waiting. She likes me, too, Dad. I can tell."

"Don't say I didn't warn you," Lee said grimly.

It wouldn't be the end of the world for Mark to get turned down when he asked Stephanie Cavanaugh for a date. His self-confidence wouldn't be dealt a major blow, nor would his self-esteem be shot to hell, the way Lee's had been. But damn, the idea of his son feeling rejected and unhappy even temporarily on Stephanie's account rubbed Lee raw.

Chapter Two

"Let's get a soft drink. I'm thirsty," Stephanie said to Candy.

"Me, too."

Carrying their purchases, the two teenage girls headed toward the food court of the mall. "Oh, look, Patricia and Lindsey and Anna are here." Candy groaned, adding, "And look who else."

Stephanie made a pained face as she identified her two enemies. "Heather and Megan."

"I'm not *that* thirsty. Are you?"

"Yes, I am," Stephanie said determinedly, tossing her blond hair. "I'm not letting them bother me. It's *their* problem if they don't like me, not mine."

"*Stephanie!*" Candy stopped in her tracks in excitement. "Do you see who I see, headed toward the food court? *Mark Zachary!*"

"It *is* him! Come on, Candy! Let's go talk to him!"

"He *sees* us! He's *waiting* for us! Oh, Stephanie, he definitely *likes* you!"

"I like him, too." Her heart beating fast with giddy adolescent pleasure, Stephanie smiled at Mark and waved a greeting.

He was with another boy, Carl, whom he introduced to them. As a foursome, they went to one of the counters in the food court to buy soft drinks. Mark insisted on paying and also bought a large order of fries for them to share. Stephanie and Candy exchanged glances the whole time, carrying on blissful, unspoken girl conversation, while their acquaintances from school observed enviously. It was the fantasy of every teenage girl in the food court to come to the mall and have a romantic encounter, like the one Stephanie and Candy were experiencing.

Finally Carl called Mark's attention to the time, and the two boys said goodbye and left. Stephanie and Candy went to the pay telephones, where Stephanie called her mother to come and pick them up. Rachel promised to be at the mall entrance in twenty minutes. With a little time to kill, they went over to visit with their friends and acquaintances from school. By now a cluster of tables were occupied.

Barraged by curious questions, Stephanie denied that she was dating Mark. When pressed, she was truthful, admitting that he hadn't actually asked her for a date yet and, when or if he did, she would probably have to turn him down, unless her mother's attitude became more reasonable. "My mom has this old-fashioned notion that I should only date boys my age," she explained.

The general response was sympathetic, but Heather Smith piped up in a catty tone, "Well, if you can't date him, why lead him on, Stephanie?"

Heather's sidekick, Megan Trent, added snidely, "Yes, why not leave the field open for someone who *can* go out with him? Unless you just can't resist flirting with anything in pants."

Stephanie remembered her mother's advice not to descend to their level. It wasn't easy, but she managed not to retaliate with a cutting remark of her own. Instead she loftily ignored Heather and Megan.

"Did you see their faces when you didn't answer them?" Candy demanded when she and Stephanie were hurrying toward the mall entrance shortly afterward. "They looked like they'd gladly kill you."

"Let's don't repeat what they said to my mom," Stephanie replied. "About me leading Mark on. I'll get another lecture about not encouraging him."

"You're going to tell her that we ran into Mark, aren't you?" The question was rhetorical. Candy knew her best friend didn't make a habit of deceiving her mother.

"Just that we saw him here at the mall with another boy." Stephanie's voice reflected her guilt and her defiance. "There's nothing wrong with meeting Mark places and having a soft drink with him. But my mom probably wouldn't want me to, if she knew. Just because her parents were strict with her, she thinks she has to be strict with me."

"I doubt my parents would let me date a senior, either," Candy pointed out with a sigh of commiseration. "They're strict, too."

"I wish my dad were alive. I'll bet he would take my side."

"As a general rule, my dad sides with my mom. When they argue, it's never about letting us do stuff."

"My parents didn't ever argue. They were always hugging and kissing each other—and me," Stephanie recalled wistfully.

"Your mom doesn't go out on dates, does she?"

"Oh, no. My dad will always be her husband, just like he'll always be my father."

The two girls had reached the glass-walled entrance where they were to wait for Rachel. They came to a standstill, keeping a watch for her car.

"Does your mother still feel real unhappy and cry when she thinks about your father?" Candy asked.

"Not in front of me. She probably does cry some, though, like on their anniversary."

"It's so tragic to lose your one true love and then be alone the rest of your life."

"But you have your memories...." Both Candy's eyes and hers were glazed with tears. "And in my mother's case, she had me. She wasn't all alone."

"That's true. But someday you'll grow up and get married."

"I won't move away, though. She can still see me every day. And when I have children, they can stay with her sometime at her house. My mom won't be lonely.... There she is now."

They dashed outside and their pensive mood evaporated in the late-afternoon autumn sunshine.

"What did you buy?" Rachel asked with interest, and they interrupted each other in their eagerness to narrate their great finds. Next she asked without any suspicion, "Who did you see at the mall?"

Candy and Stephanie named the whole list of people, including Mark and Carl. "Mark was shopping for socks," Candy divulged with a titter.

"He and Carl had played golf earlier," Stephanie put in.

"I guess his car is being repaired and he's having to catch rides," Rachel commented, and then changed the subject.

Stephanie's relief that her mother's suspicion hadn't been aroused was mixed with guilt. Maybe later the opportunity would arise to make a full confession. If not, Stephanie assured herself, she hadn't done anything wrong, other than being secretive. And it was her mom's own fault that she had to be.

"Magnolia Realty is off to a good start," Rachel summed up at the regular Monday-morning meeting. "Among us, we've listed seven properties in two weeks and have written up sales contracts on two properties listed by other agencies."

"We are off to a good start," Mary Lynn concurred. "And all three of us have big prospective clients. Yours is the biggest, though, Rachel. If you can sell Zachary on listing with Magnolia Realty, we're on our way to being the top real-estate agency on the Mississippi Gulf Coast."

Rachel had related to Mary Lynn and Alice the chance meeting with Lee and Mark at the restaurant on Friday night. In their eyes, it had been a stroke of good fortune.

"That's a big *if*," Rachel stressed. "Though I certainly intend to do my best selling job." Her best wouldn't be good enough with Lee. Knowing that, why was she so eager?

"When do you plan to follow up and try to corner him at his building site?" Alice inquired.

"Today." Rachel's windpipe had closed, making her voice husky. She cleared her throat and elaborated briskly, "After we're finished with our meeting, I'll drive over there and patrol the place all day, if necessary."

"Good girl." Mary Lynn applauded. "I'm betting on you."

"I am, too," Alice assured her.

"Thanks for the vote of confidence, but your odds might not be a whole lot better than feeding quarters into the slots at our gambling casinos." The state legislature had licensed casino gambling on the Gulf Coast, against the opposition of many residents, and floating casinos were now sharing the coastline with scenic marinas and other harbor businesses.

The meeting was concluded, and Rachel set out on her mission to track Lee down. She took the highway along the beach, heading west. Plantation Village was between Gulfport and Long Beach, the adjacent small town. It was a lovely tract of land with big live oaks. Lee was taking the necessary precautions to protect them, she noted approv-

ingly as she drove onto the building site from a side street.
Around each tree a fence had been built at the drip line of
the outer branches, preventing workmen from parking ve-
hicles or driving heavy equipment over the tree's extensive
root system.

A large crew of workmen was there at the site, digging
footings and laying reinforcement rods for concrete foun-
dations. A man obviously their foreman was supervising the
labor. Lee was looking on. When Rachel spotted him, her
heart leapt and then sank. She was in luck, she told herself,
heading over toward him.

Friday night his outfit had been in tune with Mark's. Today he was wearing what she guessed was his working attire—jeans and boots and a long-sleeved cotton shirt with
the cuffs turned back. Even from a distance she responded
to his rugged masculinity.

Several of the workmen facing in her direction glanced
curiously at her. Alerted by their reaction, Lee turned and
saw her when she was still twenty yards away. His surprise
showing on his face, he gave her a quick male once-over.
Rachel had never felt sexy before in her tailored navy skirt
teamed with a white silk blouse and red blazer, but suddenly she was all thighs and hips and breasts.

The fact that he stood and waited, giving her his full attention, was disconcerting, but seemed somehow a point in
her favor.

"You said I was welcome to track you down," she reminded him when she'd reached him. "Here I am." She held
out her hand.

He hesitated before he shook hands with her, his big fingers engulfing hers. "Hello, Rachel," he finally said in
greeting.

Rachel's palm tingled from the warm contact with his
toughened skin, and her breathing had become shallow. She
blamed the latter on nervousness as she sucked in a lungful

of air and gestured toward the workmen. "You're moving right along here."

"Day after tomorrow we should be pouring concrete."

"Is this the foundation for the clubhouse?" Rachel was relying on the information she'd read in the newspaper article.

"No, it will be over here." Lee led her away from the activity and indicated the exact spot. He pointed out the planned location of the swimming pool, then took her over to a large sign showing an aerial view of the property and the layout of the buildings. Enthusiasm crept into his deep voice as he discussed with her the concept behind Plantation Village: convenient, safe community living with a measure of privacy.

The lawn and grounds would be maintained by gardeners. A gated entrance would be manned by a security guard at all times. The clubhouse would serve as a social center for card parties and club meetings and various recreational and educational events. Owner-residents would elect from among themselves a clubhouse board to oversee the use of the facility.

"They might also want to purchase a Plantation Village van for excursions," Lee said.

"It sounds like a wonderful place to live, as you envision it," Rachel declared in all sincerity. "You've obviously put a lot of thought into the project and want it to be something good for the community. There's more than a profit motive involved, and I admire that."

"Do you?" he asked cynically.

Rachel's cheeks grew hot at his skepticism. "That wasn't a sales pitch to butter you up. I like the whole concept and would feel good giving prospective buyers my personal stamp of approval, if the quality of construction measures up."

"It'll measure up."

She summoned all her courage and dignity. "Well, then, let me take the bull by the horns. My two partners and I would like for you to pick Magnolia Realty as your official real-estate agency for the Plantation Village development. Could we set up a meeting to present you with our ideas and outline our special qualifications?"

He shook his head abruptly. "That would be a waste of your time."

"You've decided on an agency?" Rachel couldn't hide her disappointment.

"No, but when I do, it won't be yours. I owe you an apology for letting you come here," he admitted tersely.

"In other words, you're ruling out Magnolia Realty because I'm one of the owners. It has nothing to do with professional qualifications."

"That's right."

His bluntness made her speechless for a second. "You still have hard feelings after all these years because of what happened when we were teenagers?"

"You mean because of what *didn't* happen when we were teenagers."

"Okay, what *didn't* happen. You asked me out and I said no, after giving out signals that I would say yes. Would it do any good to say now that I regret having been a bad experience for you?"

"Being sorry after the fact never changes anything," Lee stated, unmoved. "I was damned sorry at the time that I'd made a total ass of myself. I knew better than to think that you and your parents were a cut above other people and were judging me by what I was, not who I was. It's old history, but what happened hurt a hell of a lot. I'm glad I finally got a chance to say that and get it off my chest."

Rachel sighed. "I feel horribly guilty. I never intended to be cruel, but I was. I knew full well my parents wouldn't let me date you."

He shrugged his broad shoulders and replied brusquely, "You were just a typical teenage girl. It wasn't your fault I'd put you up on a pedestal. At any rate, I apologize for not being more straightforward on Friday night. You took me by surprise at the restaurant when you came over and made your pitch."

Rachel's gaze took in the sign and the workmen. "I'm very disappointed," she said truthfully. "Frankly, I was just going through the motions Friday night and today. My partners originally pushed me to contact you after they learned that I'd once known you. I had little confidence that I could sell you on choosing Magnolia Realty. There was the grudge factor and, also, we're an all-female agency."

"I have no problem doing business with a woman un-less—" He broke off.

"Unless what?" Her heartbeat suddenly picked up its pace as he gazed at her. Rachel looked away, shocked by her own flare of sexual excitement.

"Unless I want to take her to bed," Lee explained flatly. "Which happens to be the case with you. So Magnolia Realty wouldn't be in the running anyway."

"I see." She couldn't meet his eyes for fear of revealing that his plain language wasn't as offensive as it should be. She felt more complimented than insulted.

An automobile was turning in from the side street, pro-viding a welcome diversion. The driver parked next to her car and got out. Rachel recognized him immediately. He was Jim Hagen, a real-estate rival, obviously coming to call on Lee to make his selling pitch.

"You have another visitor," she said to Lee. "I'll go now and leave the coast clear for him. Thank you for your time, and I hope everything goes well with Plantation Village." She offered him her hand again in parting, as she would have done with any other developer.

Again he hesitated briefly before he clasped her hand, but this time Rachel had to end the handshake. Conscious that her cheeks were flushed and her entire body was suffused with warmth, she departed hastily, greeting Hagen in passing. "Hello, Jim. How are you today?"

"Just fine, Rachel," he returned in his unctuous baritone, his voice pitched loud enough for Lee to hear. "You're looking lovely, as usual."

Chauvinist, she uttered silently. Jim Hagen invariably commented on her appearance, using his compliments to put her down as a fellow professional. The implication was always clear that she could chalk up any success to her looks.

He'd reached Lee and was shaking hands with him as she started her car. The men stood side by side, talking and watching her as she drove away. Lee was frowning. Somehow his sour expression put Rachel in an even lower frame of mind as she returned to the office to report her failure.

Why the hell couldn't Hagen have waited another thirty minutes before showing up? Lee wondered angrily. He probably wouldn't ever have another conversation with Rachel. Certainly they wouldn't ever resume the same conversation that had been interrupted. He'd wanted her to make some response to his admitting that he found her very desirable.

"Pretty woman, isn't she?" Hagen commented.

Lee didn't reply. He wasn't going to discuss Rachel with the man.

"Good agent, too. But there's a big difference between showing houses and running a real-estate agency. Told my wife, and she agreed with me—it's a man's world, and men do business with other men. A real-estate agency run by three women just isn't going to make it on the Gulf Coast. They'll go belly up in a year." Hagen made a *tsk-tsking* sound. "It's a shame, all right."

"It would be a shame if Mrs. Cavanaugh and her partners fail simply because they're women," Lee said curtly.

"Personally, I was very impressed with her professionalism. For one thing, she didn't bad-mouth her competition."

"You misunderstood me! I admire Mrs. Cavanaugh a great deal. But enough small talk. I see you've begun construction. Your general contractor, Carl Beatty, is the best."

"Yes, he is," Lee concurred. He gave Hagen a much-quicker guided tour of the premises than the one he'd given Rachel. Then he got rid of the man, whose efforts to undercut her had backfired, instead bringing out Lee's sense of fair play.

He'd been an underdog himself. It had been tough going to make something of himself, coming from a poor background with no pull, no family connections with the right people in the right places. The thought of Rachel's putting herself on the line and failing for no valid reason didn't make him feel good at all. In fact, it made him feel lousy, because he would have done his part in denying her an equal playing field.

There wasn't any justifiable reason to deny Magnolia Realty a fair shot at his business along with the other agencies who were vying for it. Lee came to a decision: he would give Rachel and her partners a chance to sell him on choosing them.

It was noon by now. The rumbling in his stomach told him he was hungry. Lee got in his car and headed toward Gulfport. He would grab some lunch and then pass by the Magnolia Realty office. Rachel or one of her partners should be there.

No, he would reverse the order and pass by Magnolia Realty first.

What the hell, if Rachel were any other agent, male or female, Lee wouldn't feel any hesitation about extending an impromptu lunch invitation if the notion hit him. Why treat her differently?

As he turned off the main highway onto the same narrow, tree-shaded side street where Mark's accident had occurred, Lee's thoughts turned to his seventeen-year-old son. The attraction between Mark and Rachel's daughter actually hadn't crossed his mind all morning until now.

Lee's guess was that Rachel had nipped the romance in the bud. Sure, that bothered him—bothered him a lot. But how Rachel raised her daughter was her own affair and not a criterion for judging her as a real-estate professional. In all honesty, Lee couldn't be objective about Stephanie. He assumed she was a heartless little flirt, and she might not be. So how could he condemn Rachel for assuming Mark was a carbon copy of his father at seventeen? Lee had done his best to nip the romance in the bud, too.

Rachel's car was parked at the Magnolia Realty office alongside a small economy sedan that had seen a lot of use. *Good. She's here*, Lee told himself matter-of-factly to counteract his gut reaction, which wasn't nearly so calm.

He was favorably impressed with the agency building, a nice old cottage. It showed a touch of class. The interior lived up to the outside, he saw when he entered and found himself in an inviting reception room. A plain but pleasant woman in her late twenties who was busy at work at her desk looked up and welcomed him. Lee deduced that the economy sedan probably belonged to her and that she was a secretary, not one of Rachel's partners.

Her face showed respectful recognition of his name when he introduced himself and stated that he was there to see Mrs. Cavanaugh.

"Rachel's in her office," she replied readily. "Through that door and to your left."

Lee thanked her, annoyed with himself for his stir of anticipation. This was business, not pleasure.

The door to Rachel's office stood open. Lee could hear her voice before he reached it. She was talking on the phone to a client. That was obvious from the conversation, which was about real estate.

Pausing in the doorway, Lee saw that she was gazing out the window, which afforded a view of the side yard. With his hand raised to knock and alert her to his presence, he treated himself to a few seconds of looking at her unguardedly. She'd taken off the red jacket. Her white silk blouse revealed the slim shapeliness of her figure above the waist. While Lee watched, she lifted her arm and massaged her neck, lifting her breasts in the process. Male pleasure curled through him. He rapped hard with his knuckles against the wooden doorframe.

"Lee!" she blurted in midsentence when her head jerked around. Quickly she terminated the phone call and stood up, her right hand pressed to her chest. "You gave me quite a start. Come in."

"Sorry," he apologized brusquely, taking a step inside.

"This is totally unexpected," Rachel said foolishly, trying to recover from her surprise. She indicated a chair. "Won't you sit down?"

Lee shook his head, glancing around her office. It was tastefully decorated, like the outer room. On the wall were certificates and awards. "I don't intend to stay long. I came by to set up that meeting with you and your partners that you asked for."

Rachel sank weakly into her chair. First there was his unexpected appearance and now his sudden change of mind. "But an hour ago you turned me down," she reminded him.

"For no good reason. I was letting personal feelings interfere with running my business. You and your partners have an equal chance. That is, if you still want to be considered," he added.

"Of course we do. If I seem unenthusiastic, it's because I'm very surprised. You were so definite earlier, and I'd accepted the fact that we'd lost out."

"Well, you haven't. Nor do you have an edge." Lee was making the declaration to himself as much as to her. She was so damned lovely to look at. Her hint of uncertainty made her seem vulnerable and feminine.

"It goes without saying that we wouldn't have an edge. We're a new agency and have to prove ourselves." Rachel picked up a pen and inquired, "What day would be convenient for you? How about Wednesday or Thursday?"

"Make it Thursday."

"Morning or afternoon?"

"Afternoon. Three o'clock."

Rachel made a notation on her desk calendar, as though there were actually a possibility that she might not remember the appointment. She needed desperately to slip into her identity of agent broker-agency owner. Maybe then her pulse would settle down and she would feel in control.

"Would you like to come here to our office?" she inquired. "Or have us come to yours?"

"I'll come here."

"Very good. We'll see you Thursday at three then." She dropped the pen and stood, wishing she were wearing her jacket. Her simple, modest white blouse seemed far too revealing in his presence. "My partners are both at lunch with clients. Otherwise I'd introduce them to you now."

"Have you eaten?" Lee asked.

"Why, no, I haven't. I brought my lunch today, but I—I haven't gotten around to eating it," Rachel stammered. She needed to sit down again and recover from still another unexpected move from him.

"I was headed to a restaurant. Would you care to join me? The meeting Thursday is still on, either way," he added bluntly, making it clear that she was under no pressure to accept.

She hadn't interpreted his invitation as sexual harassment, and his sensitivity to the issue came as one more surprise. Sensitivity wasn't a quality Rachel would have associated with Lee Zachary. "I'd be happy to join you, as long as you let me pick up the check," she stipulated. "We can talk more about Plantation Village." Feeling as though what was happening wasn't quite real, she donned her jacket and got her purse from a drawer.

Lee returned to the outer reception room while she briefly visited the bathroom to freshen up and try to adjust mentally to the events of the last ten minutes.

Magnolia Realty actually had a fighting chance to be picked as Lee's exclusive-listing agency for his Plantation Village development. It was quite incredible, but true. During lunch with him today and at the all-important meeting scheduled later in the week, she simply *had* to put aside guilt, conquer physical attraction and concentrate on what was important—selling him on her and her partners' abilities as a team to do the job for him. She bore an enormous responsibility to Mary Lynn and Alice and owed it to herself not to blow this golden opportunity.

He was Lee Zachary, major developer and prospective client. That was his identity now, not would-be boyfriend.

With her perspective in order, Rachel went to collect Lee and take him to lunch. She expected to find him prowling the outer room. Instead, he was gone. Rachel's mouth fell open and disappointment surged through her.

"He's waiting for you outside," Cindy explained.

"Oh. For a moment I had doubts about my sanity."

Rachel had interpreted "outside" to mean on the porch, but Lee was sitting in his car, talking on his car phone. As she approached his automobile, he swung the passenger door open, evidently intending for her to ride with him to the restaurant.

That arrangement hadn't occurred to Rachel. She'd envisioned them driving separate cars. Mentally composing a polite excuse for sticking to her plan, she headed for the open door and, reaching it, leaned down. Lee was in the middle of what was obviously a business call. He gestured for her to get in.

She hesitated and then slid in, her straight, tailored skirt riding up on her thighs. Settled in the comfortable leather seat and intensely conscious that he was watching, she tugged the skirt down as far as it would go before closing her door and fastening her seat belt.

Lee started the car and shifted into gear as he made concluding remarks. "Any particular restaurant?" he asked, looking over at her as he replaced the phone in its niche between the seats.

"I'll leave the choice up to you."

Without any further discussion, he backed out onto the street and drove toward the beach. Rachel searched for a topic of conversation. His car was a full-size luxury model, but it seemed close quarters, perhaps because he filled the space so well. She was conscious that the denim of his jeans hugged hard, muscular thighs, that his shoulders were broad and powerful and his hands big and strong. The impact of his masculinity was almost overpowering.

"You've done very well for yourself," she said. "When I read the article in the newspaper, I was sincerely glad for you."

"In my business, you can't rest on your laurels or you'll land on your backside," Lee replied. He knew he was resorting to crudeness deliberately to hide how enormously pleased he was by her commendation. At this point he was having serious doubts about his commitment to fair play. Who was he kidding? How could he keep his mind on business around her? "I've got more than my credibility invested in Plantation Village. I'm one of my own backers in this venture."

"It should pay off. From what I saw and learned today, Plantation Village should be a very successful venture."

They'd reached the highway and were having to wait for a break in traffic. The scent of her perfume in his lungs, Lee looked over at her as he said flatly, "I intend to make sure it's successful. I started right by picking one of the best architects and best general contractors on the Gulf Coast. Now I've got to pick the best real-estate agency."

"The *right* real-estate agency to do the best job for you. That's not necessarily the largest agency or the oldest, is it?"

"No," he conceded. "But sympathy can't enter into my decision. I can't afford to be a good guy. And I'd be a damned fool to be ruled by anything other than sound judgment."

A horn tooted. Lee glanced in the rearview mirror and verified that a car had driven up behind his. He'd been too absorbed in the conversation, too caught up in being with her to notice. "Keep your pants on, buddy," he muttered. After checking traffic, he stepped hard on the gas pedal and pulled out onto the highway.

Rachel held on to the sides of her seat, drawing in her breath audibly. Her purse slid to the floor. She picked it up and settled back again once they were riding along in the right lane, the white sand beach and open expanse of the Gulf visible through the windows on her side.

"Sorry," he apologized gruffly. "You can't poke around at those intersections."

"No, not unless you're willing to sit all day and wait." After a few seconds of silence, she inquired, "Did Mark suffer any injuries from his accident? He seemed fine on Friday night, and Stephanie mentioned seeing him at the shopping mall Saturday."

Lee deduced that his driving had made his son come to mind. Like father, like son, she was probably thinking. "Fortunately, he walked away without a bruise. He was very upset, though, about the damage to his car and about ruining his perfect driving record. It was his first accident." Catching her surprised expression, he stated, "Mark's a very good driver."

"Most teenagers are probably better drivers than the average adult," Rachel said diplomatically. "Their reflexes are faster. It's their lack of maturity that gets them into trouble and makes them a danger on the highway. I'm not looking forward to Stephanie's getting her license when she's old enough."

"How old is she?"

"She's only fourteen."

Lee caught the emphasis on *only*. "I would have guessed fifteen or sixteen," he admitted. "But with girls in their early teens, it's hard to tell."

"You can't lump them all into one age category, though. Each year represents a stage of mental and emotional development. Fourteen is very young. Stephanie is allowed only to double date and go out on group dates—with boys her age. They don't drive yet, either."

Lee was remembering Stephanie's flirtatious manner toward Mark on Friday night. "I don't think she has conveyed that message to my son," he said.

"I had a talk with her Friday night."

"I figured you had. I had one with Mark, too. But the next day he was off to the mall hoping to run into Stephanie. I hope your talk carried more weight." Lee didn't hide his skepticism.

"Apparently it did. Stephanie would have given herself away if she'd been overly excited about seeing Mark. She and I are very close," Rachel explained. She wished she could say to Lee that it was fine with her for Stephanie and Mark to be friends, but in all honesty she couldn't say it, not when she remembered the rough language Mark had used in front of her and the older woman who'd been driving the luxury sedan.

It was a relief to arrive at the restaurant and let the conversation die. After Lee parked the car, Rachel opened her own door and got out. People were exiting as she and Lee approached the door of the restaurant, so they walked single file, with her reaching it a step ahead of him. She opened it herself instead of waiting for him to act the gentleman, as she would have done at one time.

A hostess greeted them and inquired, "A table for two, sir?"

"Yes. That table by the window," he replied.

"Certainly. This way, please."

As she followed the hostess, Rachel thought of how Blaine would have exuded his southern charm in the same situation. Oddly, she found Lee's brusqueness almost pleasing in contrast. There was no pretense with him, and he evidently didn't feel any compulsion to make conquests of every female who crossed his path.

At the table, she pulled out her chair and sat down. It was time to focus on her purpose, selling Lee on Magnolia Realty.

Their waitress came soon after the hostess had presented them with menus and left. "Can I get you something to drink?" she asked.

Rachel requested ice tea, her usual beverage with a meal, and Lee ordered a beer, which she guessed was his usual choice, too. He'd been drinking beer with his dinner on Friday night when she'd gone to his table. Blaine hadn't been fond of beer, Rachel recalled as she studied her menu. His taste had been more that of the southern gentleman, his preference a whiskey old-fashioned made with a specified fine bourbon.

Why was she comparing Lee and Blaine? Her mind should be on real estate, Rachel reminded herself. She should be ordering her thoughts even while she made social small talk, as she would do with any other prospective client. But there *was* no small talk with Lee. He hadn't once smiled at her. The realization prompted a disturbing wistfulness.

Rachel put her menu aside. "Let me tell you a little about my two partners, Mary Lynn Porter and Alice Kirkland. They're both million-dollar agents, too."

Lee tossed his menu to one side as well, and gave her his attention. The waitress returned, interrupting briefly to deliver drinks and take the food order. Rachel resumed talking as she sweetened her ice tea and sipped it. Through the salad course, she covered her partners' credentials and her own. Through the main course, she explained the cooperative concept behind Magnolia Realty that fostered teamwork, not competition. "So, in effect, any property owner who lists with us gets three full-time listing agents, not one," she summarized.

Lee had put in a few questions, but otherwise listened closely as he ate. Now he put down his fork. "I would want one of you in charge as the person who kept in close communication with me."

"Surely, and that person wouldn't have to be me. When you meet Mary Lynn and Alice, you might really click with one of them."

"What if I wanted you?" he asked bluntly. "How would you react to the idea of having lunch with me every now and then? Of going with me to a business dinner or two? Also, there'll be a trip to Pensacola, Florida, with Livingston, my architect, and Beatty, my general contractor, to visit a retirement-home development there that's been very successful."

Rachel swallowed hard, conscious of her pulse fluttering in a very unprofessional way. "It doesn't present me with any problems to have a business relationship with you, Lee. I would go all out on your behalf, with my partners' full support, if you went with our agency."

"I like everything I've heard," he said soberly, balling up his napkin. "But the whole time I've been conscious that you're Rachel Preston."

"But I'm not Rachel Preston," she retorted. "I'm Rachel Cavanaugh." A faint tinge of bitterness had crept into her voice, and he hadn't missed it.

"I wasn't around when your husband was shot. I was offshore. What happened?"

Rachel had a reprieve in answering. The waitress had come to clear away their plates. They both refused coffee and dessert. "Just hold the check," Lee instructed. "We're not in a hurry." He leaned forward, resting his elbows on the table, and prompted without any gentleness, "So what happened?"

"Blaine was murdered by his receptionist's fiancé, who was insanely jealous. The man was convicted of manslaughter and is still serving his prison term. It was all quite tragic and horrible."

"You haven't remarried."

"No, I wasn't interested in remarrying. My life is full with rearing Stephanie and earning a living in real estate."

"Your husband had life insurance?"

"Oh, yes, Blaine was well insured. I wasn't left a rich widow by any means, but neither was I in dire financial straits. Fortunately, our house was paid off by a mortgage insurance policy. I wasn't forced to get a job immediately. Real estate suited my situation. It didn't require a college degree, which I don't have. It allowed me to benefit from having lived on the Gulf Coast my entire life. Most important, I could arrange my work schedule to be a full-time mother to Stephanie, who was only five at the time and attending kindergarten." Rachel hesitated before she added, 'My parents were very supportive and always willing to act as sitters when they were free. Of course, they also passed out my cards at the pharmacy and referred customers to me. But I give myself credit for turning those contacts into repeat clients. Now I've been in real estate almost nine years and feel very good about it as a profession."

Lee apparently didn't have more questions for her. He caught their waitress's eye and signaled for the bill.

"You agreed to let me buy lunch," Rachel reminded him.

He pulled out his wallet and extracted a couple of crisp bills. "I didn't agree to anything," he said. "Lunch is on me."

She gave in gracefully without haggling. "Then thank you. Next time I'll know to get a verbal commitment."

Lee looked at her. "That 'next time' hinges on whether you're my real-estate agent, doesn't it?"

Rachel didn't hold his gaze. She didn't dare, for fear that he might read messages she didn't want to send. "Lee, I don't date."

"Cavanaugh must have been some man," he mused harshly. Dropping the bills on the table, he stood up. "Let's go. That'll cover it."

The money was far too much for the bill and a generous tip, but she stood, too, and accompanied him out to the car. He opened her door for her and slammed it shut after she'd gotten in, her narrow skirt riding up on her thighs again. He slammed his own door, too, and jammed the key into the ignition.

"Just a minute, please," Rachel pleaded, reaching over impulsively to place her hand lightly on his. He grew tense at her touch. "Explain why you're so angry at me. I thought we were both clear on why I accepted your lunch invitation today."

Lee sat back. "I'm not angry at you. I'm mad as hell at myself."

"For what reason?"

"For being a damned fool again. I'm actually tempted to make you my real-estate agent so I'll have an excuse to see you. Don't tell me you don't realize that."

"I certainly *will* tell you! If I'd had any inkling that you weren't weighing my abilities as an agent and broker, I wouldn't have wasted my breath trying to sell you on Magnolia Realty!'' Now Rachel was angry, and not just at him, but at herself, because his admission pleased the woman in her.

Lee rubbed his hand roughly on the spot where she'd touched him. "I owe you an apology."

"Just consider that we're even now. Years ago I raised false hopes and now you've paid me back."

The drive to her office was a silent one. Rachel tried to start up a polite conversation, but met with no cooperation from him. So she gazed out her window, coping with deep disappointment and a sense of guilt. She'd let her partners down. They would have to suffer the consequences of her old acquaintanceship with Lee Zachary.

"I wish you great success with Plantation Village," she told him, unbuckling her seat belt when he'd pulled in next to Alice's dove gray sedan. Mary Lynn's dark blue luxury model was also there, along with two other unfamiliar cars, presumably those of clients. "When your Realtor holds an open house, you can count on one of us being there." It wouldn't be her.

"Best of luck to you in getting Magnolia Realty off the ground," Lee replied with gruff sincerity. "If I can send any business your way, I will."

"That will be appreciated." She said goodbye and opened her door and got out. By the time she'd reached the sidewalk, he'd backed his car out and was headed toward the beach again.

Rachel's disappointment hit her full force as she gazed after him. There was a disturbing personal sense of letdown she could acknowledge now that she wasn't in his presence.

A big part of her excitement over the idea of being the exclusive broker for Plantation Village had stemmed from the fact that she would see him regularly.

Chapter Three

"I'll be in my room, Mom. I have a paper to write for English class." Stephanie made the announcement when she'd helped her mother clean up after supper.

"Okay, dear. If you'd like, I'll proofread it for you when you've finished writing it," her mother replied.

It was Stephanie's practice to do her homework in her room. She liked being close to her telephone, so that she could answer calls from her friends and chat with them while she did assignments. Since her preteen years, she'd had her own private telephone line, thanks to her mother's being in real estate and needing to keep a home phone free for business use. Therefore Stephanie enjoyed the luxury of carrying on lengthy phone conversations without ever being lectured.

Actually, she got very few lectures, because she was an obedient daughter. Her mom's rules were pretty reasonable except for one—her strictures about dating. Those were seeming more and more old-fashioned. Stephanie couldn't see waiting until she was sixteen to go out on real dates. Of course, she hadn't actually been asked out on a date by a boy old enough to have his driver's license, but it was only a matter of time until she was.

The subject was so much on her mind that she wrote her English paper on the topic Maturity in Teenagers. She'd just finished recopying her rough draft and was about to go and have her mother read the final copy—and, Stephanie hoped, broaden her narrow thinking—when the phone rang.

To her extreme delight, her caller was none other than Mark Zachary. "Could you hold on just a moment, Mark?" she asked when the sheer thrill subsided enough for caution to assert itself. Her bedroom door was open, and her mom might walk in without warning.

"Sure," he answered, and Stephanie went quickly to close the door, suppressing pangs of guilt. There was nothing wrong with talking to Mark on the phone, just as there'd been no harm in having a soda with him at the mall, but her mom probably wouldn't approve. It was her closemindedness that was forcing Stephanie to be secretive.

Settled comfortably on her bed, she resumed the conversation. They talked about school, about music and then about movies they'd seen and wanted to see. Mark took the opening and asked casually, "Want to take in a movie this weekend? I'll have my car back on Friday."

At his words, Stephanie's heart leapt with pure ecstasy. A high school senior was asking her out, and not just any senior. Mark Zachary was surely the handsomest boy on the Gulf coast. Every girl at school would love to be in her shoes.

Was there any chance that her mother would let her go on a date with him? No, probably none, and it would be so embarrassing to have to tell him that she wasn't able to get permission. He would lose all interest in her. "I'm sorry, but I really can't," she said, trying to tone down her overwhelming regret. "Not this weekend."

"That's the way it goes," he said offhandedly. "Maybe another time when you're not busy. Now I guess I'd better hang up and do my math homework."

"Maybe I'll see you at the mall," Stephanie said hopefully. "My girlfriend Candy and I are going tomorrow afternoon after school to exchange a blouse she bought."

"I have golf practice tomorrow afternoon. But I'm sure we'll run into each other sometime."

He said goodbye and hung up. Stephanie held the phone to her ear, listening to the click cutting the connection. Tears of utter misery welled up and ran down her cheeks. She just *hated* her mother for doing this to her! It was so humiliating to be treated like a twelve-year-old!

The only bright spot was being able to tell her friends all the thrilling details. Stifling a sob, Stephanie picked up the phone and called Candy. "You'll *never* guess who just asked me to the movies. Oh, I *despise* my mother...."

At nine o'clock Rachel decided to go and check on Stephanie's progress with her English paper. Perhaps she'd run into problems and could use some input.

Outside her daughter's bedroom, Rachel noted the closed door with mild surprise. Stephanie never closeted herself in her room when there were just the two of them in the house. After tapping lightly, Rachel entered.

Stephanie was sprawled on her bed, talking on the phone. Her tear-stained face gave rise to instant concern strong enough for Rachel to interrupt the conversation. "Darling, what's wrong?"

"Candy, my mother just walked in. I'll see you tomorrow." The words were spoken in an aggrieved tone that added to the mystery, but also brought a measure of relief. Nothing tragic was wrong.

"What's the matter?"

"I can't wait until I'm sixteen! That's what's the matter!" Stephanie blurted out resentfully, fresh tears spilling down her cheeks. "Mark Zachary asked me out, and I had to say no."

Rachel confirmed the obvious, asking, "You talked to him tonight?"

"Yes. He called me. Mom, if he asks me out on another date, can I *please* go? I'll just *die* if I can't." Stephanie sat up cross-legged as she pleaded, looking woefully young.

"No, darling, you can't go on a date with Mark Zachary." Rachel's refusal was gentle, but definite. "I hope you explained that to him."

"But *why* can't I? I'm very mature for my age."

"The fact remains that you're only fourteen. Have you finished your homework?"

Stephanie crossed her arms defiantly across her chest in response to the change of subject. "When have I ever *not* done my homework? When have I ever gotten into any trouble? Why don't you *trust* me?"

"Darling, I do trust you." It was Mark Zachary she didn't trust. "I also love you and want only what's best for you. Now why don't you change into your nightgown and get ready for bed while I proofread your paper?" Rachel started toward the bed, intending to sit down.

"I don't want you to proofread my paper. I'll get Candy to do it for me." Stephanie scooted off on the opposite side and flounced over to her closet, where she jerked her nightgown off a hook.

"Then may I read it out of interest? I always enjoy reading your compositions. You inherited your father's talent for language."

"I wish Daddy were alive," Stephanie said piteously, some of her rebelliousness crumbling. "I bet he would side with me." She trudged over to her desk, got the paper and brought it to Rachel, who put her arms around her daughter and hugged her.

"Darling, I'm so sorry you're unhappy. But you'll grow up soon enough, I promise. Enjoy being fourteen."

After a moment of stubborn resistance, Stephanie hugged her back, and the rift between mother and daughter was healed.

Lee stuck his head in the open doorway of Mark's bedroom and frowned at the sight of his son lying on his back on his bed, gazing morosely up at the ceiling.

"Hey, what's the matter?"

"Oh, nothing," came the dejected reply.

"Sure, something's the matter." Lee walked over and sat on the edge of the bed. "You look like you lost your best friend."

Mark rolled over on his side, propping his head on his hand. "I just got off the phone with Stephanie Cavanaugh. She turned me down when I asked her out this weekend."

Lee cursed, partly in sympathy and partly in anger. "Damn it, Son, I warned you not to waste your time with Stephanie Cavanaugh."

"I know you did, Dad. But I was so sure she liked me, too. When Carl and I ran into her and her girlfriend at the mall Saturday, Stephanie acted real friendly toward me, just like she had at the restaurant. She and her girlfriend went to the food court with us and sat down and had sodas. Tonight on the phone she seemed glad I'd called. I was expecting her to say yes."

"And then she lowered the boom," Lee said grimly, knowing exactly what his big, strapping son was feeling. "Did Stephanie explain to you that she's not allowed to date boys older than her?"

"No, she didn't give any reason." A frown of puzzlement creased Mark's brow. "Is that true? How could you know that, Dad?"

"It so happens I talked with Mrs. Cavanaugh today, and she told me herself."

"Stephanie didn't mention anything about needing to ask her mother's permission. She just put me off, saying she couldn't go out with me this weekend."

Like mother, like daughter. Stephanie couldn't resist stringing Mark along, knowing good and well that she couldn't date him. Rachel had done exactly the same thing to Lee.

"If you have anything more to do with her, I'll kick your butt."

"Don't worry, Dad. This time I'll listen to you."

"Good." Lee slapped him on the leg. "How about some warmed-over pizza?"

"Sure."

Father and son went out to the kitchen together and heated up the leftover pizza from their supper. It was painfully obvious to Lee that Mark was putting up a brave front for his benefit, but underneath the poor kid was still feeling down in the dumps.

This whole thing would blow over. Mark would snap back. Lee didn't have any worries on that score, but, damn, it galled him that he'd been helpless to prevent history from repeating itself.

The damage was done, but Lee was going to burst if he didn't have one more conversation with Rachel and get some things off his chest. Pride had held him back today, but to hell with pride.

"Want to watch a little TV?" he asked when he and Mark had finished their slices of pizza.

"No, I think I'll listen to some music in my room for a while and then go to bed. I'm okay, Dad. Honest."

Lee put his arm around his son's shoulders, which were almost as broad as his own, and gave him a rough, fatherly hug. "Don't try to fool your old man. He's been there."

"Pretty funny, huh? You fell for Stephanie's mom a long time ago and now I fall for Stephanie."

"Pretty funny, all right."

"See you in the morning, Dad."

"Good night, Son."

Lee went into the living room, flipped on the TV and tuned in a cable news channel, but he couldn't concentrate. Inside he was fuming. To hell with it, he decided. He would call Rachel right now at home.

Her business card was in his wallet. Lee extracted it and read the home phone number printed on it.

Rachel answered on the second ring. "Hello."

"Lee Zachary here," he said, identifying himself grimly.

There was a startled pause. Then she echoed his name in a soft, surprised voice that did things to him. "Lee."

"This is a personal matter, not business."

"A personal matter?"

"Yes, regarding my son and your daughter." Lee was furious with himself by this time for responding with male pleasure to her presence on the phone. He was a good one to give Mark advice.

"Oh. He told you that he'd asked Stephanie for a date, I suppose, and you aren't any more pleased than I was."

"'Not pleased' doesn't express my feelings strongly enough. It's a bitter pill to swallow for my son to be duped just like I was by a replica of you."

"Stephanie's not a replica of me," Rachel denied. "She's her own person and a lot more strong willed than I was. If it's any consolation, Mark's asking her out caused quite an emotional storm here at our house tonight. I hope he doesn't persist in showing her attention."

"He won't, but that's no thanks to Stephanie."

"What do you mean?"

"I mean she didn't cut him loose. He didn't have a clue about why she'd turned him down. It's pretty damned heartless, even for a fourteen-year-old, to keep a guy dangling."

"Are you certain of your facts, Lee?" Rachel questioned stiffly. "I got a different story from Stephanie, who was heartbroken because she'd had to discourage Mark's interest in her. She's certainly no more at fault than he is. After all, he's old enough to realize that she's too young for him."

"Mark's the same age I was," Lee stated angrily.

"And I was Stephanie's age. You were too old for me. My parents were wise not to let us date, and I think I'm being equally wise to follow their example." Her tone of voice revealed that she was threatening to lose her temper.

"There was more than a difference in age involved. Your parents didn't think I was good enough for their daughter."

"My parents weren't snobs," she exclaimed heatedly. "Lee, you were sexually active by the age of seventeen! Admit it! You'd dated girls by then who'd let you sleep with them. I couldn't have handled you."

"Sure, I'd had sex with girls by the time I was fifteen. But I didn't have any thought whatsoever of getting you in the back seat of my old car. I knew you were innocent."

"Inexperienced, yes, but I had hormones raging. So does Stephanie now."

Lee had momentarily forgotten about Mark and Stephanie. It took a second for him to switch gears. "She could wind Mark around her little finger and keep him in line, just like you could have done with me back then." And could still do. The realization filled him with self-disgust. "But that's neither here nor there. It just rubbed me raw for my son to follow in my footsteps and let your daughter shoot him down. For some reason, I thought saying that to you would help, but it hasn't," he admitted harshly.

"Stephanie's not a Lolita, and for that matter, neither was I," Rachel protested indignantly. "She's attracted to Mark, the same as I was attracted to you. It's a major tragedy in her life that she isn't allowed to date him, but she'll soon get over it and so will Mark. We did."

"You might have gotten over it soon after it happened, but I didn't," Lee said. Hell, it must be pretty obvious to her that he hadn't ever gotten over it completely. "But you're right on one count. Mark will be fine. Now that I've spilled my guts, I'll hang up."

"Wait..."

Lee waited.

"I wouldn't have had this happen for anything. I'm truly sorry that Mark had to experience rejection in connection with my daughter. I hope you believe that."

"Whether I do or not doesn't really matter, does it?"

"It does to me. That was what I wanted to say," she added.

"Then I guess our conversation's over. Good night, Rachel." He hung up, cursing himself bitterly for being every kind of a fool. He was a fine one to give his son advice about girls. He had seized on the excuse to talk to Rachel again because any excuse was better than none.

Rachel had just stripped down to her bra and panties when the phone had rung, and the caller had turned out to be Lee. During the entire conversation she'd felt a ridiculous self-consciousness as she perched on the side of her bed, as though talking to him in her state of undress were inappropriate.

After he'd hung up, she sucked in a deep breath and held the phone to her ear for a few seconds, listening to the electronic buzz and combating a sense of letdown that had nothing to do with Stephanie and Mark.

In the past four days, she'd spoken to Lee three times face-to-face and now once on the telephone, and every time she'd been left feeling as though she'd survived an ordeal. It was such a struggle for her to hold on to her identity as Rachel Preston Cavanaugh, mother and real-estate professional being the main components.

Lee brought out adolescent urges and responses that were unacceptable. Her heart had leapt at his words, *This is a personal matter, not business*. To her utter shame, she hadn't instantly put two and two together and comprehended that the personal matter had to do with Mark's phoning Stephanie earlier. Her first thought had been that Lee might be leading up to asking *her* for a date.

If he had, she would have had no choice except to turn him down. This *wasn't* and couldn't be the second time around for her and Lee.

The grown-up Rachel Preston wasn't ever getting emotionally and physically involved with a man again.

The next morning at breakfast, Stephanie didn't bring up Mark Zachary's name. Neither did Rachel, who had pondered about whether she should press her daughter to confirm that she had indeed told Mark exactly why she couldn't date him. According to Lee, she hadn't, but then it was altogether possible that Mark hadn't confided fully in his dad.

Aside from harmless fibs, Stephanie hadn't ever lied to her. It might seem that Rachel doubted her honesty if she questioned her. Better to let the whole matter die down.

"Bye, Mom." Stephanie hurriedly gathered up her books when a horn tooted outside.

"Bye, love." Rachel offered her cheek for her daughter's goodbye kiss and got in a quick, affectionate hug before Stephanie dashed out to catch her ride to school. Today Candy's mom was playing chauffeur.

Rachel made quick work of clearing the table. Then she gathered up her briefcase and handbag and left the house, too, with no premonition whatever that a major disaster might be brewing.

"Excuse us."

"You're blocking the sinks. Why don't you have a little consideration?"

Heather Smith and Megan Trent rudely elbowed their way through the knot of Stephanie Cavanaugh's friends surrounding her in the girls' bathroom. Sharing a mirror, the two girls took their time combing their hair and applying lipstick while they eavesdropped on the conversation punctuated with squeals of excitement.

"I can't *believe* Mark Zachary really asked you out!"

"Tell us every word, Stephanie! What he said and what you said!"

Heather met Megan's eyes and said loudly, "I think I'm going to be sick to my stomach."

"Me, too. Let's get out of here."

Candy Wakefield spared them a scornful glance. "You're both just green with jealousy."

Outside Megan muttered, "I can't *stand* her. I'd like to slap her face."

"Her head will really be swelled now. What do boys see in her?" Heather muttered back.

Seething with their dislike of Stephanie Cavanaugh, they headed down the corridor toward their next class. Both of them were relatively attractive girls. Heather had brown hair and brown eyes and was only a few pounds overweight. Megan's hair was a lighter shade of brown, and she had blue eyes and a trim figure. Each of them got a reasonable share of attention from boys—except when Stephanie entered the scene. Then it seemed that every boy's eyes were glued on her.

All day Heather and Megan were forced to put up with the hubbub over Stephanie's being asked out on a date by a senior. That afternoon when they were picked up at school by their mothers, who were longtime best friends and had been shopping together, the girls climbed into the car in a sour mood. When questioned, they erupted with catty comments about their hated classmate, Stephanie Cavanaugh.

Rita Smith, Heather's mother, was driving. "Sound familiar?" she asked Kay Trent dryly.

Kay grimaced. "Very familiar. But Rachel got hers when she landed Blaine Cavanaugh."

"Did she *ever*. Even I had to feel a little sorry for her."

"Liar," Kay accused, and Rita laughed.

In the back seat Heather and Megan were all ears. Sensing that they might learn something scandalous, they stayed absolutely quiet.

"Do you suppose the rumor was really true that he was buck naked when his receptionist's boyfriend burst into his law office and shot him dead?" Kay mused.

"Cliff's uncle was on the police force at the time." Cliff was Rita's husband and Heather's father. "He told his wife—and, of course, Aunt Mary wasn't supposed to breathe a word—that they suspected strongly Blaine had been partially undressed and someone had put the rest of his clothes back on him after he was dead. The police figured he'd probably been caught in the act with that cute, sexy young receptionist of his."

"I remember your telling me that. Everybody else figured the same thing—that he'd gotten his just desserts."

Rita nodded. "Where there's smoke there's usually fire, and he had the reputation of liking women."

"And it stood to reason that the receptionist's boyfriend wouldn't have gotten off with manslaughter if Blaine had really been innocent." Kay looked over her shoulder, suddenly mindful that they had an audience. "You girls are awfully quiet back there."

"Don't either of you repeat any of that," Rita admonished, glancing into the rearview mirror.

"We won't," Heather and Megan chorused together, their eyes meeting gleefully.

Since grade school they'd yearned for ammunition to hurt Stephanie Cavanaugh. Now, finally, they had it.

In whispers, they rehashed the shocking information and relished spreading it all over school. "I'll call Monica and Christie and Anna," Heather said, formulating her list.

"I'll call Jennifer and Darleen and Karla."

None of the classmates mentioned was a member of Stephanie's inner circle, but by tomorrow at noon her

friends would have gotten wind of the scandalous story that
was circulating and would report it to her. Let Little Miss
Popularity see how she liked this kind of attention. For the
first time ever, Heather and Megan were looking forward to
seeing Stephanie occupy center stage.

The following afternoon Rachel was about to leave the
office to pick up Stephanie and Candy and drop them off at
the mall when the phone rang. She was instantly alarmed
when she answered and her daughter's best friend identified herself in a tearful voice.

"Mrs. Cavanaugh, this is Candy Wakefield."

"Candy. Is Stephanie all right?"

"She's real upset and crying. Could you come home right
away, Mrs. Cavanaugh? We're here at your house."

"At our house? You're not at school?"

"No, ma'am. We left school before sixth period. Stephanie was too upset to go to class. But she'll tell you about it
herself."

"I'll be right there."

Rachel was still very concerned, but her worst anxiety had
been eased. Stephanie hadn't suffered any physical injury
and wasn't at the hospital. Something had obviously happened at school, something that she hoped wasn't all that
serious. What could be minor to an adult could take on
major importance to a teenager.

She expected to find the two girls in her daughter's bedroom, and, sure enough, they were huddled together there,
sitting on the bed. Candy's arm was around Stephanie's
shoulders, and Stephanie was clutching to her breast the
framed photograph of her father that she kept on her
dresser.

"It's all lies about your dad," Candy was saying in a tone
that indicated she'd been repeating the same assurances over
and over. "Your mom will probably bring a lawsuit for
slander."

An icy hand closed around Rachel's heart.

"Mom..." At the sight of her mother, Stephanie began to sob, tears welling in eyes that were already swollen from crying.

"Oh, darling, don't cry...." Rachel went quickly to sit beside her and gather her into her arms. "I'll take over, Candy. Why don't you go on home, dear?"

"Yes, ma'am. I'll call Stephanie later." With a compassionate look at her wounded friend, Candy left.

"Oh, Mom, they're saying the most awful things about Daddy." Between sobs, Stephanie blurted out the sordid story about her father's death that was all over school.

Rachel embraced her tighter, a terrible anger at Blaine mixed in with her pain for her vulnerable child. The hard edge of the frame protecting his photograph cut into Rachel's breast.

What he'd done to her was unforgivable. Now Stephanie was subjected to shame because of his weak character.

"Now, now, darling, please don't cry," she crooned. "You'll just have to hold your head high, like your mommy had to do years ago. That same story was making the rounds when I buried your father. People are very suspicious and cruel, but gossip can't hurt you if you don't let it." It was the same comforting wisdom Rachel's own mother had uttered to her.

Stephanie had grown very still. Now she raised her head and gazed at Rachel's face. "Mom, it's all lies. Daddy wouldn't do anything like that."

Her daughter wanted her to say, *No, of course, he wouldn't,* but Rachel couldn't speak those words honestly or convincingly. The best she could do was not say, *Yes, he would and did.* "Your daddy loved you very much. It's right that you should be loyal to his memory."

"He loved you, too. He was always hugging and kissing you."

"Yes, he was, darling."

Stephanie was shaking her head. She pulled away from Rachel, hugging the photograph protectively. "No, it's *not* true. It's *not* true!" she repeated shrilly. "I'll stand up for Daddy even if you won't!"

"Put the whole ugly thing out of your mind, darling. The gossip will soon die down. Gossip always does." Rachel lovingly smoothed her daughter's tumbled, silken blond hair.

Stephanie jerked her head away. "I want to spend the night at Candy's," she said in a choked voice. "She believes in Daddy, too, and she didn't even know him."

Rachel couldn't really defend herself, not without incriminating Blaine. "Please don't be angry with me. Wash your face and you'll feel better. We'll go out to a restaurant for supper."

"I'll have supper at Candy's house. Her mom is a good cook. She doesn't work at a job all the time." Stephanie spoke the deliberately hurtful words as she went over to her closet.

"Mrs. Wakefield doesn't have to support herself and her children," Rachel pointed out quietly. "Mr. Wakefield earns a good income."

"If he died and people said horrible things about him, I'll bet she would sue them."

Rachel sighed, watching as her daughter assembled clothes. At least she was composed and not in hysterics. Stephanie hadn't asked for or gotten permission to spend the night at her girlfriend's house, but under the circumstances, Rachel thought it better to overlook the atypical, defiant behavior.

"I wish you wouldn't go to Candy's tonight," she said. "I wish you'd stay home with me."

"You can make telephone calls to clients and work on real estate," Stephanie snapped, taking down her overnight case. "You won't miss me."

"That's not true and you know it."

"All I know is that I wish my daddy hadn't died," came he broken, reproachful reply.

The overnight stay with Candy was arranged, and Rachel dropped Stephanie off. Her emotions raw, she returned home. It hurt unbearably to have her daughter turn on her, even though she understood that Stephanie was in a state of denial and needed someone to blame.

The guilty person was Blaine, who'd let them both down with his infidelity. That thought like an abscess in her mind, Rachel went into the family room and took down the wedding portrait. Her hands trembling, she removed the photograph from the frame and tore her likeness from his. Then she wept bitter, angry tears of catharsis.

Thursday afternoon Lee picked up Mark at school to take him to L.J.'s Body Shop to get his car, which was good as new now. "How'd it go today?" he asked. "Aced that algebra test?"

"Was there ever any doubt?" Mark shot back with a cocky grin. "Say, Dad, did you know Stephanie's father?"

Both the question and the casual mention of Stephanie Cavanaugh took Lee by surprise. His son hadn't mentioned her since Monday night, when he'd been so down in the dumps. Nor had he seemed to be moping about her or about anything.

"No, I never met him. He was from northern Mississippi." That bit of information Lee had probably gleaned from the newspaper account of either Rachel's engagement or marriage. He'd read both. "Why do you ask?"

"Well, there's this story going around about how he was fooling about with his secretary, and her boyfriend caught them doing it and shot him. I wondered if it was true."

"You heard this story at school?"

"Yeah, from some guys on the golf team who knew I kinda liked her. Was Mr. Cavanaugh shot?"

"Yes, he was shot, and the man who shot him was the boyfriend of a woman who worked in Cavanaugh's law office. The rest is speculation. Whatever took place, it all happened nine years ago. You'd think people would let it lie and let him rest in peace," Lee said, shaking his head disgustedly.

"Poor Stephanie. I feel sorry for her. It's got to be rough having your dad's name smeared like that."

"Very rough." Lee's sympathy wasn't just for Stephanie. He was thinking about Rachel. She'd already been through the gossip mill.

They arrived at the body shop, and he tried to put the matter out of his mind, but it nagged at him off and on until he went to bed that night. Then the next morning Jim Hagen, the broker who'd shortened Rachel's visit on Monday, came calling again at the Plantation Village site. The man brought up Rachel's name and alluded to the fresh outbreak of gossip about Blaine Cavanaugh's death, which had obviously spread to the real-estate community.

Lee cut him short and sent him packing. Still steaming, Lee got into his car and headed for Magnolia Realty.

She was there and so were her partners, he gathered. The same dark blue and dove gray sedans were parked in front of the agency, along with her car.

"Hello, Mr. Zachary," the secretary said, greeting him when he entered.

"I'm here to see Mrs. Cavanaugh," he explained briefly and continued on through the outer room to Rachel's office.

As on his previous visit, she was seated behind her desk and in the midst of a phone conversation, but she glanced toward the door and saw him immediately. Lee looked closely at her face and saw evidence of strain and worry.

"Hold on, please, Mr. Connors," she said, and covered the mouthpiece to greet him. "Hello, Lee. I'll be with you in just a minute."

"Take your time." He was aware that she probably meant for him to wait outside in the reception room, but instead he entered and closed the door. While she was concluding her conversation, he sat in the chair nearest her, looking at her and listening to her voice and facing up to some truths. He was going to keep finding reasons to see her, talk to her, maintain contact with her. Either he'd fallen for her again or else he'd never gotten her out of his system.

"I'm sorry," Rachel said, hanging up the phone. She glanced at the closed door and sighed wearily. "I hope this isn't about Mark and Stephanie. Quite frankly, I have more pressing problems."

He shook his head. "That subject is closed. I came to tell you that tongues are wagging about your husband's death. Mark heard about it at school, and it's being passed around by your real-estate colleagues, too. I thought you needed to know."

"Oh, God . . ." Rachel buried her face in her hands.

Lee clenched his fists and glanced away, the sight of her distress making him feel helpless and angry. "Is there any truth to the gossip?" he demanded harshly.

"Yes," she confirmed with bitterness and shame. "That's the worst part."

"Cavanaugh fooled around on you?" Lee's incredulity quickly turned to fury on her behalf. "Why, the dirty bastard! So he really did deserve to be shot."

Rachel dropped her hands, but didn't look at him. "His receptionist called me that day, in hysterics. It was noon. I rushed to Blaine's office. He was dead of a bullet wound through his back. Fortunately, he'd kept his shirt on while he made love to her. She helped me dress him before she put on the rest of her clothes." A shudder of revulsion went through her.

Lee cursed Blaine Cavanaugh savagely. It required all his control not to get up and go to her and offer comfort.

"I don't know why I'm telling you all this," she said. "Except that some part of me wishes I could shout it from the rooftops. I hated having to live a lie and pretend to believe my husband was faithful to me. But for Stephanie's sake, I had no choice." Her composure crumbled at the mention of her daughter. "Forgive me," she said thickly. "I appreciate your coming here."

"How is Stephanie holding up?" Lee asked gruffly.

"She's very unhappy and is taking her feelings out on me. She idolized her father and wants to cling to her belief in him."

"You didn't refute the gossip."

"No, and she's having trouble forgiving me. It's very hard, because we've always been extremely close. If her grandparents were here, I could count on their support. But they're off traveling around the country." Rachel drew in a deep breath, squaring her shoulders. "I didn't mean to burden you with my personal problems. How is the progress on Plantation Village coming along?"

"It's coming along well." Lee shifted in his chair. "Are your partners here?"

"Yes, they're both here."

"Well, why don't I meet them?"

Rachel gazed at him uncertainly. "They would be delighted to meet you. Lee, you're not doing another about-face, are you?"

"What if I am?"

"I wasn't working on your sympathy."

"It's your call. Are you or aren't you still interested in being my Realtor?"

"Of course I'm still interested."

He shrugged. "Then let's get on with it. I don't have all day."

"Excuse me. I'll invite Mary Lynn and Alice to come in and join us." She rose from her chair and left the room, returning in minutes with two women in tow that Lee vaguely recognized from the picture accompanying the newspaper article about Magnolia Realty.

He sized them up while the introductions were being made. At the same time, they were sizing him up. Unless Rachel had cued them in, they both knew from their initial impressions to cut the small talk. Surprisingly, Alice Kirkland, a short, plump, grandmotherly type, took the lead.

"Mr. Zachary, I was excited about Plantation Village when I first heard about it. It sounds perfect for me. I'm rattling around in a big house that's much too large and expensive to keep up. What could I expect to pay in a monthly fee?"

She asked him questions from the standpoint of a retirement-age person, cleverly reinforcing that she was in that age group herself and could relate to their interests and needs. Then she suggested, "If I were you, in planning your advertising, I wouldn't leave out those senior citizens like myself who aren't in any hurry to retire. Plantation Village will be very attractive to them, offering convenience and security and social opportunities."

Mary Lynn Porter, a thin, redheaded woman bristling with nervous energy, jumped in next and quoted statistics about the popularity of the Mississippi Gulf Coast as a retirement spot, showing that she'd done her homework.

Ideas flew fast, and at the end of thirty minutes of give-and-take, Lee was sold. His only qualm arose from knowing what fierce pleasure he took in seeing the animation return to Rachel's blue eyes, the pink color return to her cheeks. She'd participated, while saying the least. Yet there wasn't any doubt that she carried the most weight with him.

Lee was fully aware that he *should* designate one of the other two as his liaison person, but he wouldn't. He was going with Magnolia Realty for the wrong reasons as well as the right ones.

Chapter Four

Lee stood, and Rachel reacted with that involuntary little tightening in her midriff that was a female response to his masculinity.

"Let's get a Magnolia Realty sign up on the building site right away," he said.

His words sank in, and jubilant smiles broke out on her partners' faces and on her own, too. She took her turn at shaking Lee's hand and tried to ignore her pleasure in feeling her fingers engulfed in his big, strong ones.

Before her skin had stopped tingling, Alice and Mary Lynn departed, apparently under the assumption that she would take matters from there.

"You seem to have struck a chord with Alice," she said, feeling him out. "It wouldn't insult me if you wanted to put her in charge."

"I don't," he replied in his blunt way.

"Very well."

"Tomorrow night I'm having dinner with Livingston, my architect, and Beatty, my general contractor, and their wives. Can you join us?" He added, giving her an out, "I realize it's short notice."

"I don't have plans." Rachel sighed, remembering the scene at breakfast that morning, when she'd broached weekend plans with her daughter and been given the cold shoulder. "Under normal circumstances, I might have to refuse because I was doing something with Stephanie. What time and which restaurant?"

"I'll pick you up at your house at seven-fifteen."

"It isn't necessary for you to pick me up," she protested weakly in surprise. She'd assumed she would drive her own car.

"Do you object?"

"No, I don't object."

Her honest admission obviously settled the issue for him. He turned to go.

"Lee," Rachel said hesitantly, stopping him. "Saturday night isn't a date. I wouldn't have agreed if you hadn't been proposing a combination business and social dinner. As I told you, I don't date."

"If it were a date, there sure as hell wouldn't be four other people there," he replied flatly. "Let's get something straight, Rachel. I won't be asking you out. This time around, you'd have to do the asking."

Not giving her an opportunity to answer, he strode out of her office, leaving her feeling foolish and sorry that she'd offended him. She'd just needed to set parameters, mainly because the idea of going out on a date with him was anything but distasteful to her.

Thanks to his candor, she now knew she didn't need to worry about keeping up her defenses and being prepared to have to turn him down. Rachel should have been relieved, but relief wasn't among her emotions.

She had no time to sort out those emotions because her two partners came back into her office, and the mood was one of elation. To celebrate, the three of them went out to lunch at an elegant restaurant and took Cindy along, locking up the office and leaving the answering machine to record messages.

Several times during lunch and throughout the rest of the day, Rachel thought about Stephanie. It was normal for her daughter to come to mind often and for Rachel to mention her in the course of conversation, but it wasn't normal to feel this aching little sense of worry that now accompanied any thought of her. Sadly, Rachel felt little eagerness about going home and divulging the exciting events of the day to the now-hostile fourteen-year-old. She dreaded Mark Zachary's name coming up, as was inevitable with the announcement that his father was a client.

Apparently as a kind of punishment, Stephanie was making a point of excluding her mother from her daily routine. Rachel wasn't being allowed to play chauffeur, for example, as she was used to doing gladly and without complaint. Stephanie arranged for rides with her friends' mothers. Also, she confined herself to her room in the afternoons and evenings, depriving Rachel of her company and depriving herself of watching TV. There'd never been any need for her to have her own set, since the one in the family room was at her disposal.

Rachel had decided to be patient and loving while she and her daughter worked through this temporary rupture in their formerly close relationship. At least Stephanie, while antagonistic, wasn't rebelling against Rachel's parental authority, which she'd always exercised gently.

Time and patience and love would restore the closeness and trust, Rachel firmly believed.

She took it as a good sign when she arrived home and found Stephanie watching TV. "Hi, darling," she greeted her, acting as though nothing were out of the ordinary.

"Hi."

"How was school?"

Stephanie answered with a shrug. She turned up the volume slightly.

"I have the most wonderful news to tell you." Rachel sat down on the opposite end of the sofa. "Mrs. Porter and Mrs. Kirkland and I are beside ourselves with excitement. Magnolia Realty has landed a huge listing."

"That's nice," Stephanie said without interest, keeping her gaze directed toward the TV.

Rachel continued, pretending not to notice the cool response. "I'm sure you remember my telling you that Mr. Lee Zachary, Mark Zachary's father, is a big developer. I went by their table last Friday night when we were leaving the restaurant to give him my business card," she reminded her, leading up to her good news.

The mention of Mark had elicited Stephanie's full attention. She looked squarely at her mother, resentment shimmering in blue eyes that were carbon copies of Rachel's. "You made me wait for you," she recalled with an accusing note. "You wouldn't let me go with you to talk with Mark while you talked to his father."

"Anyway, since then I've met with Mr. Zachary and toured the building site of his residential development for retirement-age people. It's located between Gulfport and Long Beach and is called Plantation Village. Today he visited our office and has decided to choose us as his exclusive Realtors. I thought that you and I would go out for supper tonight and celebrate. You can pick out any restaurant."

Stephanie lifted one slim shoulder to express her indifference. "It really doesn't matter to me." She gazed again at the TV.

Rachel sighed, disheartened in spite of herself. "While I'm thinking about it, I'd like for you to arrange to spend the night with Candy tomorrow."

"Why?"

"I have a business dinner with Mr. Zachary, his architect and contractor and their wives."

"I can stay here by myself. I'm fourteen years old."

"You probably would be perfectly safe," Rachel agreed. "But I would feel better if you weren't at home alone." As soon as the words were out, she knew she'd pressed the wrong button.

Stephanie's chin rose a stubborn notch. "I'd rather stay here by myself. I get sick of being treated like a baby. We have a burglar alarm, and I'm certainly capable of dialing 911."

"Why don't you think about it and decide?" Rachel suggested diplomatically. "It might be pretty boring and lonely without company. Instead of your staying overnight with Candy, maybe she could come and spend the night with you. You could rent a couple of videos and make some popcorn."

"How late will you be out?"

"Not late. Mr. Zachary is picking me up at seven-fifteen. I would expect to be home by ten-thirty or eleven, at the latest."

Stephanie's head jerked around. "He's picking you up? I thought you said it was a business dinner. It isn't, though, is it? You're going out on a date with him." Her accusing glance went to the spot on the wall where the wedding portrait of Rachel and Blaine had hung. So far there hadn't been any discussion of the fact that it was missing.

"There wouldn't be anything wrong with my going out on a date with Mr. Zachary, but I would have told you the truth, if that were the case. I've never lied to you, Stephanie." Rachel added gently, "That's why you're so angry at me, darling—because I couldn't lie to you and exonerate your father, as you wanted me to do."

"I'll *never* believe bad things about Daddy as long as I live. If you'd really loved him and been a good wife to him, you wouldn't believe them, either. And it's unfair that you can go out with Mark's father and yet I can't go out with Mark. I *hate* you!'' Bursting into tears, Stephanie tossed the TV remote-control device onto the carpet and ran from the room. Even though Rachel knew she didn't truly mean those words, hearing them from her lips hurt unbearably. With her heart aching for both of them, Rachel followed after her and found her bedroom door closed and locked.

"May I please come in?'' she asked.

"Go away,'' was the muffled answer.

"You're the one who's being unfair, darling, by blaming me because your father let you down. His death wasn't my fault.''

"Daddy *didn't* let me down. He loved me.''

"Yes, he did. And so do I, very much.''

There was no answer, but there was no hostile denial, either. "Wash your face and comb your hair,'' Rachel instructed through the door panel with gentle matter-of-factness. "I'm going to freshen up, and then we'll go out to eat.''

"I'm not very hungry.'' The claim was sullen, yet reassuringly composed.

"Well, would you rather just stay home and have the two of us fix ourselves a light supper?''

"No, I'd rather go out.''

"Then that's what we'll do.''

Stephanie was ready when Rachel emerged from her bedroom. "Your new blouse looks nice,'' she said, reaching to adjust the collar.

"Don't.'' Her daughter shrank back from her touch, and Rachel dropped her hand. "I'm not a little girl. You don't have to straighten my clothes.''

"You'll always be my little girl, no matter how old you are.''

The rebuff hurt, but Rachel was thankful that they were at least back on the same strained footing as they'd been before Stephanie's emotional outburst. "Where to?'' she asked in the car, and her daughter named her choice of restaurant in a sulky tone.

Once there, Stephanie ordered a full-course meal and ate with her normal appetite, while Rachel consumed a salad. Her attempts at cheerful conversation met with no cooperation, but she didn't lose patience or hope. With love and understanding, she would eventually get through the barrier Stephanie had erected between them, and afterward they would be closer than ever before.

"Would you like to go by the video store and rent a movie?" she inquired on their way home.

"Everything new that's out has already been rented by now. I don't see why we can't subscribe to the movie channels, like most people do."

"Because a great majority of the movies are R-rated for violence and sex and bad language. You wouldn't be able to watch them anyway."

"It's not as though I haven't heard all the bad words. And I know about sex. If there was a lot of blood, I would just close my eyes." Stephanie's argument was delivered in an aggrieved voice.

"Darling, there will be plenty of R-rated movies for you to see when you're a few years older and not so impressionable."

"I can't wait until I *am* older and can finally have some fun."

Rachel smothered a sigh and let the conversation die.

Self-pity and resentment welled up in Stephanie when Rachel drove the rest of the way home without offering again to detour by the video store. Stephanie hadn't said, *No, I don't want to rent a movie.* Her mother should have asked a second time and given her a chance to say yes. There probably wasn't anything worth watching on TV.

At their house, Stephanie wrenched open the car door and stalked inside. Thoroughly miserable, she debated about whether to go to her room or into the family room. Neither place was a haven anymore. In her bedroom her daddy smiled at her from his photograph, and she wanted to break down and cry when she looked at him. She wanted to ask him in her heart, *Was it true, Daddy?* Her doubt made her feel horribly disloyal.

When she fled to the family room, there was that gaping spot on the wall where the wedding portrait of her parents had always hung. Her mother had obviously taken it down. Stephanie couldn't bear to think about what that meant—that her parents hadn't loved each other and hadn't been happy, as they'd seemed.

Nothing was the same anymore in Stephanie's world. Nothing was right or safe, and she couldn't turn to her mother because she should have prevented all this from happening.

"Have you checked the TV listing? Is anything good on?" The gentle, patient inquiry roused the longing for everything to be the same, as it never could again.

"Yes, I've checked it, and, no, there's nothing good on. We should have rented a movie." Stephanie stormed off to her room, closed the door and locked it.

Huddled on her bed, she waited for her mother's light tap on the door. When it didn't come, she felt terribly betrayed and wept defiant, anguished tears. "I'll *show* her," she whispered. "I'll make her sorry."

Mark whistled. "Boy, you're dressed up, Dad. A tie?"

"I wear a tie every now and then," Lee replied.

"Usually when you're going to some shindig with bankers, though. Are you trying to impress Mrs. Cavanaugh? She's a pretty lady."

His son's teasing had hit the nail on the head. Lee tugged at the knot of his tie and muttered, "Damned thing's choking me."

"You look sharp. Have a good time."

"The purpose of tonight isn't to have a good time. This is a business dinner. Do you have a date?"

Mark shook his head. "Nah. Carl and I talked about seeing a movie."

Lee frowned. "Why don't you have a date on a Saturday night?"

"I just don't. No special reason. Don't worry about me, Dad." Mark slapped Lee on the back. "Say, this is kinda weird, huh? I ask Stephanie Cavanaugh out on a date this weekend, and you end up having dinner with her mom. Put in a good word for me. Maybe she'll bend her rules and let Stephanie and me go out."

"My conversation with Mrs. Cavanaugh will be about Plantation Village. What I told you about her before still applies, Mark. The fact that you're my son doesn't win you any points with her."

"So why did you pick her to be your real-estate broker?"

"Because her agency can do a good job for me." It was the truth, but not the whole truth. "I've got to go. You be careful."

"You, too, Dad."

I'll try, Lee said to himself.

Fifteen minutes later, he pulled into the driveway of Rachel's house in a quiet, ultrarespectable residential area of Gulfport. The neat, one-story brick ranch sat on a nice-size lot with large shade trees and an abundance of azalea shrubs. Lee gazed at the house, realizing that it was probably the home she'd shared with Cavanaugh, the one that had been paid off at his death with the mortgage insurance.

There'd been a time in Lee's life when he'd longed to live in a neighborhood like this one. He and his mother and siblings had lived in a rental house with peeling paint and a bare yard. A vision of it flashed clearly into his mind now, bringing a grim sensation that made him set his jaw hard. Neither Rachel nor her parents had comprehended that it had taken a lot of courage for him, a kid from the wrong side of the tracks, to ask her out. His toughness and brashness had been a cover-up for his inferiority complex.

Since then Lee had come a long way, but for all his success and his cynicism, he felt a little like the seventeen-year-old he'd once been as he got out of his car and strode to the front door, where he punched the lighted doorbell button with his forefinger.

During the half minute before Rachel opened the door, he reminded himself that he wouldn't be taking her to dinner if he weren't a big client. However, the reminder didn't help much when she stood framed in the doorway, a knockout in her off-white dinner suit and pale pink blouse.

"Ready?" he asked gruffly, knowing that his eyes were paying her flowery compliments.

"Hello, Lee. You're right on time." She sounded slightly flustered. "I gather this is a fancy restaurant we're going to."

"You mean the jacket and tie. I can tell you're relieved that I look presentable."

"*Impressed* is more the word," she replied. "You certainly look like a successful businessman tonight. Excuse me just a few seconds, while I say good-night to Stephanie." Swinging the door wide so that he could step into the foyer, she vanished briefly. When she returned, she gave him a strained smile.

Lee waited until they were outside and walking to the car to inquire, "Things aren't any better with Stephanie?"

"No, but they aren't any worse, either. I'm trying to give her as much leeway as possible. For example, I'm going along with her decision to stay home by herself tonight."

"It looks like a very safe neighborhood."

"It is, and we have a burglar alarm, which my father insisted upon when he and my mother were taking off on their travels. As an added precaution, I even spoke to our neighbors this afternoon and asked them to keep an eye out for anything suspicious. I'm not worried about her safety. And I expect she'll get lonely and decide to go to her friend's house, or have Candy come over."

"Why is she staying home alone? Out of spite?" Lee's tone wasn't very sympathetic.

Rachel sighed. "Yes, she's punishing me."

They'd reached the car. She put out her hand to open her door herself.

"Let me," Lee said brusquely. "I do have some manners."

"I'm sorry," she said in embarrassment. "I don't expect men to open the door for me anymore."

Lee let his silence say *garbage*. She didn't expect male courtesy from him.

He could have told her that she'd brought out the urge to treat her like a princess when he was a callow teenager, and she still did.

At the sound of the front door closing, Stephanie jumped up from the sofa in the family room and ran quickly to the window overlooking the street. Peering out, she watched Mark's father escorting her mother to his car, where he opened the door for her.

"She's going on a date with him," she murmured aloud. "It isn't really a business dinner or she would drive herself."

When the car was out of sight, Stephanie turned slowly away from the window. Her gaze was drawn to the empty spot on the wall, and her sense of being wronged by her mother was compounded.

Tonight Stephanie could be going to a movie with Mark and having fun. Instead she was sitting home by herself, while her mother was out with his dad, enjoying herself. That wasn't at all fair.

The phone rang, and Stephanie ignored the first two rings. The call would be for her mother, not her, and probably about real estate—unless Grandma and Grandpa Preston were calling. The thought sent Stephanie quickly to the phone.

"Hello."

After a slight pause, a young male voice—Mark Zachary's—came over the line. "Could I speak to Mrs. Cavanaugh?"

"Mark?" Stephanie blurted.

"Yeah. Is this Stephanie? I was trying to get a message to my dad. Has he gotten there yet?"

"He just left."

"Oh, well. I'll try his car phone again. I tried it a few minutes ago, and he didn't answer."

"Sounds like it must be something real important," Stephanie ventured, purely for something to say.

"Probably not that important. On second thought, I'll just leave Dad a note. He probably doesn't want to be bothered tonight."

"It's nice to talk to you, anyway."

"Yeah," he said noncommittally.

"I haven't been going to the mall lately."

"Me, either." He added hesitantly, gruff sympathy in his voice, "You doin' okay, Stephanie?"

A huge lump formed in her throat. He'd heard the ugly story about her father and felt sorry for her. "What you heard isn't true, Mark. My dad wasn't like that."

"It's got to hurt for people to say things about him, though. I can imagine how I'd feel in your place."

"It hurts ter-*terribly*." Stephanie's voice broke, and she began to sob, her emotions rising up and engulfing her.

"Hey, don't cry," Mark pleaded.

"I'm just so unhappy, and I hate my mother. I'll probably run away from home before it's all over."

"You don't want to do anything crazy."

Even in her misery, Stephanie registered the hint of alarm mixed with his concern. "I might just run away tonight. I'm here at home all by myself with nothing to do. I doubt any boy will ever want to date me now."

"That's not true." He added, "I'd still like to date you."

"You would?"

"Sure, I would. I'd like to take you out tonight, for that matter."

Stephanie's heart was pounding wildly as a rebellious plan took form. Why shouldn't she go out with him and have some fun? She'd been so miserable for days. What would be the harm in it? None, absolutely none. It was cruel of her mother to deprive her of dating Mark, while she herself dated his father.

"Then why don't you come over and pick me up in about thirty minutes, Mark? I can be ready by then."

"But won't your mother be mad?"

"She can get mad, for all I care."

He objected uneasily, "I don't know, Stephanie."

"You could be saving me from making a big mistake," she pointed out dramatically.

"Okay. Give me directions to your house."

"I'm slightly acquainted with James Livingston. He and Blaine were at Ole Miss together. And I've met Carl Beatty." Rachel got the conversation on track during the ride to the restaurant, but she wasn't able to block out the awareness of how handsome and manly Lee was in his dress slacks jacket and tie. Every time he looked at her, a little shivery sensation spread through her.

This wasn't a date, and yet she was reacting as though it were her first real date at age sixteen.

The restaurant turned out to be the Blue Rose in Pass Christian, another of the scenic little towns strung together by the ribbon of white sand beaches along the Mississippi Gulf Coast. Rachel loved the Blue Rose, which was situated on a bluff overlooking a quaint marina and the open waters of the gulf. The restaurant featured not only fine cuisine, but a very intimate and romantic atmosphere.

She wished the dinner had been arranged for elsewhere. Why not be honest with herself? She wished even more that the reservations could have been for two, not six.

Lee maneuvered the car into a parking spot along one side of the narrow street and got out and came around to open her door. Then he took her arm and escorted her up the walkway.

Inside they learned that they were the first of their party to arrive. Rachel's mixed feelings deepened when she was seated beside Lee at a round table on the small, glassed-in front porch. Candles had been lit on all the tables, making each one, with its own old-fashioned bouquet of cut flowers, a private oasis of elegance and charm. Through the windows, the splendid view of the gulf, stained by the vivid colors of the autumn sunset, was fading into darkness.

"I'll have ice tea to drink," she told Lee, and was embarrassed by the wistfulness in her voice.

"Wouldn't you like a glass of wine instead?" he asked.

"I'd love a glass of wine, but it relaxes me too much. I'd better stick to ice tea."

Lee glanced beyond her. "Here's Livingston and his wife, Janet." He rose and shook hands with the architect. By the time the couple had taken their places, Carl Beatty and his wife, Louise, arrived. Again Lee got to his feet. He was obviously the host. Their waiter deferred to him when he presented menus and inquired about before-dinner cocktails.

When the other two women both opted for a white wine the waiter recommended, Rachel weakened and had the same. It didn't surprise her—or disappoint her—when Lee ordered an imported beer.

After some initial get-acquainted talk, conversation during the excellent meal centered on Plantation Village, with the two wives participating. They both were obviously taking interest in the big project in which their husbands were involved. Rachel learned that Janet and Louise were making plans to come along on the trip to Pensacola in a few weeks, the trip to a retirement development Lee had mentioned the day he'd taken her to lunch. On the one hand, she welcomed the idea of the wives coming, since it would make for a less-awkward situation than her going on the trip with three men. The drawback was that she would be paired off with Lee, as she was tonight.

Never had a drawback seemed less like one. That was her real problem. Rachel didn't dare let herself fall into being a couple with him.

Lee paid the bill, and the six of them walked outside together, the September night enveloping them. A breeze blew off the Gulf, and overhead a luminous moon hung in the sky, which formed a velvety backdrop for a myriad brilliant stars.

"What a lovely night," Janet Livingston observed with a sigh. "If we weren't such old fogies we would go walk on the beach."

"And get our shoes full of sand," rejoined her architect husband dryly.

"Of course, I meant we'd slip off our shoes and go barefoot." She hooked her arm in his. "Come on, dear. Let's go home and park ourselves in front of the TV."

Janet had expressed Rachel's own vague yearning to forget propriety and do something impulsive to seize the essence of the night. The yearning didn't dissipate during the round of convivial good-nights.

"I had a very good time tonight," she said when she and Lee were in his car. "I'm more charged up than ever about Plantation Village."

He started the engine and pulled out onto the street. "Air conditioning?"

"Why don't we just roll down the windows?" Rachel suggested, and she pressed the button on her armrest. Lee let down his window, too, and the tangy ocean breeze ruf fled her hair and caressed her skin as they drove slowly along the quiet, tree-shaded street that ran parallel to the beach highway. With a sigh, she leaned back against the headrest.

The street intersected with the highway, and soon they were riding along the beach, headed toward Gulfport. Lee settled deeper in his seat and rested his arm on his door. The silence between them wasn't relaxed, but neither was it tense. Rachel didn't feel compelled to make conversation. She was acting on the simple urge to engage him in conversation when she asked idly, "Did Janet's words hit home with you? Do you feel like an 'old fogy' sometimes?"

He shrugged. "I was always old for my years."

"Your father wasn't around when you were growing up, was he?"

"No, he took off when I was nine years old, and it was good riddance. We were better off without him. He was a no-good drunk."

"You were the oldest child?"

"Yes. My sister was seven and my brother was four."

"What's happened to them? Do they still live in Biloxi, too?"

"No. Evelyn lives in Alabama. She and her husband have three children. My brother, Jack, makes his home in Texas. He has his own auto-parts store and is married and has two children."

"And your mother?"

"She lives near my sister." He added, "My mother lived with Mark and me from the time he was a baby until she moved five years ago to baby-sit Evelyn's newborn. Evelyn's a nurse."

"So all three of your mother's children turned out well. She must be very proud of you."

"She is."

Rachel hesitated. "Is it being too personal to ask what happened to Mark's mother?"

"She left me. I was working offshore, staying away most of the time to earn big money, and she was bored. She cashed one of my paychecks, skipped town with a guy she'd met and went to California with him."

"She took Mark with her?"

"No, she'd never wanted him to begin with. She pretended to be taking birth-control pills and got herself pregnant so that I would marry her. In California she got into drugs and overdosed."

"How tragic."

"For her it was," he said cynically.

"You don't seem at all bitter," Rachel observed. He'd related the events matter-of-factly.

"At the time I was ticked that she made off with my hard-earned wages. Other than that, my attitude was that if she wasn't willing to try to make a go of marriage, Mark and I were better off without her." His voice grew gruff as he volunteered, "I've never had the least regret about being saddled with him, not since they handed him to me in the delivery room."

The image of Lee as a young man of twenty awkwardly holding his newborn infant was enormously appealing. Rachel banished it and didn't pursue the subject of Mark, whom he'd understandably indulged and spoiled. "You haven't remarried? My information was that you were divorced."

"It's wrong information. One trip to the altar was enough for me."

They'd reached Gulfport and were passing through it, she realized. "You missed the turn."

"It's early. Only ten-thirty."

"I told Stephanie I'd be home by ten-thirty or eleven."

"She may not be home herself. Call and check on her." Lee handed his car phone to her.

Rachel knew that she really should end the evening, regardless of any consideration for Stephanie, but she wanted to prolong it, just for a little while longer. She dialed her number and got no answer, then dialed Stephanie's and again got no response. "She's at Candy's house." Rachel dialed the Wakefields' number and heard a busy signal, indicating that someone was home. "I'm sure she left a note for me."

Lee drove to Biloxi along the beach highway. They passed gaudy gambling casinos built on barges. The parking lots were packed with cars. Within the town limits, fast-food restaurants and motels and souvenir shops lined the highway on both sides, their brightly lit neon signs contributing to the touristy look.

"Casino gambling has certainly boosted the local economy," Rachel remarked, noting all the No Vacancy messages.

"Yes, it has," Lee agreed. "No one can argue that point, even those who were and still are adamantly opposed to it."

"You weren't opposed, were you?" Rachel was interested in his viewpoint. She was interested in *him*.

"No, although I shared the common reservations. I approve of the state legislature's stand that no permanent structures may be built on land, to become eyesores if or when the gambling craze dies."

"I approve of it, too."

Both of them Mississippi Gulf Coast natives, they knew that all the casinos were technically "riverboats," though some of the casinos didn't resemble a boat or ship, but were huge, garish floating palaces.

Rachel confessed, "I've gone inside a couple of them, out of curiosity, but I haven't put the first quarter into a slot machine."

"Same here."

"Really?"

"That surprises you—that I'm not a gambler?"

"It wouldn't have surprised me if you visited the casinos for recreation. I can imagine you playing blackjack, with a big pile of chips stacking up from your winnings." Like all her images of him, it was an attractive one. "You must thrive on risk, being in your occupation."

"But it's calculated risk."

They'd passed through Biloxi and were headed toward the next town to the east, Oceans Springs. On their right was a stretch of white sand beach that was deserted at this hour. Rachel felt as if she would be content to drive for hours with the windows rolled down and the balmy breeze filling the car.

In Oceans Springs, Lee turned right and then right again, bringing them back to the water and more deserted beaches. Theirs seemed to be the only vehicle on the quiet street, which didn't provide access to the houses that sat high on a steep bluff. Suddenly Lee slowed and pulled over.

"The signs say No Parking After 10 p.m.," Rachel said, her tranquil mood shattered.

"I'll gamble on a parking ticket," he replied, opening his door and getting out. She opened her door, too, and got out.

A low concrete wall separated beach from pavement. They stepped over the wall and sat on it, the sand beneath their feet. Rachel reached down and scooped up a handful, letting it sift through her fingers. It felt silky and was still warm from the afternoon sunshine. At the water's edge, moonlit waves caressed the sand with gentle lapping sounds.

"We'll have red faces if a policeman comes by," she said, fighting the effects of the romantic setting. "Here we are upstanding citizens, breaking the law." He turned toward her with an abrupt movement that made her lose her breath. "Lee, you're not going to—"

"Yes, I am," he contradicted roughly. "Unless you stop me."

"I *should* stop you," Rachel murmured as he brought his mouth to hers. It was a slow, seeking kiss, not hard and demanding as she'd expected it to be. She felt herself responding helplessly, her lips clinging warmly to his. A length he sought entry to her mouth with slightly more pressure, and she opened and met his tongue with hers. He groaned her name and pulled her close, and she slid her arms around his neck. The kiss turned hot and passionate.

Lee was the one who ended it. He dragged his lips from hers. Sucking in air, he said harshly, "I want you so damned much, Rachel."

Her wild heartbeat was jarring her body, a body weak with desire to make love with him. Shame flooded her at her own irresponsible behavior. "I'm sorry, Lee. Forgive me for acting this way. Blame the moonlight."

"You blame the moonlight, if you need to blame something." He released her and sat apart from her as abruptly as he'd turned toward her before. "I'd want to kiss you in a damned convenience store under a fluorescent light."

Rachel ached to feel his arms around her again. She felt lonely and bereft with the few inches of space between them. "You're angry."

"Hell, yes, I'm angry. Anger's something I can handle where you're concerned. I know from experience," he said in a harsh tone of voice.

"Lee, there's no similarity between the circumstances years ago and the circumstances now. Then I was too young and too innocent for you. Now too much has happened in my life. I'll never trust a man again, after what Blaine did to me. And having an affair would go against my old-fashioned ideas of right and wrong, even if there weren't Stephanie to consider. I have to be a good role model for her."

"You think that I trust women, other than my mother?" Lee demanded cynically. "Hell, married women started coming on to me by the time I was fifteen. And not just low-class broads, either. Men aren't the only ones who're unfaithful. The difference between you and me is that I never had any illusions about marriage in the first place. As for being a role model, I'm just as conscious of that as you are, or maybe more conscious, coming from my background. If you think I've shacked up with women, you're dead wrong."

"I don't have a low opinion of you, Lee."

"No? That's good."

His cynicism didn't sting. "All my instincts tell me that your toughness is a protective veneer and underneath you're a very decent, good man," she said, articulating what was in her heart. "The problem is that I can't trust those instincts, because they led me so terribly wrong before."

"I trust mine, and they tell me to leave you alone. But knowing something and doing it are two different things."

"I didn't exactly have to fend you off," she pointed out. "You called a halt."

"Not soon enough. I was ready to make love to you." He stood up and cursed as he got sand in his shoe.

Rachel stood, too, new shame coursing through her because his blunt admission was titillating. He offered his hand, and she took it, letting him help her step over the concrete wall onto the pavement.

There was a heavy sense of anticlimax as they got back into the car and he drove her home.

"It was really a very productive evening," she said when he pulled into her driveway. "And the dinner was excellent."

"You don't have to make a polite speech."

"I'm *not* making a polite speech," Rachel denied. "I'm making sincere remarks and trying to get us back on the right footing. I don't know about you, but I need to put what happened in Oceans Springs behind me if I'm going to be able to function well in a professional relationship. We'll be in frequent contact." She hesitated, the next words sticking in her throat. "That is, unless you want to put Alice or Mary Lynn in charge at this stage."

"No, I don't." His answer was typically terse and definite.

"Then I'll be in touch with you early in the week." Rachel opened her door. "Good night. Please don't bother to get out."

He got out anyway and silently escorted her to her front door, where he took the key from her and opened the dead bolt.

"Good night," Rachel said again.

"I'll stay here a minute while you go inside and check things out."

"That's really not necessary."

"Maybe not, but I'll wait anyway."

"Who said chivalry is dead?" she demanded lightly, genuinely touched by his insistence. After a rapid tour of her house, she reported back to him that all was well, and he bade her a terse good-night, turned and walked toward his car with long strides. Rachel stood in the doorway and watched until he'd almost reached it. Then she closed the door and locked it, conscious of a deep dissatisfaction.

She'd just glanced into Stephanie's room on her quick tour. Now she returned to it, looking for a note. There was none. Rachel went on a search, looking in her own bedroom, in the family room, in the kitchen. No note. Trying not to entertain thoughts of kidnapping and foul play, she returned to Stephanie's bedroom. The small suitcase her daughter usually packed with clothes and toiletry items when she went to Candy's to spend the night sat on the shelf in the closet. Her robe hung on a hanger.

Becoming alarmed, Rachel hurried into the hall bathroom and verified that her daughter's hairbrush and toiletry items were all there. Dear God. Stephanie hadn't gone to Candy's. Where was she?

Rachel walked through the entire house again on shaky legs and detected no sign of forced entry, no indication that any struggle had taken place. All the windows were locked. So was the door from the kitchen to the carport, and the sliding glass door onto the patio. Opening the latter, she went outside and circled the house. Nothing seemed amiss.

There were lights on in the Carlsons' house next door and someone was up in the Struthers' house across the street. Back inside, Rachel headed straight for the phone to call both neighbors and talk to them before she called the police. She dialed the Struthers' number first, and Mabel Struther answered the phone.

"Mabel. I saw your light on. I'm starting to panic because I just got home and Stephanie isn't here. Did you happen to see her leaving the house?"

"Why, yes, I did, Rachel. I figured there must have been a last-minute change in plans. You'd said she was staying home, so I was keeping an eye on your house. About eight o'clock a teenage boy picked her up. He was driving a brand-new, little red car."

"What?" Rachel asked blankly. "A teenage boy picked Stephanie up?"

"A very nice-looking boy, about seventeen or eighteen years old."

"Mabel, Stephanie didn't have a date tonight. Did she seem to get into the car willingly?"

"I certainly got that impression. He rang the doorbell, and she came out, looking pretty as a picture as usual, and locked the door behind her. They walked together to his car. She stood there a moment and seemed to be admiring it. He opened the door for her like a gentleman, she got in and they drove away." Mabel went on apologetically, as though she were somehow at fault for not intervening. "I have to admit I was a little surprised you were letting Stephanie date a boy as mature as he was. But it never occurred to me she might be slipping out."

"I certainly don't blame you, Mabel." Rachel sighed. "Stephanie's been going through a rebellious period. You've relieved my mind somewhat. I was having nightmares about foul play."

"Do you know the boy?"

"From your description of him and his car, I think I do. His name is Mark Zachary. He asked Stephanie out once before. Tonight he must have called her after I'd gone and asked her out again." Rachel didn't fill her neighbor in on the rest of her conjecture—that Mark had probably known the coast was clear and deliberately timed his call. Lee may well have mentioned that he was having dinner out with her.

In Stephanie's resentful, emotional state, she'd obviously allowed herself to be talked into going out with Mark without permission. Rachel wasn't excusing her daughter, but she put the bulk of the blame on Lee's son, who was old enough to show more scruples than he had.

There was nothing to do except wait up, pace the floor and pray that no harm came to Stephanie.

Chapter Five

Lee was in need of the cold-shower remedy as he drove home, but sexual frustration wasn't his main malady, and he knew it. Taking Rachel to bed wouldn't cure what ailed him; kissing her and holding her in his arms had told him that. Sex would leave him only more hung up on her.

He'd gotten himself into a no-win situation and kept getting in deeper and deeper. Every time he saw Rachel, he wanted her more, and the craving went beyond the physical.

Passing the lit-up casinos, Lee thought of their conversation about gambling and taking risks. There wasn't any gamble involved in falling hard for her, because there wasn't a chance that she would return his feelings. He'd realized that at the outset, and yet he couldn't seem to help himself.

Success or no success, he was still Lee Zachary, from the wrong side of the tracks. However much Rachel might deny it, snobbery formed a barrier that he could never break down, no matter how hard he tried. And his pride wouldn't let him try.

Briefly Lee considered stopping in at one of the casinos instead of going on home, but the idea held no appeal. On his arrival at his condo, he saw that Mark's car was there. By association, Stephanie Cavanaugh came to mind, and Lee's state of dissatisfaction deepened. For all the reasonableness of Rachel's opposition to her daughter's dating his son, Lee knew damned well that Mark had a strike against him because of who his dad was.

As he mounted the stairs from the garage to the second level, he found himself hoping that Mark would have already gone to bed. Lee was in no mood to be good company for his son. But music was coming from Mark's bedroom and apparently he had a visitor. Walking down the hallway toward his open door, Lee could hear him talking to someone.

Reaching the door, he stuck his head in, expecting to see Carl or another of Mark's school buddies. Instead he stared, wondering for one crazy moment whether he'd conjured up Stephanie Cavanaugh, who sat daintily on the carpet, looking through his son's collection of compact discs. Mark was sprawled nearby, a bag of chips open between them. Seeing Lee, he sat up like a shot, blurting, "Dad, how's it going?"

"Turn that music down," Lee ordered, and his son speedily obeyed. "Now, let's hear an explanation. What the hell is Stephanie doing here with you?"

"She was home by herself tonight, Dad. We went out for something to eat and rode around awhile, then decided to come here and listen to music." He looked at his watch. "I guess I should be taking her home pretty soon."

Stephanie had turned a nervous smile on Lee. "Hi, Mr. Zachary."

"Hi, Stephanie," he responded shortly. "Does your mother know you're with Mark?"

The guilt flashing across her pretty face answered his question. Lee glared at his son. "Were you aware she didn't have permission?"

Mark hung his head. "Yes, sir."

"Stephanie, you call your mother immediately and tell her you're headed straight home."

"Use my phone," Mark said gruffly, getting to his feet with her. "Dad, you don't have to talk rough to her. Yell at me if you want."

"Don't worry," Lee snapped. "I intend to."

Stephanie sat gracefully on the side of Mark's bed. After punching the numbers, she shook back her blond hair and held the receiver to her ear. "Hi, Mom." In the same sulky, defensive voice, she carried on a conversation with her mother, every now and then rolling her eyes ceilingward. "I'm fine.... Yes, I went out with Mark. How did you guess...? Oh. Mrs. Struther. Did you ask her to spy on me...? I was going to leave a note, but I forgot.... I'm at Mark's house.... Yes, Mr. Zachary's right here.... Mark's going to bring me home now.... No, he can bring me home. Mom, *don't* come over here. Don't—" Stephanie hung up the phone and burst into tears. "Mom's driving over to get me," she sobbed. "Oh, I *hate* her for embarrassing me like this!"

Mark sat beside her and patted her back. "Don't cry, Stephanie. This is all my fault, and I'll take the blame."

Lee shook his head at the gruff tenderness in his son's voice. "Both of you, come into the living room and get ready to face the music," he said with grim weariness. "Mark, you've put me in a hell of a position."

He'd already shed his jacket and tie. Now he deposited them in his bedroom, got a beer from the kitchen and joined the two teenagers, who sat side by side on the leather sofa looking defiant and nervous.

"What's the big deal anyway?" Marked blurted out. "We didn't do anything wrong."

"Mark was a perfect gentleman, Mr. Zachary."

"Tell that to your mother, Stephanie, not to me," Lee replied sternly.

"She won't listen. She insists on making me follow the same rules about dating that Grandma and Grandpa Preston made up when she was a teenager, and times have changed!"

Lee wasn't being put in the middle. "Times may have changed, but teenagers are still teenagers," he stated neutrally.

"You're going to take Mrs. Cavanaugh's side, aren't you, Dad?" Mark turned accusing brown eyes on him. "Even though you told me yourself that she was a snob and warned me that she wasn't going to let Stephanie date me, just like her parents wouldn't let her date you because you weren't good enough for their daughter."

"My warning was for your ears alone, not for the whole world to hear."

Stephanie was gazing with incredulity at Mark and then at Lee. "Is that true? My mom just said you'd worked for my grandpa. She didn't tell me that you'd tried to date her, Mr. Zachary."

Lee downed the rest of his beer to wash the sour taste from his mouth. "Maybe she didn't think it was important enough to mention."

"Did you really ask her out on a date and get turned down?"

"You heard Mark say that I did. I never lie to him, and he doesn't lie to me."

"Then Mark's lucky," Stephanie said bitterly. "I can't believe half of what my mother wants me to believe." She huddled on the sofa, tears welling up in her blue eyes again.

Mark put his arm around her shoulders, and Lee didn't have the heart to interfere. Stephanie looked so young and vulnerable that he felt sorry for her himself, especially since he knew that she was referring obliquely to the ugly gossip

about her father. New anger burned inside him against tha
bastard Blaine Cavanaugh, who'd hurt his innocent daugh
ter as well as his wife. "I feel sure your mother's truthfu
with you, Stephanie. If she kept any information from you
it was to protect you."

Mark glanced at his father in surprise at the brusqu
gentleness in Lee's voice. At that moment the doorbel
pealed. Rachel had arrived. Lee got to his feet quickly an
went to the door, greatly disgusted with himself because th
thought of seeing her again tonight, even under these ci
cumstances, caused a stir of anticipation.

She was wearing the same outfit, but she'd combed he
hair and showed the strain of coming home and discover
ing Stephanie gone.

"I won't come in, Lee," she said with careful compo
sure. "Just get Stephanie, if you please."

Lee frowned. "Don't you want to confront both kids an
get to the bottom of this?"

"I'll deal with Stephanie's behavior and let you deal wit
Mark's, as you see fit."

He gave his head a shake, negating that plan, and opene
the door wider. "No, I think we should both hear the sam
story and lay down the law together."

Rachel stepped over the threshold. "I'm not sure I'm u
to hearing it with an audience." She seemed to be workin
up her courage before she asked, "They were here all b
themselves when you got home?"

"Yes, in Mark's bedroom..." She'd turned deathly pal
and closed her eyes. Lee grasped her shoulders, half ex
pecting her to faint. "For God's sake, Rachel, they wer
listening to music and eating chips. The door was wide ope
Don't imagine the worst."

She eyed him anxiously. "You're not covering up fc
Mark?"

Her hesitant words were like a slap in the face. Lee released her and replied curtly, "I sure as hell am not. I've raised him to be accountable for his actions."

"I'm sorry," she apologized. "Maybe it's just my own guilty conscience at work. When I learned that they'd come here to your condo tonight while we were out together—well, I did let my imagination run away with me. Why should teenagers show more control than adults would in similar circumstances?"

Lee's pulse sped up at her obvious meaning. She was questioning whether the two of them would have handled the privacy and opportunity for intimacy tonight as well as his son and her daughter had. He questioned it, too. If he'd been kissing her on his sofa instead of on a public beach—Lee cut off the thought, saying brusquely, "Nothing happened. I'd swear to that."

"Thank heaven."

She accompanied him into the living room, where Stephanie now sat apart from Mark, much to Lee's relief.

"Hello, Mrs. Cavanaugh," Mark said defensively.

"Hello, Mark." Rachel's eyes were on Stephanie's tear-stained, pouty face.

Lee took charge, both he and Rachel remaining standing. "Okay, let's hear an explanation. Mark, you go first."

"What's there to explain?" his son blustered. "I called Mrs. Cavanaugh's number and Stephanie answered. She wasn't doing anything, and we decided to go out."

"You were calling to talk to Stephanie?"

"Not actually. I was calling to get a message to you. I'd called your car phone a few minutes earlier and you hadn't answered."

"Is this really necessary, Lee?" Rachel asked, both her tone and expression saying that she put no stock in Mark's story.

Mark shot his father a pleading glance that said he'd tell him everything later. "Yeah, Dad. What does it really matter?"

"It matters to me. Was tracking me down a good excuse to call Mrs. Cavanaugh's house in the hopes of speaking to Stephanie?"

His son nodded.

"Did you have in mind asking Stephanie to slip out with you?"

"No. I mainly wanted to make sure she was doing okay. What with all the talk going around about her dad, I knew it had to be rough on her."

Rachel intervened again. "Lee, I just want to take Stephanie home and put this behind us."

Mark and Stephanie both rose quickly to their feet. She looked at him guiltily, and some silent message passed between them. Lee could damn well guess what the message was: Rachel's daughter was offering to confess her role in how the date had materialized, and his son was bidding her to be quiet and let him take the blame.

"I hope you're not going to punish Stephanie, Mrs. Cavanaugh," Mark said manfully. "It was all my fault."

"Not *all* your fault, Mark. Stephanie did wrong, too, by giving in to temptation. Worst of all, she put me through the worry of thinking that something terrible might have happened to her."

"I meant to get home before you did," Stephanie said in defense. "That's why I didn't leave a note. But I was having such fun with Mark. He's so nice." She gave him a tremulous smile.

"Let's go, Stephanie." Rachel held out her hand.

"Before you leave," Lee said, "let's get a few things settled. There won't be a repeat of this situation tonight. Right, Mark?"

"Right, Dad."

"Right, Stephanie?"

"No, Mr. Zachary." Stephanie's lip quivered. "I don't guess I'll ever get to go on another date with Mark my whole life."

"Your whole life is a long time, Stephanie," Rachel said wearily. "Come along. It's late."

Father and son accompanied mother and daughter to the door, where Stephanie turned to Mark.

"Bye, Mark," she said in a tragic tone. "I hope I haven't gotten you into a lot of trouble."

"Don't worry about it, Stephanie," he answered stoutly. "You take care of yourself."

Rachel looked at Lee and said with an air of constraint, "Good night, Lee."

"Good night, Rachel." He wanted to add words of support in the same vein as his son's. But unlike the teenagers, the two adults weren't in league with each other, though Lee had certainly meant for them to be.

He'd meant for them to handle the episode together, but she hadn't let that happen. All she'd been interested in was getting Stephanie away from Mark and keeping Lee at a distance, beyond that barrier she wanted to keep in place between them.

After the door closed, Lee led the way back into the living room. He wheeled around and faced his son. Mark held up his hand. "Dad, I'm not answering any questions until you promise me you won't blab to Mrs. Cavanaugh."

"You've just answered my first question, which was whose idea it was for you to take Stephanie out tonight. It was hers, not yours, wasn't it?"

"You give me your word?"

Lee sighed. "Yes, I give you my word."

"Then it *was* her idea. I knew I'd get in trouble, but she sounded so depressed and mixed up. She was talking kind of crazy, about running away from home. I honestly thought she'd be safer with me than home by herself. I wasn't just looking for an excuse to take her out, Dad."

"I believe you. Mark, Mrs. Cavanaugh should be told that Stephanie talked to you about running away. She might have just been playing on your sympathy, but then again she might have been serious."

"I guess you could mention that part of it."

"What you did was wrong, even though your motive was good."

Mark nodded, obviously chastened. "I'm sorry I was a bad reflection on you, Dad."

"When the whole story is told, you're not a bad reflection." Lee flexed his shoulders. "Let's turn in. I'm tired."

"You know what?" Mark asked as they were switching off the lights in the condo before retiring to their bedrooms. "I still like Stephanie, kind of like a brother. But I wouldn't really want to date her, after tonight. She's pretty and all that, but awfully young for me."

"If you got Stephanie out of your system, tonight was worth all the trauma."

"Maybe you would have gotten Mrs. Cavanaugh out of your system, Dad, if you'd gone out with her just once. She was probably too young for you, too."

"Probably she was then." But certainly not now.

"You like her a lot, don't you?"

"Yes, I like Mrs. Cavanaugh a lot," Lee admitted.

"Wouldn't that be something, if Stephanie and I ended up as stepbrother and stepsister?"

"It would be something, all right. Something that's not going to happen." Lee's bald statement came out sounding bleak.

Mark slapped him on the back. "Hang in there, Dad."

Stephanie broke her defensive silence when they were in the car. "Mom, *why* did you insist on coming over to get me? Why couldn't you have let Mark bring me home? Instead you put me through all this embarrassment!"

"As angry and disappointed in you as I am, Stephanie, you're my daughter, and I love you. I wanted to make sure you got home safely. That's why I came to drive you home myself." Rachel carefully refrained from being more explicit and saying that she didn't trust Mark Zachary's driving.

"But Mark's a safe driver. That was his first accident a couple of weeks ago in front of your real-estate office."

"Well, I didn't want his second accident to occur with you in the car. Do you have any idea how frantic I was when I came home tonight and you weren't there? I was on the verge of notifying the police that you were missing when I called Mrs. Struther."

"What time did you come home? You said you'd be home by ten-thirty," Stephanie reminded her righteously. "If I hadn't gone out with Mark, I would have been there all evening by myself while you were out on a date with Mr. Zachary. It was a date, wasn't it?"

"No, it *wasn't* a date. And if it was, there wouldn't be anything wrong with my dating him. Your father's been dead for nine years. But I haven't been interested in having a social life because spending time with you was more important."

"You let me think all this time that you were still in love with Daddy's memory. But you weren't, were you? You probably hated him because you believed all those lies about why he was killed."

Rachel took a deep breath, searching for the right words to express a painful truth that her daughter had to hear. "I adored your father when I married him, but he killed my love by not being faithful to me. You were much too young—you're too young now—for me to share my feelings with you. Someday, when you have a daughter, you'll understand that my intention was never to deceive you." She reached over and touched Stephanie's arm, offering comfort and also seeking it.

Her daughter flinched and cried out accusingly, the pain of denial in her voice, "But you've kept other things from me, too! You didn't tell me that Mark's father asked you out when you were a teenager! I'll bet the reason you won't let me date Mark is that you couldn't date Mr. Zachary! But now you can!" Stephanie broke down in sobs.

Rachel's heart ached for her. She knew the real cause of the tears was anguish over her father's not having lived up to his image. "Mark told you that his father had tried to date me?"

"Yes. His dad warned him that I wouldn't be allowed to date him because you wouldn't think he was good enough for me."

"That's not the case at all. I hope you stood up for me."

"No, I didn't," Stephanie admitted guiltily. "I thought of your letting me date Johnny Henderson, whose mom has to buy groceries with food stamps, but I would have felt funny mentioning him."

"Johnny's a fine boy."

"He's only fourteen and not nearly as tall and cute as Mark." Stephanie blew her nose into a tissue and shot a glance at Rachel. "Mr. Zachary was all dressed up when he picked you up tonight. Do you think he's handsome?"

"Yes, I find Mr. Zachary very attractive."

"If he asks you out on a date, will you go?"

"No." Rachel tried to keep the regret out of her voice. "For one thing, he's a big client. Also, I'm not interested in dating anyone. My life is full with being a mother and working full-time in real estate."

The answer seemed to satisfy Stephanie. "Am I going to be punished for tonight?"

"Yes. For the next two weeks, no telephone calls and no trips to the mall."

"Two whole weeks?" The protest wasn't strong. "Mom, could the two weeks start at noon tomorrow? I want to call

Candy first thing when I wake up. It's too late to call her tonight.''

Rachel agreed, granting her daughter that slight latitude. She felt more optimistic than she had in days about Stephanie's state of mind and emotions. If tonight proved to be a turning point back to normalcy, all the anxiety would have been worthwhile.

On their arrival home, Stephanie asked helpfully, "Want me to help you turn the lights off?"

"No, darling, you go on and change into your night-gown and get into bed."

Ignoring her words, Stephanie trailed after her into the family room. Sensing something amiss, Rachel glanced up and saw her gazing sadly at the spot on the wall where the wedding portrait had hung.

"Stephanie, I'm so sorry your daddy disappointed both of us," Rachel said, her throat suddenly tight. She held out her arms, and her daughter came to her in a rush. "I took the picture down and destroyed it, and I really shouldn't have. But I'm human and make mistakes, too," she confessed, holding Stephanie in a loving embrace.

"Every time I look at Daddy's picture, I feel so unhappy. But I want to keep it out and remember him."

"You should do both. Keep your father in your heart and feel certain that he loved you very much. That's not being disloyal to me."

It was the reassurance Stephanie wanted. Mother and daughter finished turning out the lights. At Stephanie's bedroom door, they said good-night and hugged each other again.

As she undressed for bed, Rachel offered up a prayer of thanksgiving. Her daughter's unhappiness wasn't going to magically go away, but now Rachel could help her through the crisis of disillusionment.

With this main worry alleviated, Rachel felt stronger and more in control of her life. She should be better able to cope with working closely with Lee and seeing him frequently. What had happened between them tonight *couldn't* be allowed to happen again.

The next day Rachel and Stephanie attended eleven o'clock church services and afterward had a leisurely lunch at one of the better restaurants. Stephanie wasn't her former carefree self, but neither was she the sullen, resentful girl she'd been during the recent difficult days.

Rachel didn't bring up the topic of the previous night's fiasco, wishing to convey that it was over and done with. However, she sensed that Stephanie was reliving the date with Mark Zachary whenever her face took on a dreamy expression.

Like daughter, like mother, Rachel acknowledged to herself. She'd dreamed about Lee last night, an erotic, wonderful dream, and had awakened with physical and emotional yearnings. Her mind kept returning to him, no matter how hard she tried to keep him out of her thoughts. Rachel wondered with embarrassed shame if her own expression didn't look dreamy when she visualized Lee.

She was sure her face turned red when her daughter proposed an outing for the afternoon as they were leaving the restaurant. "Let's go home and change clothes and go to the crafts fair in Oceans Springs."

"That would be fun," Rachel said. "We can look for a wreath for our front door."

Once home, they headed to their bedrooms to change. Rachel emerged from hers first. Nearing Stephanie's open door, she heard her daughter answering her phone on the first ring.

"Mark! Hi!"

Rachel stopped dead in her tracks, at once upset. This was a headache she hadn't anticipated. She'd hoped Mark would leave Stephanie alone, but obviously he didn't intend to do that.

"Oh, I'm fine. Everything's okay. I'm being punished and can't talk on the phone for two weeks, though, so I have to hang up. Are you being punished ... ? I'm glad to hear that. I would feel terrible if you'd gotten grounded or something. Bye, Mark."

So Lee's son had evidently gotten off scot-free. Rachel wasn't really surprised. Nor did she put much faith in Mark's promise that he wouldn't try to repeat the stunt he'd pulled last night. At the risk of offending Lee, she had no choice but to ask him to give her more support at his end of this problematic situation.

The good news was Stephanie's almost-cheerful obedience. Rachel tried to focus on that and be positive during the rest of the afternoon. But the necessary talk with Lee weighed on her mind.

When and where was she to have the talk with him? As soon as possible, and somewhere other than her office or his, which up to now she hadn't had an occasion to visit. The building site of Plantation Village was also ruled out. This was a personal, not a professional, matter. Rachel meant to appeal to him as a mother, not a Realtor.

She decided that she would call him at home that evening and set up a meeting.

Having come to that resolution, she felt an eagerness that she shouldn't have.

"What's the score?" Mark asked, joining Lee in the living room, where a football game was tuned in on the oversize TV.

"I think Buffalo's ahead," Lee answered, hating to admit that he hadn't been following the action of the Sunday-evening game being telecast on a cable sports channel. He'd been staring at the screen and thinking about Rachel, wondering what the status was with her and Stephanie. Tomorrow he would drop by Magnolia Realty and take the opportunity to ask.

Mark sank down into a chair. During a commercial break, he confided casually, "I talked to Stephanie on the phone this afternoon."

"You called her or she called you?" Lee asked, frowning.

"I called her. I was kinda worried about her. She sounded real good. I don't think you need to mention to Mrs. Cavanaugh that she might be thinking of running away from home."

"I'll probably see Mrs. Cavanaugh during the day tomorrow." Lee knew damn well he'd manufacture some excuse to drop by Magnolia Realty. "If she indicates that things have settled down with Stephanie, I won't mention it."

"Good. *Great* pass!" Mark exclaimed, focusing his attention on the game. During the next commercial break, he got up, announcing, "I think I'll get a soda. Can I bring you one, Dad? Or a beer?"

"No, thanks."

The cordless phone on the end table near Lee came to life shrilly in the middle of his refusal. He reached and picked up the receiver, while Mark waited to find out if the call was for him. The sound of Rachel's voice on the other end acted on Lee like a shot of adrenaline.

"Hello, Lee. This is Rachel. I hope this isn't an inconvenient time."

"Not at all. Hold on for a second, Rachel." Lee covered the mouthpiece and said to Mark, "It's not for you."

"I'm going," Mark said. "Remember, Dad, you gave your word."

Lee nodded impatiently, and Mark left the room. Lee said into the phone, "I'm back."

"What I called for won't take long. I wondered if we could meet for coffee tomorrow morning."

"Sure. At your office?" Lee couldn't think of a better way to start the day.

"Preferably somewhere else." She suggested a restaurant between Gulfport and Biloxi that served breakfast.

He took a second to recover from his surprise. "That's fine with me. What time?"

"Nine o'clock?"

"Nine o'clock's good."

"Then I'll see you tomorrow morning."

Lee wanted to keep her on the line longer. "Our meeting is about Plantation Village, I assume."

"Well, no, it isn't about real estate at all," she admitted. "But I'd rather not go into detail on the phone tonight. Stephanie is waiting for me in another part of the house to watch a TV program with her."

"How are things with you and her?"

"Much better. In fact, almost back to normal."

"I'm glad to hear that."

"I'll let you get to your football game, Lee," she said. "I can hear the TV in the background. Good night."

"Good night, Rachel."

Mark came back with his soda and a bowl of microwave popcorn and settled down to watch the rest of the game. Lee sat there, less able to concentrate than before. Why had Rachel made the coffee date with him? The whole business between Mark and Stephanie was a closed book now. There wasn't any need to discuss that further, certainly no urgent need that required a meeting first thing on Monday morning.

She wasn't acting in her capacity of his Realtor; she'd made that clear. Did she just want to have coffee with him? *Don't go raising your hopes,* he cautioned himself. But the possibility that Rachel was making a personal overture, woman-to-man, caused a warm glow inside him.

It wouldn't take much to fan that glow into a fire, he knew.

The next morning Lee donned slacks instead of jeans. Hell, he wouldn't mind making the effort to look more presentable if there was some motivation. Rachel could smooth his rough edges, if she wanted to take on the project. Lee could even clean up his language to please her.

In this mood of willingness to reform, he drove to the restaurant, taking the beach highway. The familiar sight of flocks of sea gulls soaring over the water and coasting effortlessly on stratas of morning air boosted his spirits higher.

Ninety-nine chances out of a hundred, you're going to get shot down, he told himself cynically, without any sobering effect.

Rachel was getting out of her car as he entered the parking lot. His chest tightened at her blond loveliness. As he climbed out of his own vehicle and went to her, Lee felt like the luckiest man on the Gulf Coast.

"Good morning, Lee." She greeted him with a flustered smile.

Lee swallowed compliments on her appearance that were begging to be spoken. "Good morning."

"Thank you for fitting me into your busy schedule on such short notice."

"Any time," he said gruffly. "I'm never that busy."

They went inside and took a booth. Lee tried to guard his expression as he gazed at her across the table. She turned up her cup, and he did the same, asking, "Have you had breakfast?"

"My usual bowl of cereal. But you go ahead and have breakfast, if you haven't eaten."

"I don't want to eat alone. Have some toast or an English muffin." Lee wasn't hungry himself, but he was willing to prolong the coffee date any way he could.

"I suppose I could eat some toast."

Their waitress arrived with a coffeepot, and they ordered.

"You mentioned that your parents were traveling around the country," he said, taking charge of the conversation. "Are they on an extended trip?"

"Yes, they're traveling in a motor home. My father retired and sold the pharmacy."

"So I'd heard."

"Yesterday they called from Yellowstone National Park. They both said to tell you how pleased they are that you've made such a great success of yourself."

Lee nodded to acknowledge the message. He couldn't quite bring himself to reply in kind and ask her to give her parents his best wishes. It would be too hypocritical.

"You still have hard feelings against them, too?" Rachel asked regretfully.

"It was no thanks to them that I amounted to something," he answered bluntly. "Though maybe they can take some credit along with a lot of teachers and other upstanding citizens who saw no potential in me. I was bound and determined to prove them wrong."

"But my father did see potential in you," she objected. "When you worked for him, you impressed him as being bright and hardworking and honest. I remember him saying that to my mother. You don't know how much he hated losing you when you quit in anger."

Lee shrugged. "I won't argue the point. My grudge against your parents isn't so strong that I couldn't get over it. When will they be returning to Gulfport?" The question he really wanted to ask, but wouldn't at this point, was whether the elderly Prestons had belatedly given him their stamp of approval. Was there a connection between Rachel's having a long-distance conversation with them about him and her calling Lee and making this date?

If there was, he was ready to forgive and forget.

The waitress served their food as Rachel finished outlining her parents' travel itinerary, which wouldn't bring them home until Christmas.

Lee picked up his fork to eat his pancakes, and she nibbled at a piece of toast. At a nearby table four men were carrying on a debate about the various national health-care plans that Congress was considering. Lee asked her opinion on the issue and explained his views between bites. She became engrossed in their discussion and ate her toast while he cleaned up his plate, conscious of the pleasure of being with her.

"This was a good idea you had," he declared, sipping a fresh cup of coffee after the table was cleared.

"I don't know about that," she said, sighing. "It's been so enjoyable that I'm thinking it would have been better to ask you to have coffee with me at the office. We could have closed the door and talked."

"About what?"

"About Mark and Stephanie."

Lee sat back, feeling as though a fist had suddenly been rammed into his full stomach. So she'd had a purpose in meeting him for coffee other than wanting to see him. This wasn't a date, as he'd fooled himself into thinking it might be. "What is there to talk about concerning them?" he asked flatly.

Rachel reached her hand across the table toward him in a gesture of appeal. "Please don't get hostile on me. I need your support. Mark phoned Stephanie yesterday after he'd given you his word that he wouldn't persist in trying to date her."

"I was aware that he phoned her. He mentioned to me that he had. He was worried about her and wanted to reassure himself that she was all right."

"Lee, it's only normal that you want to see your son's behavior in the best light. But what he did Saturday night was irresponsible and wrong. According to what he told Stephanie, you didn't even punish him. What kind of message does that send?"

"Mark won't call Stephanie again," Lee answered shortly. His son had sealed his lips, so he couldn't come to his defense with an explanation of why no punishment had been deserved. "You can put your fears to rest."

"I hope so," Rachel said in a troubled voice. "If they're not put to rest, I can't go off to Florida and leave her three weeks from now. She has a real crush on Mark. I'm afraid she wouldn't be strong enough to refuse him if he pressured her into going out with him again on the sly."

"I don't believe he pressured her into going out with him on Saturday night. It could be that you're seeing *Stephanie's* behavior in the best light. Have you questioned her about it?" Lee asked harshly.

"I'm not excusing Stephanie," she said, not answering his question. "She *is* being punished. Part of my concern is for Mark."

"Don't waste your concern on him. He's a hell of a good kid, and I couldn't be prouder of him. He makes good grades in school. He doesn't use drugs. He's planning to go to college. You seem to have some misguided idea that he's wild and not to be trusted, but I won't have one qualm about going away to Florida for a few days and leaving him on his own."

"More coffee?" their waitress asked, depositing a small plastic tray with the bill near Lee.

"No, thanks," Lee answered. "I've had enough."

"None for me, either," Rachel said in a disheartened tone.

She reached for the bill, but he picked it up first, and she didn't haggle over who would pay.

"Have a nice day," the waitress called out as they left.

"Lee, I'm terribly sorry you're so offended," Rachel said, once they were outside.

"I'll get over it," he replied tersely, not correcting her wrong interpretation of his reaction. He was more deeply disappointed than offended. He'd gotten his hopes up over nothing and been shot down.

Chapter Six

"Just once I wish we could part company on friendly terms," Rachel said in frustration and dismay. "But we don't seem to be able to do that."

"No, we don't," Lee agreed tersely.

"Next time, let's both make a concerted effort."

"Next time," he repeated, with a kind of bleak skepticism.

"I hope your appointment goes well," she remarked, fighting a sense of futility.

"My appointment?"

"Yes. You're not wearing your usual work clothes. I assumed you had a meeting with someone...." She let her voice drift off as she realized her mistake. He'd dressed differently to have coffee with her.

His expression had hardened with an emotion like self-contempt. "I didn't want to embarrass you," he said, the self-derision evident in his voice.

"Embarrass me? I wouldn't have been embarrassed to be seen with you, no matter what you were wearing! You always look..." Her brain failed to produce any acceptable adjectives, only those that were too revealing, like virile and manly and ruggedly handsome. "You always look fine to me."

"You always look so damn beautiful."

His harsh compliment flustered her even more. "I should be getting to the office. Thank you for breakfast."

"You're more than welcome."

Rachel hurried to her car. Glancing over her shoulder, she saw him striding to his own, a big, tall, overwhelmingly masculine man. Didn't he realize that she found him just as attractive as she had when she was a teenager? If he ever stopped resenting her for the past and set out to storm her defenses, she didn't know if she could resist him. Fortunately, he kept up a barrier. He didn't even seem to like her, and any male interest on his part was grudging. She should be glad and yet she wasn't.

The talk with Lee about Mark hadn't been productive. That failure added to Rachel's mental and emotional turmoil as she drove to the office. All she could hope was that Lee's undisciplined son lost interest in Stephanie so that her crush on him could die.

Another troubling concern was whether Rachel was being unprofessional by not insisting that one of her partners take over the role of liaison person working closely with Lee. Clearly Rachel was too personally involved with him. The question was whether he would agree to let Alice or Mary Lynn replace her.

And she didn't really want to be replaced, which added to the complication. She was excited about Plantation Village and eager to play a major role in making the venture a big success—for Lee, for Magnolia Realty and for herself. Also, she needed to face up to her feelings for him, not avoid dealing with them by avoiding him.

Mary Lynn and Alice were both waiting for her at the office, ready to begin the weekly Monday meeting. Rachel put aside her qualms, both personal and professional.

The meeting had just broken up at one o'clock when Kim Lamberts called. Kim was the interior decorator Lee had hired to furnish and decorate a model house and a model condo unit. Rachel was acquainted with her and knew she was a vivacious brunette woman in her mid-thirties, a real extrovert.

"This is short notice," Kim said, "but I'm meeting Lee at Plantation Village at four-thirty. By then the workmen should be gone. Could you possibly be there, too? I just spoke with him, and he wants you to have input."

"Why, yes, I can be there," Rachel replied, her mouth suddenly going dry. She would get her chance to start out on a different footing with Lee much sooner than she'd expected.

"By the way, congratulations on landing his listing. That was quite a plum to snatch from the bigger, older agencies."

"We're very pleased and excited."

"Isn't he a hunk? And on his way to being rich, to boot. I'm between husbands and would love to land *him*. How 'bout you?" the decorator asked frankly.

"Excuse me, Kim, but I have another call," Rachel said, not about to make a reply. She was left feeling something disturbingly akin to jealous dislike for the other woman.

It was a ridiculous reaction, since she certainly had no claims on Lee.

At four-fifteen Rachel drove to the Plantation Village site to keep her appointment. The workmen had gone, and Lee and Kim Lamberts had both arrived ahead of her and stood together by his car. Carpet samples and wallpaper books were spread out on the hood.

Rachel parked a short distance away and got out. Kim was telling him an anecdote, apparently about some disastrous paint job. "... the most bilious shade of green you've ever seen! The painter was halfway finished with the upstairs when Mr. Plume and I came by the house. Well, Mr. Plume almost had a cardiac!"

"I don't blame him," Lee said, amusement in his deep voice. "I'd have hit the roof myself."

Rachel stood transfixed for several seconds, the groundless, jealous dislike for Kim curling through her. She slammed her door harder than necessary. Lee turned around, and his wry smile faded from his mouth. He hadn't smiled at Rachel once on any of the occasions she'd seen him, the first being the encounter in the restaurant.

"Hi, Rachel," Kim called in greeting. The decorator was wearing a bright red suit with a short, tight skirt, and her white knit shell had a V-shaped neckline. She looked stylish and sexy. In comparison, Rachel felt like someone's maiden aunt in her knee-length suit and silk blouse with its modest neckline and scarf.

"Hello, Kim. Lee," she responded as cordially as she could manage.

"You just missed a funny story," the other woman said.

"So I gathered."

Lee finally spoke up. "Now that Rachel's here, why don't we see what you've got, Kim?"

"I've got some *fabulous* wallpapers!" the decorator declared. "First I'll show you what I have in mind for the house." She opened up the wallpaper books and held paint chips and carpet samples next to the designs she'd selected for various rooms. "That's the house. Now the condo." She went through the same process. When she'd finished, she looked inquiringly at Lee. "So what do you think?"

Lee shrugged and looked to Rachel for an answer, as though her opinion would double for his. Kim's eyebrows raised a notch. "Is Rachel pinch-hitting for the boss's wife?" she quipped.

"Nothing like that," Rachel declared, her cheeks warm. "I just see the interiors of a lot of houses and hear the reactions of wives. I like the colors you've put together very much. But I might choose wallpapers that were slightly less bold."

Kim nodded and flipped several pages in the sample book that lay open. "Something more like this?"

"Exactly."

"That gives me a frame of reference. I'll work up some other combinations. This is all preliminary, anyway. I like to actually walk around inside the rooms before the decorating scheme is finalized." She began to close the books and stack them.

"Let me carry those for you," Lee said.

Kim smiled at him and batted her eyelashes. "Just what the doctor ordered—a big, strong male to carry my heavy wallpaper books. But who's going to carry them when I get to my apartment? Say, why don't you both come to my place and have a drink?"

"Thank you, but count me out," Rachel said quickly. "Before I go, though, I'd like to check on the building progress. I won't be long, Lee. Don't wait on me." She called back over her shoulder, "Bye, Kim."

"Bye, Rachel."

There was no response from Lee.

She could hear their voices as she walked at a brisk pace along the rough path, not being as careful as she needed to be, since she was wearing pumps with heels. When her left foot came down on a clod of dirt and twisted sideways, she let out a little gasp at the pain, but kept walking, gritting her teeth. When Lee and Kim were gone, she would limp back to her car.

A skeletal wooden structure had been erected on a concrete foundation that had been poured since her previous visit to the site. Rachel stepped up onto the concrete through a gap between upright studs and leaned against one of the posts, taking the weight off her left ankle, which throbbed painfully. Reaching down, she rubbed it.

Only one car had started up and left. Lee had probably ignored her words and was waiting to see her safely off the premises before he went to Kim's apartment. With a sigh, Rachel straightened and swiveled around on her right foot, not at all looking forward to the return trip.

Her heart skipped a beat and she quickly lowered her raised foot when she saw that Lee wasn't waiting at his car. He had come to get her, a frown on his face.

"I was just coming back," she called to him. "Don't let me hold you up."

"You're not holding me up," he answered, not slowing. "I don't have anywhere to be."

Rachel tried not to wince as she started toward him with careful steps. "I assumed you would accept Kim's invitation."

"Why would you assume that?"

"The two of you seemed to be very friendly. I almost felt like I was intruding when I drove up." The truthful words, which would have been better left unsaid, came out of her set mouth.

"I've known Kim a long time."

Lee had reached her. Rachel paused, needing a rest. The physical strain seemed to unleash her tongue again. "You've probably known me longer, and you aren't at all friendly to me."

"I can't be."

"But why? Wouldn't it make for a better working relationship if we could be more congenial? Maybe it would relieve some of the tension if we got to know each other. I'm on pins and needles when I'm around you." She took a step and winced.

"What's wrong? Your ankle? I saw you rubbing it," Lee said.

"I twisted it a little. Nothing serious." Rachel took another step, favoring her left foot. Now that he knew her problem, she could limp along next to him.

"You might have sprained it. Is it swollen?" Lee took her arm, stopping her, and squatted down. His fingers probed gently at her injured ankle. "No, there's no swelling."

"The pain isn't excruciating. I can walk. When I get home, I'll use an ice pack."

He rose. "It's quite a distance to your car. I'd better carry you."

"No, indeed not!" Rachel objected. "That would be too embarrassing! Lee..."

He picked her up in his arms over her protests. Blushing hotly and conscious of a pleasure as great as her embarrassment, she wound her arms around his neck and submitted to be being carried.

When he stood her on her feet beside her car, Rachel was breathless, as though she'd been the one exerting herself. "I hope *you* didn't strain something," she said.

Lee hadn't stepped back. He held her by the shoulders, looking down at her, his chest rising and falling. "Any excuse to get my hands on you." His grip tightened, and Rachel gazed at him helplessly, witnessing the battle he was waging with himself not to lower his head and kiss her. It was a battle she should help him to win, but she couldn't get out a word.

He released her and opened her car door, saying harshly, "You need to get your weight off that ankle. Go straight home and ice it down."

"I will." To her own ears, she sounded disappointed.

With his help, Rachel got behind the wheel. She tingled from his strong, gentle touch, which was so at variance with his exterior hardness and toughness. "Thanks very much for coming to my rescue, Lee. Next time I promise not to be such a klutz."

"Accidents happen. I could follow you home and get you inside your house."

"That's very kind, but I can manage to hobble inside from the carport."

He didn't insist. Closing her door, he lifted his hand in an abrupt farewell and walked to his car.

Rachel sighed as she started the engine, more conscious of the poignant ache in her chest than of the throb in her ankle. If only things were different. If only she could afford to trust a man again.

But she couldn't . . . not ever.

Rachel's words, *I hope you didn't strain something*, echoed in Lee's head as he drove from the site back toward his office in Biloxi. He'd strained his self-control to the limits when he hadn't taken her in his arms and kissed her. It would have snapped if she'd made the smallest move to encourage him, but she hadn't. She'd stood there on her injured ankle, at his mercy. Concern about the pain she was suffering had saved him.

Lee had never wanted a woman the way he wanted her. His desire was mixed with an unfamiliar yearning for her to want him the same way. He was really the one at her mercy, today and every time he was around her. He didn't like the feeling one bit.

You've known me longer, and you aren't friendly at all, she'd reproached him. Maybe he should try treating her the way he treated Kim Lamberts and other women he knew professionally and liked. Maybe getting to know Rachel on a more casual basis would cure his problem with her.

If Kim had twisted her ankle, Lee would have shown his concern openly, instead of hiding it. While he was carrying her to her car, she would probably have made wisecracks about being crippled for life and hiring an ambulance-chasing lawyer to bring a lawsuit. He would have threatened to drop her and probably would have teased her about being a deadweight. It would have been a whole different episode from start to finish, and tonight he wouldn't have hesitated to call and inquire about how she was doing and whether she needed anything.

Maybe Lee's mistake was keeping such a tight lid on himself around Rachel. Maybe if he unbent, she could relax and be herself. Once he got to know her, he might get over her. There was a good chance that Lee was hung up on some creation in his mind.

So tonight he *would* call her, and starting now he would do his damnedest to unbend, as much as his personality would allow. Lee wasn't a jocular, life-of-the-party type any more than he was a flowery-talking Casanova.

Stephanie opened the kitchen door seconds after Rachel pulled into the carport. She ran to get their pair of crutches and, after seeing that her mother was settled comfortably on the sofa in the family room with her foot propped up, she filled up the ice bag and put it in place on Rachel's ankle.

"Thank you, darling. You're a good nurse," Rachel declared, appreciative of the solicitous attention.

"I'll fix supper," Stephanie volunteered.

"That's sweet. How was your day at school?"

"We got back our math tests. I made a *B*."

"Good. Math isn't your favorite subject."

"No, but it's Mark's. He makes all *A*'s in math." Rachel didn't reply, reaching down to readjust the ice bag. Stephanie went on, "In phys ed class, I got all sweaty. Mrs. Ames made us run laps around the gym. Heather Smith and Megan Trent made nasty comments about me that I could hear in the dressing room."

"I hope you ignored them."

"I did." She sighed. "Mom…" The hesitant tone of voice signaled a change of subject. "My punishment is not talking on the phone and not going to the mall, right?"

"That's right."

"Then can I go to a movie Saturday night with Michael Curtis and Candy and Barry Yates? Michael's never asked me out before and I'm afraid if I turn him down, he won't ask me again." She added as persuasive information, "He's a sophomore."

Rachel didn't need any time to think over her decision. If she let Stephanie go out with a boy her own age on Saturday night, her daughter wouldn't be moping over Mark Zachary. "Yes, darling, you can go. Not dating wasn't a part of your punishment."

"Thank you, Mom! Oh, it's going to be so much fun!" Stephanie hugged her and then, insisting that Rachel stay put, danced off to the kitchen to heat up leftovers for their supper. She brought their plates into the family room, and they ate watching a game show on TV and being home participants.

Afterward Stephanie took away the plates and went to her room to do homework. Rachel's ankle didn't hurt at all, but she kept it propped up as she sat on the sofa, her open briefcase beside her while she did some real-estate paperwork and made several calls to agents and clients. She was about to make another one when the phone rang and she answered, expecting the caller to be either an agent or a client.

"How's the ankle?" Lee asked without identifying himself.

Rachel felt little shock waves of surprise. It registered that, despite his typical brevity, his manner of speaking to her was different, not terse and guarded. "I've mostly stayed off it since I got home. But I think I'll be able to walk without much problem tomorrow."

"I'm glad to hear that. If you decide to see a doctor and have an X ray, give me the bill."

"At this point, I doubt seeing a doctor will be necessary, but if I do, I have good medical insurance. You're not afraid of a lawsuit, are you?" she asked, being facetious.

"You were married to a lawyer," he retorted.

Rachel blurted out candidly, "Lee, have you had a couple of drinks tonight? I can't believe this is really you talking to me."

"I'm cold sober. You just made a good point this afternoon, and I decided to turn over a new leaf."

"In other words, you're making an effort to be more friendly." Rachel hesitantly spelled it out.

"To let bygones be bygones."

Rachel was completely nonplussed. "I won't know how to act, not walking on eggshells."

"Just treat me as you would any other big client who expects you to work for him twenty-four hours a day."

"A deal," she said cheerfully. "While I have you on the phone and in such an agreeable frame of mind, let me run an idea past you. Mary Lynn and Alice and I have been discussing an open house for agents at Plantation Village, which would be held as soon as the models are finished. What do you think of sending invitations that are lottery tickets and having a drawing at the open house for an expensive prize? Not just a small TV set or a microwave oven, but something that would bring them out in force. The winner would have to be present."

"I like the idea a lot. What do you have in mind for the prize? Maybe a big-screen TV? Or his-and-hers gold watches? Or how about a cash jackpot to fit in with the gambling craze on the Gulf coast? Say, a thousand bucks?"

"A cash jackpot would be perfect! I'll start working on the invitations. We want to set the right tone in all our promotions and printed matter, not be stuffy and pretentious, but definitely classy."

"I'll let you have the final say-so on brochures and ads. By the way, you weren't just being diplomatic this afternoon with Kim, were you?" he asked. "You did basically like her decorating scheme?"

"Yes, I did. I wasn't being tactful. I have too big a stake in Plantation Village to be anything but frank. From your viewpoint, how is the construction progressing? I wanted to ask you that this afternoon. It seems to me to be going fast."

He answered in some detail, and Rachel listened with avid interest, conscious of her pleasure in hearing his deep voice, which emanated masculinity.

"Beatty's a good contractor," he concluded as Stephanie came in and sat down and flipped on the TV, muting it.

Rachel glanced at her watch and noted that she'd been on the phone with him for thirty minutes. The conversation had come to a natural lull, but she hated ending it. "I'm sitting here in the family room, and Stephanie just came in to watch a TV program before she goes to bed," she said. "So I'll let you go. Thanks so much for calling."

"Take it easy on that ankle."

"Tomorrow I expect it to be in good shape." Rachel added on impulse, "We usually have a pot of coffee brewed in the office, since Mary Lynn is a coffee addict. If you're in the neighborhood, stop in any time."

"I may take you at your word."

She told him good-night and hung up, feeling a warm glow inside.

"That was Mr. Zachary on the phone?" Stephanie asked.

"Yes, he was checking to find out whether my ankle was injured badly. Then we discussed real estate."

"I don't like him much. He talks so rough. And I can tell he doesn't like me."

"You've only been in his company twice, that night at the restaurant and then Saturday night, when he could hardly have been expected to be pleasant."

"He doesn't have nice manners like Daddy did." Stephanie turned up the volume of the TV, saving Rachel from having to reply.

No, Lee didn't have Blaine's suave manners, and he was rough spoken, but he had genuine kind, considerate instincts, she reflected, coming to his defense mentally. Loading Kim Lamberts' heavy wallpaper books into her car for her this afternoon had been an act of consideration, plain and simple, performed in his own style. It had been concern that made him pick Rachel up and carry her rather than risk having her do worse injury to her ankle.

For a man who could easily have been a macho type, he showed respect to women by his directness. Rachel liked the absence of the "good ole boy," condescending bowing and scraping. She liked . . . Lee.

And she wanted him to like her.

The next morning Rachel's ankle was stiff and there was some soreness. She wondered about the wisdom of wearing heels. After walking around her bedroom in a pair, she decided to wear flats and dispense with her usual career-woman attire for one day. Instead of a suit, she slipped on a skirt and blouse with a coordinating vest, a new outfit Stephanie had talked her into buying.

"Mom, you look cute!" her daughter exclaimed when she saw her.

"I feel short and underdressed," Rachel confessed laughingly.

At the office she met with similar reactions to her appearance. "In that outfit you could be Stephanie's older sister," Alice declared, and Mary Lynn seconded the sentiment.

"I think you both need glasses," Rachel said, seriously considering going home and changing. But her partners pooh-poohed her self-consciousness, and she stayed, intending to hole up in her office.

Settled at her desk with the door closed, she began working on the invitation for the agents' open house at Plantation Village, last night's conversation with Lee playing over in her mind. Phone calls kept interrupting.

"Darn!" she murmured in exasperation, tossing down her pen when the phone rang again after she'd just hung up. "Hello. This is Rachel Cavanaugh speaking."

"I'm in the neighborhood," Lee said. "A cup of coffee sounds good."

"Why, then, by—by all means, stop in and have a cup," she stammered, her toes curling in her flats. "I have to warn you, though. You may not recognize me today in my sensible shoes and clothes to match. I'm the partner with the blond hair."

"Your ankle is okay?"

"A little sore and stiff, but otherwise okay."

"That's good. See you in a couple of minutes."

It was no more than two minutes. Rachel met him at the door of her office, trying for a dignified air. He was wearing jeans and boots today and loomed over her. His eyes took in her outfit. She could feel herself blushing.

"It's already been said that I look 'cute' and could pass for Stephanie's older sister."

"Then I won't make either of those comments, though I might agree with both of them," Lee said. He was thinking to himself that adorable described the way she looked more than cute.

"I never fully realized before how important shoes and clothes are to one's image. But enough on that subject. I'll get your coffee. Black with one sugar?"

"I can get my own coffee, if you'll lead me to the kitchen." Lee wasn't craving a cup of coffee. He'd just given in to the urge to see her. Since he would stay only a few minutes, he didn't want to let her out of his sight.

"A man after my own heart. Follow me." She led the way. They passed her partners' offices, which she pointed out in turn, explaining each woman's whereabouts. "They'll be sorry they missed you."

Lee wasn't sorry, so he made no reply.

In the kitchen, Rachel indicated the coffeemaker with a glass carafe half-full of dark brew, the collection of mugs neatly arranged on a shelf and a bowl of sugar packets. "I hope the coffee isn't too strong."

"It can't be too strong for me if it pours," he answered, taking a mug and filling it. "You haven't drunk strong coffee until you've worked out on the rigs offshore with a bunch of Louisianians."

She was lighting the burner under a kettle sitting on the stove. "How long did you work offshore?" Her voice was full of interest.

"For fourteen years. I was on a crew boat headed out into the open gulf the day after my high school graduation. I was hung over and in no shape for a boat ride," he recalled, stirring sugar into his coffee while she opened a tea bag and dangled it into a mug.

"What kind of job had you been hired to do?"

"I started off as a roughneck and worked my way up to platform foreman." Lee sat down at the table. Prompted by her questions, he began telling her about his offshore employment. The conversation was one he would never have expected to have with her, but she seemed fascinated and even lost her self-consciousness about her appearance. After she'd made her cup of tea and added artificial sweetener, she sat down across from him.

"What kind of schedule were you on?" she inquired. "You stayed on the rig for a certain number of days and then came home for the same period of time?"

"No, I never took equal time off. Until I was married, I would stay out two or three months at a stretch. It was hell, but I wanted to make the money."

"And after you got married?"

"I worked twenty-one and seven. Sometimes twenty-eight and seven," he admitted.

"I'm trying to put myself in your wife's place and to imagine having a brand-new husband gone for three or four weeks," she reflected.

"She knew what I did for a living and what my ambitions were when she made her bargain," Lee replied unsympathetically. He took a sip of his coffee, which had cooled. "The marriage ceremony says 'for better or worse.' If she'd stuck it out, I would have stuck by her."

"Excuse me, Rachel." The receptionist spoke apologetically from the kitchen door. "I hate to interrupt, but Mr. Payne is on the phone and insists on talking to you."

"Mr. Payne is well named," Rachel said with a sigh. "Tell him I'll return his call in a few minutes."

Lee rose from the table and took his mug to the sink, where he dumped out the rest of the contents and rinsed the mug. "Thanks for the coffee. I didn't mean to overstay my welcome."

Rachel had gotten up, too. "You didn't. We'll have to continue this conversation when you drop by for coffee again. The next time you come I promise I won't entertain you in the kitchen. That's not very good treatment for our biggest client."

"I liked the treatment fine," Lee said. It was the understatement of the year. He'd thrived on having her undivided attention, the attention of a woman interested in a man. They'd both forgotten they were broker and client. He would gladly have kept on forgetting it for hours.

"Alice is back," Rachel said, leading the way toward her office. "I hear her talking to Cindy."

Lee heard the voices in the outer reception area, too. Alice Kirkland entered the hallway and paused to greet him and chat amiably. He was cheated of any private parting words with Rachel.

Outside in his car, Lee sat a moment before starting up the engine. *So much for getting to know her better and getting over her,* he thought. Last night he hadn't wanted to hang up the phone, and today the time spent in her company only made him hungry for more. He wished he could call her on his car phone now and say, "How about taking the rest of the day off?"

The urge was so strong that Lee struck the steering wheel hard with his fist.

Chapter Seven

She'd completely forgotten to mention to Lee that he'd interrupted her in the midst of designing the invitation for the agents' open house, Rachel realized as she sat down once again at her desk. She'd meant to show him her rough version.

Instead she'd become intrigued with learning more about the man. There was so much more she wanted to know about his experiences and his rise to success. Cindy's intrusion hadn't been at all welcome.

Remembering Mr. Payne, the reason for the intrusion, Rachel dutifully called him. Then she tried to settle down to work again, but without much success. It was a beautiful September day. The sun shone outside, bathing the world in mellow golden light. A breeze ruffled the shrubbery outside her office window. She visualized the white sand beach and the open water spreading out to the horizon just a short block away and felt very much as she'd felt years ago in high school when she sat in a classroom, longing to be somewhere else, anywhere else, having fun.

No one was keeping her prisoner today in her office except herself. Where would she like to be? What would she rather be doing? *I'd like to be in some pleasant outdoor setting with Lee, away from Gulfport and Biloxi. Maybe a sidewalk café in New Orleans...*

"That's not a pleasant setting, Rach. That's a romantic setting." Rachel scolded herself out loud. "You're Stephanie's mother, remember—not her older sister."

But it was another phone call that served to douse her in the icy water of reality, a long-distance call from her former in-laws in northern Mississippi. Relations had been strained between Rachel and Blaine's parents since his death. She'd thought that they deserved honesty from her, and she'd disclosed the whole story to them of his manner of dying. They'd been horrified and had taken the stance that she must somehow have been to blame by failing to be a good wife, because otherwise their son wouldn't have lapsed from being a faithful husband. Rachel had sensed that they held some private belief that she was lying to them.

She sent them cards on major holidays and a gift from Stephanie at Christmas. They sent Stephanie gifts and phoned her occasionally. When she was younger, they'd invited her to come for a week during the summer and once a year had taken her on a trip with them. The last few years there'd been no trip or summer visit. Blaine's sister lived in the same town and now had a son and a daughter. Rachel suspected that they satisfied the Cavanaughs' need to be indulgent grandparents.

The only times she'd seen them was when they'd picked up Stephanie and returned her home or when Rachel met them halfway. Her conversations with them in person or on the phone were polite and devoid of any affection. The spoiled relationship was just another casualty of Blaine's dishonorable conduct.

Rachel understood that his parents wanted to cling to their good memories of him, but understanding didn't keep her from resenting them for their treatment of her. She was the victim, not the guilty party.

For the Cavanaughs to call her long distance during the day at her office could only mean that some family tragedy had occurred. That was Rachel's first thought when first Eleanor said hello tearfully and then Charles greeted her solemnly, obviously on a different phone.

"Have you heard that they're letting that murderer out of prison on parole?" Eleanor blurted out.

"We just got word," Charles put in.

"He kills our son in cold blood and they lock him up for only nine years!"

"Now he'll be back out on the street, a menace to society."

"No, I hadn't heard," Rachel said.

Eleanor was weeping. "He should have been found guilty of first-degree murder, not manslaughter."

"This justice system of ours is a sham. A *sham,*" Charles repeated, his own voice trembling with emotion.

Rachel had been through essentially the same conversation nine years ago, when twenty-five-year-old John Partridge had been sentenced at the conclusion of his brief trial. Today she reminded them of what she'd told them then. She'd gone to the district attorney, whom she'd known all her life, and confessed her role in tampering with the scene of the crime. She couldn't have lived with her guilt if she hadn't and the accused had gotten a harsher sentence than he deserved.

But there'd been a self-serving motive, too. She hadn't wanted John Partridge to testify at his trial and tell his true version of his crime of passion—that he'd gone to Blaine's office with the gun to threaten him, not to kill him. Bursting in and finding his girlfriend—Blaine's pretty young receptionist—and Blaine in the act of having sexual intercourse, Partridge had pulled the trigger in a fit of jealous outrage.

The ugly story had been hushed up, and John Partridge had been convicted of manslaughter, the sentence that fit the crime. Justice had been served.

"Partridge wasn't a cold-blooded murderer, Eleanor," Rachel said, her own raw emotions stirred up by the recollection. "Nine years in prison is a long time. He's lost a big chunk of his youth for a crime of passion. I can't begrudge him his freedom. I hope he makes something of his life now."

"I think you would have liked him to get off scot-free," her former mother-in-law accused bitterly. "It really makes me wonder what kind of marriage—"

Her husband broke in, his tone stiff and reproachful. "We just thought we should pass along this information, which we find very upsetting. There may be some mention in your local newspaper, since Partridge was from Gulfport. It could be unpleasant for Stephanie."

"You should both know that recently she found out about the circumstances of Blaine's death," Rachel informed them evenly. "There was gossip going around at school. Maybe Partridge's being up for parole stirred it up."

"Surely you denied the gossip!" Eleanor demanded in an appalled voice. "You didn't let Stephanie believe those horrible things about her father!"

"No, I didn't deny it, Eleanor. It would have been lying to her, and that would have come back to haunt me."

The shocked silence was full of recrimination.

"What kind of mother—"

Charles cut off his wife again. "Don't expect us to support you in shattering our granddaughter's innocence."

"Why should I expect you to show any sort of support at this late date?" Rachel asked him, her own voice reproachful. "My only sin was in believing your son hung the moon. I *was* a good wife to him, and I'm a good mother."

"We're going to hang up now, Rachel. Hang up, dear," Blaine's father instructed.

The line went dead.

Her anger and resentment were softened by pity for the elderly Cavanaughs. Blaine had let them down terribly, too.

The sunlight outside had lost its golden aura, and the beach didn't beckon. Rachel's dreamy mood was gone. She settled down to work on the invitation for the open house with businesslike purpose.

Lee's words, with their underlying idealism about marriage, played in her memory: *The marriage ceremony says 'for better or worse.' If she'd stuck with it, I'd have stuck by her.* "She" being his deceased ex-wife.

The marriage ceremony also contained vows of fidelity. Rachel had believed completely in Blaine's sincerity when he'd repeated those vows after the minister. He'd broken them with more than one woman during the six years of their marriage, during which time she'd been wholly confident of his love and devotion.

Was Lee a better man than Blaine, capable of being faithful to a wife? He might be, but Rachel would never find out through personal experience. She was shocked to find herself even thinking about Lee in those terms. Rachel was never trusting her heart to any man again.

Rachel waited until after supper that evening to tell Stephanie about the phone call from her grandparents in north Mississippi. She and her daughter had finished cleaning up after the meal. "Could we sit down and have a talk before you go to your room to do homework?" she requested.

"Sure. About what?"

"Grandma and Grandpa Cavanaugh called me at the office today. I think I should tell you about our conversation." Rachel intended to recount only part of it—the news that Partridge was getting out on parole. Stephanie needed to be forewarned in case there was publicity.

"Oh. Okay. I hope they don't want me to visit them at Thanksgiving. Not with Grandma and Grandpa Preston out of town."

Rachel was touched. "That's sweet of you not to want to leave me without any close family, darling. But your grandparents didn't have a visit on their mind. They were very upset. I'll explain."

Stephanie was greatly disturbed by the news that the man who shot her father was being released from prison and might possibly receive some media attention. She asked numerous questions about the trial and sentencing and about John Partridge. Rachel didn't back away from the discussion, feeling that it wouldn't be good for her daughter to close it off.

"You don't think he still hates Daddy, do you? He wouldn't kidnap us or something like that?"

"No, I don't believe we're in any danger from him." Rachel soothed her daughter's irrational fears, and her more plausible ones about scandal. "If there's publicity, we'll just hold our heads high together."

Stephanie seemed reassured as she went to her room to study for a quiz.

Rachel sat a moment, wishing that her own mother were near and could reassure her.

Then she got her briefcase.

Taking out her completed, hand-done version of the open-house invitation, she studied it with satisfaction. Mary Lynn and Alice had both given it their stamp of approval. Now she needed to get Lee's okay before she took it to the printer. That afternoon she'd tried to reach him at his office, but he hadn't been there. Nor had he answered his car phone.

Should she call him at his home tonight? If he were any other client, she wouldn't hesitate to do so.

Rachel looked up his number in her client book. She recognized Mark's voice when he picked up on the second ring and mumbled an ungracious, "H'lo."

"Hello, Mark. This is Mrs. Cavanaugh. Could I speak to your father, if he's there?"

"He's not home."

"Would you give him a message that I called?"

"Yeah, sure."

"Thank you very much."

"Oh, no problem."

Rachel gave her head a little shake over his poor telephone manners as she hung up.

Where was Lee tonight? she wondered. Was he with Kim Lamberts? Or with some other woman? He hadn't mentioned being involved with anyone, but surely he had a social life. And a sex life, although he'd stated bluntly that he didn't "shack up" with women and set a bad example for Mark.

Rachel closed her briefcase. Tonight was one of those rare times when her motivation was lacking. She felt depressed and lonely, emotions she couldn't share with her daughter.

Even if her parents had been in town, Rachel wouldn't have wanted to turn to them for comfort. It was hardly fair to worry them, at their age. And while Alice and Mary Lynn were friends as well as business partners, she hadn't ever told them the whole story of Blaine's death, about her trip to his office the day he'd been killed or her visit with the district attorney just prior to the trial of Blaine's accused murderer.

The only person she had told, other than her mother and father, was Lee, oddly enough. Instinctively she'd trusted him to keep it confidential.

"Would you ask me these civics questions, Mom?" Stephanie's voice interrupted Rachel's thoughts.

"I'd be happy to." Rachel took the sheet, glad for her daughter's company.

After they'd gone over the list of questions, they watched TV until it was time to go to bed.

Rachel took a long soak in her tub, partly for the benefit of her ankle. The bath did wonders for her body, but not her morale. Gloomy thoughts crowded her mind as she got into bed and turned out the light. The years would pass. Her parents would age and lose their health and eventually die. Stephanie would grow up and have her own life and family. Rachel would still have her real-estate career. She would stay busy and productive, continue to be a member of her church, perhaps join a travel club, develop hobbies.

But she wouldn't have a companion, someone who cared and wanted to share life's ups and downs. She would go to bed at night and rise in the morning alone.

It was the future her bitterness toward her dead husband and her fear of ever trusting another man made inevitable. "Blaine, how could you do this to me?" Rachel whispered into her pillow, tears welling up and running in hot streams down her cheeks.

As though in response to her question, the phone beside her bed shrilled in the darkness, making her jump. Rachel's low mood made her an easy prey for alarm. Had something happened to her parents? A glance at the clock told her it wasn't the dead of night.

"Hello." Her voice came out nasal and husky.

"Rachel?"

The caller was Lee. Relief flooded through her, that a stranger wasn't phoning long distance with tragic news.

"Hello, Lee."

"You don't sound like yourself. Have you been crying?"

Rachel answered simply, "Yes."

"What's wrong?" His concern came over the line, cheering her somehow. "Something to do with Stephanie?"

"It affects Stephanie. Today my former in-laws phoned to report that the man who shot Blaine is up for parole." She found herself telling him everything, except about her depression over her future.

"I wouldn't expect any news coverage of Partridge's release," Lee remarked thoughtfully. "He's just another ex-convict getting out on parole. It happens all the time and seldom gets any attention, unless the case was really sensational. Publicity is probably the last thing he wants. He'll have a hard enough row to hoe without his crime being rehashed in the media."

"That's true." His analysis was greatly reassuring to Rachel. "I hadn't really thought of it from his angle."

"Try not to worry about it."

"I feel a hundred percent better. Thank you for listening. I guess you didn't have much choice, except to hang up," she added ruefully. "There's something about you that acts on me like a truth serum. With the information you know, you could blackmail me."

"What you've told me will go no further." He added just as soberly, "Anything I might want from you, I'd want to come willingly."

Rachel gripped the phone hard. "I wish I had something to give, Lee, but I don't, other than being a good Realtor for you. And a friend, if you could use a friend. Today stirred up all the awful memories and brought home the fact that my marriage to Blaine killed my ability to trust, to...love again."

His silence was heavy with disappointment, his voice harsh when he spoke. "What did you call about? There's a message here from Mark and there was also a message at my office. I saw it when I went by there a few minutes ago on my way home from my poker game."

Rachel couldn't answer for several seconds, and her silence was heavy with disappointment, too, because he hadn't responded to her words. What had she wanted him to say?

"I need to get your okay on the invitation for the agents' open house. Do you have any time free tomorrow?"

"I'm booked up all day," he replied tersely.

"What about lunch?"

"Yes, I could manage lunch, I guess, if you can be flexible about the time."

"I can be very flexible," Rachel assured him. "Just give me a call fifteen minutes in advance, and I'll meet you at a restaurant. And this time, can I please pay?"

His answer was terse, like his other replies had been. "I'm not promising that."

"Have we lost ground, Lee?" she asked regretfully. "You've gone back to seeming hostile and touchy."

"Don't let it keep you awake. Good night, Rachel. See you tomorrow." With those gruff words, he cut the connection.

"Good night, Lee," Rachel said softly, although he couldn't hear her, and hung up with a sigh.

She drifted off to sleep thinking about her lunch tomorrow with Lee. Would he show up in his jeans or in slacks? It didn't matter in the least to her. What was important was seeing him.

Lee hung up the phone in his bedroom and sat on the side of his bed, his head in his hands, and swore at himself. Of the long string of curses, "you stupid jackass" was one of the kinder descriptions he applied to himself. In his own mind, every maudlin country-and-western song about men making total fools of themselves over women might have been written about him.

Raising his head, he stated wearily, "It's hopeless, Zachary. You've got to stop acting like a damn puppy with its tongue hanging out."

Beginning tomorrow, he decided, he was going to turn over yet another new leaf with Rachel. He was going to keep his distance from her, starting with canceling the lunch date he hadn't even been free to make, since he already had lunch scheduled with a couple of bankers. It wouldn't have mattered if he was having lunch with the president of the United States. He'd have wanted to renege on it for a chance to be with her. That was the kind of shape he was in.

He had to get control of himself and salvage what little was left of his pride. Rachel had been out of his reach when he was a dirt-poor seventeen-year-old. He couldn't have her for his girlfriend then, and he sure as hell couldn't have her for his wife all these years later. That was what he wanted, so why not admit it to himself?

Rachel wearing his ring on her finger and changing her name to Mrs. Lee Zachary—that was never going to happen. Rachel loving him and wanting him to be her husband? *Never.*

He needed to face up to reality and move on.

"You look like you today, Mom," Stephanie commented the next morning.

"I feel like me," Rachel replied cheerfully. She was wearing one of her suits and pumps with heels. "Yesterday I didn't."

"We have to pick up Candy," her daughter reminded her as they got into the car. Rachel had resumed playing chauffeur this week, much to her pleasure.

After she'd dropped the girls off at school, she drove to the office and dealt with a stack of mail. Then she worked on the budget for the agents' open house at Plantation Village, calling caterers and florists and getting prices. At this stage especially, Plantation Village was going to demand most of her time and attention. That had been agreed upon among her and her partners.

They'd also discussed the fact that down the line Rachel would probably need to set up temporary office quarters on the premises of the development and be on hand daily to accompany agents with clients on tours and to finalize sales contracts, as Lee's official broker. He would surely be around often. She'd see him daily, more than likely. The prospect awoke eager anticipation.

At eleven-thirty, Rachel glanced at her watch, aware of a growing sense of expectation. Lee had said he'd call to let her know when he would be free for lunch, and she was certain he would live up to his word. He was that kind of man, one who didn't commit himself lightly.

If only—

Rachel cut off the thought without finishing it, just as footsteps sounded in the hallway. She glanced up and experienced a jolt of surprise and gladness when Lee appeared in her doorway. He was dressed nicely in slacks and a dress shirt with a tie.

"Lee! I was just thinking about you...." She stood up and came around her desk. "But I thought we agreed that I would meet you."

"I'm going to cancel lunch. That's why I came by."

"Oh." The one word conveyed her disappointment. "You're too busy after all to fit me in."

"I have a lunch date with some bankers."

Rachel nodded understandingly. "That's more important. I guess I forgive you for canceling on me," she said lightly. "Do you have time to take a look at the invitation now?"

He gave an abrupt nod. "I have a few minutes."

"Are things not going well on the financial end?" she asked in concerned. "You didn't have this bankers' lunch planned last night."

"Oh, but I did," he corrected her grimly. "I was going to cancel on them. And everything's fine on the financial end." He closed the door.

Rachel gazed at him uncertainly. "But why—"

"That's what I'm here to explain." His gaze traveled down her figure to her feet. "Is your ankle okay?"

"Yes, it's fine." She sighed. "I thought everything was fine. I woke up today in such an optimistic frame of mind. Let's have lunch tomorrow."

"Tomorrow nothing will have changed." Lee shoved his hands into his pockets. "You want to show me the invitation first, before I spill my guts?"

Rachel silently went around behind her desk again. He followed her and stood beside her as she picked up the sheet of paper. "Lee, please don't tell me anything that's going to make our relationship awkward," she begged. "Sometimes it's better to leave things unsaid. I realize that we could very easily get involved with each other if we say too much."

"Do you realize that it's sheer hell for me to be this close and not touch you?" he demanded harshly. "I don't mean grab you and paw you." Rachel turned her face slowly and looked up at him. He raised his hand and caressed her cheek with his fingertips. "Just *touch* you, like this...."

She closed her eyes, shutting out the raw yearning in his hard-featured face and bearing down on her own powerful longings. "Please don't, Lee."

His hand dropped and he moved away from her abruptly. "Go with the invitation," he said.

Rachel sat down, struggling to contain her overwhelming regret. "But you haven't looked at it."

"I glanced at it. It's good, just like I figured it would be." He spoke with his back to her.

"Thank you. Is there a certain printer you like to use?"

"Yes." He told her the name of a local company.

"They do excellent work. We use them ourselves." Rachel couldn't seem to get the disheartened tone out of her voice. "What about a caterer and a florist for the open house?"

"You can pick those yourself." He turned around. "Anything else?"

She shook her head. "That's about it for the information I need from you. By the end of the day, I should have an itemized breakdown of expenses."

"Fax it to my secretary."

"In other words, communicate with you through her, not directly. That's what you're saying, isn't it?" Rachel went on, not hiding her frustration, "I thought we were supposed to work closely together. If we can't, then Mary Lynn or Alice should take over my role."

"Could either one of them have designed that invitation? Or plan the kind of open house that you can? I doubt it. Your partners are top agents, Rachel, but you're the key to big-time success for this agency. I knew that when I picked Magnolia Realty, when I specified that you would be in charge. And you're staying in charge."

"It's very flattering to my ego that you have such confidence in me," she replied. The heavy atmosphere in the room kept his words from being as thrilling as they should have been. "Of course, you have the final word."

He glanced at his watch. "I'd better shove off."

"What about the trip to Florida?" she asked, addressing his back as he reached the door in a couple of long strides.

"It's still on."

"Have your secretary fax me the travel itinerary." Her request, with its hint of a rebuke, made him pause a second before he opened the door with a vigorous twist of the knob. But he left without looking back at her or answering.

Rachel slumped in her chair. She lifted her hand to her cheek where his fingertips had gently stroked her skin. The longing she'd suppressed welled up strongly again.

"Hold me, Lee," she whispered, uttering the words she wished she could have said to him. For just a moment she allowed herself to imagine his arms closing around her tightly, enveloping her in his strength, his rugged maleness.

Even the fantasy helped a little to ease the aching need inside her, a need that Lee had brought to life—to love and be loved by a man.

Chapter Eight

"Hello. Rachel Cavanaugh." Rachel consciously tried not to sound mechanical as she answered the phone on Friday afternoon, knowing that the caller wouldn't be Lee.

He'd canceled lunch with her two days earlier, on Wednesday. Since then he'd transmitted messages through his secretary, Eileen.

"Rachel, Eileen here." The secretary's voice, by now familiar, came through on the line. "Lee just came into the office and looked over the budget for the open house. He's approved it, so you can go ahead with the arrangements."

"Good." Rachel wished that she were free to say, *Is he there? Could I speak to him?* She wanted to hear his voice, wanted to sense his presence. It felt so wrong to be cut off from him like this. "Tell him that we have four appointments to take couples to the site this weekend. I'll be surprised if we don't make our first sale."

"I'll tell him. Maybe the news will sweeten his disposition. The man's been a bear the last couple of days," Eileen complained with good humor.

"I hope everything's going well with the construction."

"Carl Beatty was in here today, all smiles."

"There's nothing the matter with Mark, is there?"

"No, Mark's fine. Lee's probably just having a case of male PMS. He'll get over it. You have a good weekend, Rachel."

"You, too, Eileen."

The insight that Lee hadn't been acting very happy didn't make Rachel any happier herself. His secretary was undoubtedly right, though. He would get over it. Obviously his method was to avoid personal contact with her.

What was to be her method to ease the ache in her heart when she thought about him? Certainly not moping and feeling sorry for herself. Rachel noted the time. She needed to straighten her desk, load up her briefcase and go pick up Stephanie.

Her two partners were still in their offices. She stuck her head in Alice's door first and then in Mary Lynn's to bid them goodbye for the day and also to ask whether they'd like to see a movie on Saturday night. "Stephanie's going out on a date," she explained twice.

Both had to refuse. Mary Lynn was driving over to Baton Rouge to take her college-age twin daughters, who were students at Louisiana State University, out to dinner. Alice was going to New Orleans to attend a birthday party for her daughter-in-law.

The names of several other single-women acquaintances—either widowed or divorced—came to mind as Rachel drove to the high school. But all of them had children, and probably had some sort of plans, too.

Rachel resigned herself to going to a movie or somewhere else alone or to staying home. As Stephanie's social life got busier, there were going to be a lot of these Saturday nights.

"What was Zachary's reaction when you told him we'd made *three* sales this weekend?" Mary Lynn demanded, her shrewd green eyes alight with triumph. "Four sets of clients and *three* purchase contracts. That's worth a bottle of champagne, ladies."

"Better still, a torte cake from Pierre's Confections." Alice closed her eyes in a swooning expression. Opening them, she smiled expectantly at Rachel. "Tell us what he said."

Rachel and her two partners were gathered in her office, having their scheduled Monday-morning meeting. She opened a folder and riffled through the contents as she admitted, "I haven't talked to him. I faxed a note to him at his office first thing this morning."

Alice and Mary Lynn said together in astonishment, "You *faxed* a note to him?"

"Yes, he prefers not to be bothered at his home."

"My goodness," Alice declared, almost indignant at the notion of a client imposing a restriction on phone calls.

Mary Lynn frowned. "Zachary didn't strike me as a privacy nut."

Rachel looked up from the folder and stated simply, "He isn't. He just has a problem with working closely with me. I suggested that I take a back seat and let one of you step into my shoes, but he's adamantly against that. We communicate through his secretary."

"Does he want to date you? Is that his 'problem'?" Mary Lynn asked bluntly.

"I'm sure it is," Alice said before Rachel could answer. She made a *tsk-tsking* sound. "I was afraid of something like this. I saw how he looked at you."

Rachel felt compelled to clarify her position honestly. "The attraction isn't one-sided. If I were open to the idea of ever remarrying—which I'm not—I would want to date Lee."

"Some people do have good marriages, Rachel," Mary Lynn pointed out.

"Not everyone's as unlucky as the three of us have been," Alice agreed.

That was as close to any advice as she would get from either woman, Rachel knew. A basis of their original friendship, aside from full-time careers in real estate, had been their total disillusionment with marriage. They'd shared their stories in general, though not in great detail. Alice's husband of thirty years had left her for a younger woman when she turned fifty. Mary Lynn had been married to two ne'er-do-wells. The second one had turned out to be homosexual.

Rachel got the meeting back on track. "Lee and I can handle the situation. It won't blow up in our faces. I just felt that candor was in order here."

"You have my vote of confidence," Alice said.

"Mine, too," Mary Lynn agreed. "And obviously you have Zachary's. The man's no fool in love, anyway. He's smart to lick his wounds and keep you on the job for him."

"Thank you both."

The discussion turned to other clients, listings, sales, open houses. The gossip was kept to a minimum, and the subject of Lee's and Rachel's personal feelings about each other was closed. Her partners took her at her word that she wouldn't allow her effectiveness to suffer. She would honor their trust.

Just as the meeting was breaking up, Cindy appeared at the door with a huge bouquet of flowers that had just been delivered by a florist. The card was addressed to Magnolia Realty. Rachel guessed that the flowers were from Lee even before Mary Lynn opened the card and read, "Great going, Lee Zachary."

"That's a nice gesture," Alice said approvingly.

Mary Lynn also seemed genuinely pleased.

Rachel's appreciativeness was undermined by the thought of how much she would have liked to hear those words, *Great going,* spoken by him. She faxed back a note, "Thank you for the beautiful flowers. Magnolia Realty."

Later in the week Kim Lamberts called to arrange another decorating conference. She inquired, "Rachel, could we get together soon? I've picked out some different wallpapers and need to run them by you."

"You mean run them by me *and* Lee?" Rachel verified, her pulse quickening. It seemed a century since she'd seen him.

"No, he came by my shop earlier today and took a look." Kim sighed with exaggerated wistfulness. "I looked at *him.* The man's *so* gorgeous to be loose on the streets with no wife. Tell me honestly. Are you two an item?"

Rachel's throat hurt as she squeezed out her truthful reply, "No, Kim, we're not." Her disappointment was overwhelming. She wouldn't get to see Lee. He was continuing to avoid her.

The assurance was obviously what Kim had hoped to hear. She got down to business cheerfully, asking, "When and where would you like to get together? I could meet you at the site after the workmen are gone, like we did before. Or I could come by your office."

Rachel might encounter Lee at the building site. But that shouldn't be a consideration. Angry at herself and disturbed by the intensity of her longing for even a glimpse of him, she suggested, "Why don't I save you the trouble of lugging all those heavy wallpaper books and come by your shop, too?"

"You're a doll!"

"How's four-thirty this afternoon?"

"Perfect."

As she hung up, Rachel realized that she wasn't just angry at herself. She was angry at Lee because he'd gone to Kim's shop, angry at Kim because she'd gotten to spend time in his company, angry even more because her anger was so futile. It wasn't going to solve a thing.

Yet it didn't fade away entirely. Nor did the nagging disappointment or the longing to see Lee and talk to him. Her emotions mixed together into a vague unhappiness that gradually bred resentment.

It was a ridiculous situation she found herself in, acting as Realtor for a client who lived in the immediate area and yet who might have resided on the other side of the continent and been an underworld kingpin for all the contact she had with him. Rachel was thoroughly tired of using Eileen as a go-between by the time Lee's secretary called to discuss travel arrangements for the upcoming trip to Florida.

"I can book a commuter flight for you from New Orleans to Pensacola. You can take a limousine from the Pensacola airport to the hotel."

There was no mention of riding to the New Orleans airport with Lee and the Livingstons and the Beattys. "Are the others driving?" It was only about a four-hour drive from Gulfport and Biloxi. The New Orleans airport was an hour's drive in the wrong direction, and between arriving and taking off, she'd have to add another thirty minutes.

"Yes, they're going in two different cars. The Beattys and the Livingstons are leaving a day ahead of time. They're making a vacation trip out of it. Lee isn't leaving until late afternoon on Thursday. He won't be arriving in time to have dinner with the rest of you."

"I see." Rachel saw very clearly, and her resentment, which had been simmering for a couple of weeks, flared up into a sharper emotion. He meant to avoid any travel time with her and probably would avoid as many meals with her as possible. "That same itinerary would suit me very well," she said briskly. "I don't suppose he mentioned possibly giving me a ride in his car and saving me all the hassle of taking a flight?''

"No, he didn't," Eileen admitted. "I'm just the secretary, Rachel."

"I'm sorry. I shouldn't take out my annoyance on you. Is Lee there? I'd like to speak to him."

"Just a second. Let me check on whether he can take a call now."

Much more than a second elapsed, time enough for Rachel's courage to waver and be bolstered again by righteous indignation.

"Hello, Rachel." Lee's voice came over the line, terse and reluctant. "Eileen says you have a bone to pick with me."

"I've had it with going through Eileen, Lee! Enough is *enough!* This is getting on my nerves! And I'm not going off to Florida and have you treat me like I have a contagious disease!" Rachel was trembling as she ended her tirade.

"You have a temper," he said, his tone odd.

"Yes, I have a temper. I have feelings. I'm human."

"It's good to hear your voice. How have you been?"

"Just okay. How have you been?" Her resentment had melted away.

"Not too good. Do you want to ride to Florida with me?"

"Yes, if you wouldn't mind the company."

"I'll pick you up at your house around three o'clock on Thursday afternoon."

"I'll be packed and ready to go."

Rachel hung up, conscious of a warm happiness.

It had been arranged considerably in advance for Stephanie to stay with Candy Wakefield while Rachel was away. Stephanie hadn't expressed any qualms about the brief separation, nor did Rachel feel any strong qualms herself. The two weeks of punishment had ended. Stephanie had regained her telephone privileges and was allowed to go to the mall. She'd had another date with Michael Curtis, and there was no sign that she was pining for Mark Zachary.

Rachel hated to mention Lee's name and bring up the subject of Mark, but there was no getting around it without withholding the information that she was riding to Pensacola with Mark's dad. She didn't even consider doing that. Openness between mother and daughter was too important.

Stephanie's reaction to the travel plan was plainly negative. "Just the two of you are going in Mr. Zachary's car?"

"It would be silly for both of us to drive," Rachel pointed out, emphasizing the practical aspect.

"Why don't all six of you rent a van or something? It would save on gas."

"Because Mr. Livingston and Mr. Beatty and their wives are leaving a whole day earlier. We'll meet up with them at the hotel. The drive isn't that long—about four hours." Four hours with Lee. She was so looking forward to it.

"Who is Mark staying with? His friend Carl?"

"I really don't know Mark's plans. I didn't ask." Her guess was that he was staying at their condo without any adult supervision. Lee had stated in an earlier conversation that he wouldn't hesitate to leave his son on his own for several days. Rachel wasn't about to share that conjecture with Stephanie, though. "I'll bring you a present from Pensacola," she promised, hoping to get her daughter's mind off Mark.

Stephanie pouted. "I could have gone along and ridden with you. It wouldn't have hurt me to miss two days of school." She was back on the subject of Rachel's and Lee's riding together to Pensacola. "While you were away from the hotel during the day, I could have swum in the pool and done my school assignments."

"There's no way I would leave you by yourself at a hotel all day," Rachel exclaimed. "My mind would be on you, not on real estate, and Mr. Zachary wouldn't appreciate that, since he's paying my expenses."

Everything she said was true, but Rachel was guiltily aware that as much as she adored her daughter's company, she wouldn't want to give up the trip to and from Pensacola with Lee.

"Is that a new sport jacket?" Mark inquired. "New slacks, too?"

Lee had a busy day tomorrow and was packing for the trip to Florida tonight. He glanced at his son, who was lounging in the open door of Lee's bedroom, watching him. "You taking inventory of my clothes?" he evaded dryly.

Mark grinned. "You'd better watch out, Dad, or you're going to become a real dude, trying to impress Mrs. Cavanaugh."

"Did you decide whether you're going to stay at Carl's house?"

"Changing the subject, huh, Dad? Yeah, I guess I'll stay over at Carl's. I figure you'll probably feel more easy, even though you left it up to me."

"I will feel more easy," Lee admitted readily. "Not that I'd worry about coming home and finding the place trashed."

"I know. You don't like to think about me rattling around by myself. It's kinda the way I'm gonna feel when I go off to college next year."

Lee paused in the act of zipping his leather garment bag. "I won't know what to do with all that uneaten food in the refrigerator, that's for sure," he said gruffly. It was one of those heartfelt communications between father and son.

"Back to Mrs. Cavanaugh—is she still bent out of shape about me and Stephanie going out?"

"I think she considers the episode water under the bridge. But I wouldn't put her down as a character reference, if I were you."

"She thinks I'm a real bad guy?"

"Well, you insisted on taking the rap, and Stephanie let you." Lee had gotten clean underwear from a bureau drawer. He stuffed it into a pocket of the bag.

"It bothers you that Mrs. Cavanaugh sees me as some kind of punk kid."

"Hell, yes, it bothers me. You're my son, and I'm damned proud that you're anything but a punk kid."

"You raised me, Dad. With Grandma's help. I had a good shot at turning out okay." He asked casually, steering them into less-emotional territory, "How is Stephanie doing, anyway?"

"I assume she's fine. Otherwise I'm sure Mrs. Cavanaugh wouldn't go out of town and leave her." Lee added, "Mrs. Cavanaugh and I haven't been on the most friendly terms lately."

"So that's what was eating at you," Mark commented. "You must have made up, since she's riding with you to Florida."

"I don't know if we 'made up.' The term hardly applies, since Mrs. Cavanaugh and I have never dated."

Mark pressed, "But you'd like to date her."

"Yes, and that's about all I have to say on the subject."

"Just one last thing, and I'll shut up. You'll have a lot of time with Mrs. Cavanaugh on this trip. Go for it, Dad. You didn't get where you are by hanging back."

Lee had finished packing. "Relationships with women are more complicated than that. Right now I'm ready to 'go for' getting something to eat. Let's try that new seafood restaurant that just opened."

"Fine by me. I'm starving."

Father and son went out to supper together. "Got a date this weekend?" Lee asked, and Mark answered in the affirmative. He'd started dating a girl who was also a senior. The one date with Stephanie Cavanaugh had effectively cured his crush on her, so history wasn't repeating itself.

It wasn't a case of like father, like son, and Lee was glad.

He was conscious on the eve of his trip out of town of treasuring the company of his son, of treasuring the special relationship they had. And yet there was a need in him, a void that the relationship, as special as it was, didn't fill.

In the back of his mind, Lee kept hearing his son's well-intentioned and youthful advice, "Go for it, Dad. You didn't get where you are by hanging back."

Should he "go for it" with Rachel? Did he have the nerve to put all his emotional chips on the table, win or lose?

Rachel parked her garment bag, small suitcase and briefcase by the kitchen door and watched for Lee through the window of the family room, taking occasional deep breaths to calm her nervousness. It was so silly of her to have the jitters. She was going on a three-day business trip by car, not off on a safari or an ocean cruise with Lee.

His car pulled into the driveway, and she hurriedly collected her luggage, briefcase and purse. Exiting through the carport, she paused long enough to lock the door. He'd gotten out, having first popped open the trunk of his car, and came to take the luggage from her hands.

"You're right on time," she said, needing to say something. His fingers brushed hers, adding to the intense pleasure of seeing him again. She wanted to gaze up into his face.

There was the additional treat of hearing his deep voice as he replied, "If you'd waited a minute, I would have come inside and carried out your luggage for you."

"I'm just so used to carrying it myself. It isn't heavy."

Her neighbor across the street, Mabel Struther, had walked out of her house to her mailbox. Rachel had been too wrapped up in Lee to notice. It had slipped her mind to inform her neighbors that she would be away several days on business, she realized with chagrin as she waved to Mabel and Mabel waved back, casting a curious glance at Lee.

"Well, there goes my reputation," she commented as, seated in the car, she fastened her seatbelt.

"The same nosy neighbor who spotted Stephanie leaving with Mark?" Lee asked, starting up the car.

"She has a heart of gold, but she doesn't miss anything that goes on in the neighborhood. I hope she noticed I brought along my briefcase and that we're both dressed for a business trip." He was wearing a handsome sport jacket and slacks and a tie. Rachel glanced down at herself. "Unfortunately, it won't escape her that this suit I'm wearing is new. Or that you're an extremely good-looking man. Oh, well." She settled back in her seat. "Enough about Mabel. Tell me about how the construction is going on the model units."

He went along readily with her change of subject, bringing her up to date. Rachel angled her body sideways so that she didn't have to turn her head far to gaze at him. Soon they were on Interstate 10 headed west. Lee settled back with the cruise control turned on.

"Music?" he asked, looking over at her.

"Some music would be relaxing. What kind of music do you like to listen to?"

"That was *my* next question."

Rachel smiled at him. Her heart stopped beating when he smiled back. "Let's see if we can guess each other's taste," she challenged impulsively. "I'll bet you like country and western."

"I do, but not the cry-in-your-beer variety. I'll bet you like Elvis and the Beach Boys and all those oldies-but-goodies."

"How did you know that?" Rachel exclaimed.

Lee shrugged, reaching to turn on the radio. He tuned in a station that played rock-and-roll classics, adjusting the volume to a level that allowed for conversation.

"I don't dislike country and western," she assured him. "I've never listened to it much."

"We'll give you a chance between here and Pensacola." Lee unbuttoned his shirt at the throat and loosened the knot of his tie.

Rachel kicked off her pumps and shifted a little more toward him so that she could gaze at his profile. "How did you get to where you are today? Going from offshore worker to property developer? And I don't want the condensed version." She was eager to know everything about him.

"I went offshore to work because it was a way to make money that I could use as capital. An honest way that wouldn't land me in prison," he added. "It was pretty clear to me that ordinary working people are at a disadvantage in accumulating wealth because it takes most of what they earn just to subsist."

"You'd decided you wanted to be wealthy?"

"I'd decided that at a young age. When I got the offshore job, I set a goal for saving up a certain amount by the time I was twenty-five. But then having to get married set me back."

"Getting married wasn't in your plan?"

"Not until I could afford a wife. I figured that wouldn't be until I was about thirty. But things happened the way they did. I got Lisa pregnant and became a father. Then I had a kid to raise. That meant renting or buying a decent house for him and my mother to live in, and supporting the three of us. So it took me ten years to accumulate fifty thousand dollars to invest."

"You were twenty-eight." He'd told her when he came by the office for coffee that he'd gone offshore the day after graduating from high school.

"That's right. I had the money invested in CD's in a Biloxi bank. One of the vice presidents was Hal Kemp, who was my age. His father was chairman of the board, which had helped him to get his position." Lee was cynically matter-of-fact. "I went to Hal and asked him for financial advice. He told me about a group of local businessmen who were forming a limited partnership to build a beachfront condominium complex. The shares were a hundred grand, but they let me buy a half share.''

"So you risked your entire savings."

"Every penny of it."

"What condominium complex? Not the one you're living in?"

Lee looked over at her and nodded. "It's survived hurricane-force gales. Before I bought in for my half share of the limited partnership, I looked carefully at the plans and talked to the architect and contractor to satisfy myself that I wasn't backing some shoddy eyesore."

"That's a very commendable attitude. I wish all property developers had it."

He shrugged. "It just makes good sense to build something that adds to the community."

"So your first venture was successful. You took your profits and invested them in another one," Rachel said, prompting him to go on with his story. "What was it?"

"A hotel." Lee mentioned the name. "It was the same group of businessmen, but this time a limited partnership wasn't formed. We leveraged our equity in the condominium and built the hotel with a bank loan."

"And you said you weren't a gambler!"

"I said I took only calculated risks."

"So the hotel earned you more profits for your original fifty thousand, which was soundly invested in the condo complex. This is fascinating," Rachel declared. "And meanwhile you were still working offshore."

"I continued working offshore until I was thirty-two. By then I was platform foreman and pulling in big pay. Even though I was tired of the life, I probably wouldn't have quit for a number of years, but Mark was growing up and getting to be more of a handful for his grandmother. I needed to take over raising him and relieve her of the responsibility. Plus I wanted to be around for his football and baseball games. I knew how important it was to a boy for his dad to be watching from the bleachers."

"You knew that because your own father hadn't been on the sidelines watching you." Rachel's voice was soft with understanding.

Lee nodded.

"So you quit your job," she prompted. "You had a big enough income from your investment in the condo complex and the hotel to live on?"

"The hotel had been bought by a big national hotel corporation after it was built. And I'd liquidated my interest in the condo complex. The limited partnership was set up for five years, and that five years was up," he explained. "Using part of the combined profits from both ventures as a down payment, I bought an apartment building." He mentioned it by name, and Rachel recognized it as being a nice complex in Biloxi. "I had rental income, plus more leveraging power as an owner of commercial property. When I stopped working offshore, I had already invested in another venture with two of my original partners—a shopping center."

Rachel was familiar with the center when he identified it. "I shop there. It's charming because it isn't large and has architectural interest. So far I admire every single project that's made you into a big success, Lee. But please tell me more," she urged. "What came next? What did you do with your time now that you weren't employed?"

He fiddled with the radio, bringing the station in more clearly. "We don't have to talk about me all the way to Pensacola," he said gruffly, and Rachel realized that her words may have embarrassed him. Or pleased him.

The insight was disarming. "I'm *not* just making conversation. I find your rise to success truly fascinating and amazing. Most women do, I would expect." The revealing conjecture popped out, and it was her turn to be embarrassed as he shot her a searching look. She added, "Like me, they probably also find it rather incredible that there isn't a Mrs. Lee Zachary. But please go on, where you left off. If you don't mind, that is."

"Mind?" he scoffed cynically. "At this rate there won't be room in this car for both of us and my male ego."

Rachel smiled at him. "When it gets too crowded, we'll have to call a halt. You quit your offshore job at age thirty-two," she prompted. "You owned an apartment building and were involved in your third real-estate venture...."

He resumed his narrative, and she plied him with questions. They digressed periodically and got involved in discussions of local politics and local personalities. There was another interlude when she insisted that he tune in a country-and-western station, the station they'd been listening to having faded out.

Daylight also began to fade as the car sped along the interstate, eating up the miles much too fast for Rachel, who absently noted the names of towns on signs that whizzed past. She didn't want to arrive in Pensacola and meet up with the others. She wished that she and Lee could keep driving and talking for hours and hours.

"That brings us up to the present," Lee said, putting on his turn signal as they approached an exit from the interstate. "I wouldn't go broke if Plantation Village were a bust, but I'd be darned close to it."

"We're stopping for gas?" she asked.

"I might top up the tank, but we have plenty of fuel. I thought it would be good to stretch our legs and have something to drink."

Rachel readily agreed, then returned to the conversation. "You're not in any danger of Plantation Village being a money loser, but knowing how much is riding on its being profitable makes me feel a little nervous as your Realtor. I'll work twice as hard."

"Twenty-four hours a day is all I ask," Lee replied, and they smiled at each other, Rachel's heart giving the same leap of pleasure she experienced every time he smiled at her.

"Do you know that you're downright likable?" she commented lightly. "I'm seeing a whole new side of your personality." A side of him that she could so easily love.

They'd reached the stop sign at the end of the exit ramp. Lee was checking for traffic and didn't respond, no answer really being called for.

He turned right and drove past several fast-food places, where the service was sure to be speedy, to a chain restaurant, where their stop would be longer. While Rachel was finding her shoes and slipping them on, he came around and opened her door. She took his hand and let him help her out. His fingers were strong and warm, clasping hers. When he released her, she felt an ache at the separation.

They walked inside together, and Rachel excused herself to go to the women's room. As much as anything, she wanted a few moments to get a firm hold on reality. It was wonderful to be on friendly terms with Lee, but that was all she could allow.

He'd waited for her to join him rather than taking a table without her. Rachel's pulse quickened at the sight of him, tall and ruggedly attractive in his sport coat and slacks and dress shirt with the two top buttons undone. Earlier he'd discarded the tie, tossing it into the back seat.

When he turned toward her, his gaze full of unspoken compliments, Rachel's pleasure caused a giddy sensation. "You didn't have to wait on me," she said, reaching him. "Though I guess the whole idea of stopping was to stretch our legs, wasn't it?"

"You want me to answer that honestly?" Lee asked.

"No, I don't think you have to." For both of them, the real idea behind stopping had been to prolong the trip.

A waitress acting as hostess bustled up with two menus in her hand and spoke to Lee. "Would you and your wife like smoking or nonsmoking, sir?"

"Nonsmoking," he replied, letting the error go uncorrected.

She led the way to a table for two. When they both refused menus and ordered coffee, the waitress hurried over to a nearby coffee station and brought back filled cups. After setting them down, sloshing the contents in the process, she rushed away to tend to other tables.

"Sugar, dear?" Rachel inquired wryly, moving the sugar caddy closer to Lee.

He took a packet, ripped it open and dumped the contents into his cup. "She wouldn't do very well on that TV game show where the audience picks out the couple who're married, would she?"

"The poor woman hardly glanced at us. She seemed terribly overworked." Rachel sipped her coffee. "I'm surprised you're familiar with that show. Have you ever watched it?"

"Not more than a minute or two when I was passing through the room and it was on. My mother liked it, along with almost any other kind of game show."

"My mother always liked it, too."

With her left hand, Rachel rearranged the salt and pepper shakers. She wanted to tell him that she hadn't minded in the least being mistaken for his wife, but it wasn't a conversation she should begin.

Lee stilled her hand with his, then held it loosely, his thumb caressing the spot where she'd worn her wedding rings. "Did Cavanaugh buy you a splashy diamond engagement ring?" he asked. His thoughts had veered to the past, while hers had been very much on the present.

"It was a diamond solitaire, but not splashy. When he gave it to me I thought it was the most beautiful ring in the world."

His left hand was resting on his paper place mat. "Did you wear a wedding ring when you were married to Mark's mother?" she asked. She reached out and touched his bare ring finger, and he flattened his hand and moved it toward her.

"Yes, when I was home, I did. I didn't wear the ring at work, for safety reasons, so I never got used to it."

"Did you keep it?" Rachel stroked the spot between his knuckles where a gold band would have announced to the world that he wasn't free.

"I have it somewhere." He stopped her stroking motion, clasping her hand. Now he was holding both her hands, though not tightly. She could pull free at any time, and she would soon. Somehow the discussion made it all right to briefly enjoy the intimacy of holding hands with him in a public place.

"I had to keep my rings," she volunteered, "though I wanted to get rid of them. I'll give them to Stephanie someday."

Their harried waitress approached with the coffeepot and the check. "More coffee?" she inquired, laying down the check and seeming oblivious to the fact that her interruption was ill timed for her customers.

"None for me," Rachel answered, regretfully placing her hands in her lap.

"You can heat mine up," Lee said, reaching into his pocket for his wallet. He extracted a ten-dollar bill and handed it to the waitress with the check. "Keep the change for your tip, and we won't be wanting any more coffee."

"Thank you, sir. You and your wife be sure to come back and visit us," the woman gushed, dashing away toward the cash register.

Lee stirred his coffee, took a taste of it and grimaced.

"Not sweetened quite right, dear?" Rachel guessed, her irony tinged with amusement this time.

He drawled, "No, darling, it isn't." Shaking his head, he grinned ruefully. "I guess it's pretty safe for her to assume that most couples who walk through the door are married to each other."

Rachel glanced around the restaurant, which was full. "I would make the same assumption about every other couple I see. It just came as a shock for her to mistake us for being husband and wife, because I feel so *un*married."

"Same here. Of course, I wasn't really a husband long enough to get used to what it felt like."

"I loved being a wife," she recalled with a matter-of-fact bitterness. "I hate to admit how blissfully content I was."

Lee reached across the table again. She gave him her hands, and he squeezed them and held them in a tight grip this time. "Cavanaugh had to be the most stupid man on the face of the earth not to appreciate what he had."

"No more stupid than your wife was. Lee, you would make some lucky woman a wonderful husband."

"Some woman besides you, you mean."

"I wish things could be different...." That she could be the woman he loved. But she couldn't be.

"So do I. Then I would take some advice my son gave me." He released her hands. "Shall we get back on the road?"

Chapter Nine

"Why don't you let me drive and you take a turn sitting back?" Rachel suggested when they were outside.

"Do you feel like driving?"

When she assured him that she did, he surprised her by handing her the keys. She'd expected him to refuse.

Before he got into the car, he removed his jacket and laid it on the back seat. Rachel decided to follow his example, encouraged by the fact that dusk had fallen and it would soon be dark. She took off her suit jacket and laid it in the back seat, too.

Static came from the radio when she turned the key. When she insisted that he tune in another country-and-western station, he didn't argue. On the interstate, he settled back comfortably, his long legs sprawled apart. Rachel noticed that he wasn't facing forward, but had angled his body so that he could look at her easily. Under his gaze she felt sexy in her long-sleeved silk blouse. She was conscious of her breasts, conscious of the hem of her skirt against her nylon-clad thighs.

"Did you start college and drop out to get married?" he asked, his tone indicating that the question had formed in his mind as he thought about her.

"No. Blaine and I had a whirlwind courtship and became engaged the summer after I graduated from high school. It would have been a waste of my parents' money for them to send me to college for a year, I thought. The wedding was set for the following June."

"You must have worked at some kind of job."

"I worked in the pharmacy and saved my money to go toward the down payment on a house and buying furniture. We were having a big church wedding, which takes a lot of planning."

"Cavanaugh had finished law school when you met him?"

"No, he had one more year. But he'd already been assured of a position as an associate in a local law firm."

"Were you sleeping with him during that year?"

Rachel answered readily and without emotion, the memory seeming very distant when the present was so immediate. "No, I was a virgin on our wedding night, though I wasn't totally innocent, of course. It's so ironic that I admired him because he didn't pressure me. As likely as not, he may have had a girlfriend on the side while we were engaged." She glanced at him. "In case you're wondering, Blaine's the only man I've ever slept with. And the sex was good, from my standpoint. Of course, I equated sex with love. Men don't, do they?"

"I can't speak for men, just for myself."

"Well, is sex an expression of love for you?"

"It never has been, since I haven't been in love with any of the women I've slept with."

Which meant he hadn't ever been in love. That was partly what she'd been wanting to know. "There've been a lot of women?" It was more statement than question.

"I haven't kept count, but there've been quite a few."

"Are you seeing someone now?"

"No, not for about six months."

"Isn't that a long time for a man to go without sex?"

"Again, I can't speak for men in general. I wasn't having any problem until I ran into you."

Rachel's cheeks were warm, but more with guilt than embarrassment. His blunt answer was both pleasing and titillating. "There must be something about riding along at night and listening to country-and-western music that encourages conversation that gets down to the nitty-gritty," she remarked. "In the light of day, I would never have probed into your sex life."

Lee shifted in his seat, hitching his slacks higher on his thighs. "Maybe we'd better change the station. For me the conversation is getting a bit too stimulating."

She managed not to look over at his groin for any verification, but her imagination wasn't so easily controlled. "Let's just change the subject. I'm enjoying the music."

"Are you?" he asked, without any cynical inflection.

"Yes, along with your company. You're about the most direct man I've ever known. I'm tempted to think that you would answer any question I asked you with total honesty or else tell me that it was none of my business."

"There aren't any questions that are off bounds for you."

"Like everything you say, that rings so true. And yet for all I know, you could be handing me a big line. Common sense tells me that you should be married, if you were husband material." Rachel shook her head. "I just can't trust my instincts, Lee, not where men are concerned."

"I don't buy that, Rachel," he stated flatly. "You're not nineteen years old now. You're a highly intelligent woman. Am I anything at all like Cavanaugh?"

"Nothing at all like him," Rachel answered bluntly, stung by his skepticism. "Not in looks or personality or temperament. He was the master of small talk. He was completely at home in a suit and tie and very fastidious and vain about his appearance. He took being a southern gentleman to the extreme, even to kissing a woman's hand. Whereas you—"

He cut her off, saying in the same flat tone, "I know what I'm like. You don't have to describe me for myself."

"You certainly don't suffer in comparison, not in my eyes," Rachel assured him. "Quite the opposite." She wanted badly to go on and describe him the way she saw him, but it was better not to. Her description would have revealed what there was no point in revealing.

"He must have been your type of man. You married him."

"As you just pointed out, I was nineteen."

"Pull in at the rest stop up ahead," he instructed her with his old abruptness. "I'll drive the rest of the way."

"Is there something wrong with my driving?" she asked.

"There's a hell of a lot wrong about this trip, but not with your driving. And I'm sure Cavanaugh wasn't so crude in his language, was he?"

Rachel sighed audibly, switching on the turn signal. "No, he never said hell or damn in my hearing. His failings weren't so trivial."

What would be accomplished by convincing Lee that he stood head and shoulders above Blaine, in her estimation? It really didn't matter what he believed the obstacles between them to be. The real obstacle was her inability to trust her heart to him.

And he hadn't exactly tried to bash through it. If he really wanted a relationship with her, surely he would press for one more aggressively. Lee hadn't gotten where he was by taking no for an answer. At the rest stop they exchanged places. Before she got out, Rachel adjusted the seat for him, giving him the maximum amount of leg room.

She was half expecting the rest of the trip to be silent, but Lee questioned her about her real-estate career and listened intently to her answers. She found herself talking on at length, sharing the high points of her rise to success in her profession and also some of the headaches. Most of her anecdotes had their humorous side, and several times he chuckled in amusement. Rachel felt richly rewarded at having entertained him.

As they neared Pensacola, she regretted that the trip was ending and they would be meeting up with the others. Her voice was full of that regret as she read from a sign looming in the headlights, "Ten miles."

"We'll soon be there," Lee said with a note of resignation. "The trip seemed very short to me. I could drive for another four and a half hours easily." *With you for company,* he added with his eyes.

"So could I." Rachel looked at the clock on the car dashboard. "Seven-thirty. Do you suppose the Livingstons and the Beattys are waiting for us to show up so that we can all go to dinner?"

"With any luck, they won't be."

It was her sentiment exactly. She mentioned the obvious reluctantly. "I guess we could call the hotel and let them know we'll be arriving within the half hour."

"We could do that," Lee agreed. "But let's don't."

"Whatever you say. You're the boss."

"I wish," he said. "If whatever I said went, we wouldn't be in separate rooms the next couple of nights. That's for damned sure."

"One night would probably be enough for you," Rachel replied. "You would find me a very inexperienced bed partner. If I could afford to be kind, I guess I'd let you get me out of your system."

"I've never played on a woman's kindness before, but in your case I just might."

She didn't answer his cynical warning, but turned her head and gazed out at the dark terrain flying by. The thought of one night of lying in bed next to him with his arms around her filled her with such stark longing.

"You're not going to have to deal with my inviting myself to your hotel room, so don't worry about it." Lee's gruff assurance held an underlying gentleness that intensified her emotions.

When she could trust herself to speak, she said, "I'm not worried."

"There's a message here for you, sir," the front-desk clerk said to Lee. He was an officious young man in his twenties.

Lee scanned the note and summarized the contents for Rachel. His architect and contractor and their wives had gone out to a dinner-theater club and would be holding seats for them in case they arrived in time to join the foursome.

"Would you like to?" he asked, afraid that she'd say yes. She'd hardly said another word after the tense discussion about separate hotel rooms. "If so, we should probably get directions and go straight there. It's almost eight o'clock."

"Do you think we should? I mean, would it seem unsociable not to?"

The slight indecision was all Lee needed. "I'm sure they'll understand that we might be tired from traveling and might rather stay here at the hotel and have a quiet dinner. That's what I vote for."

"Then let's pass on the dinner-theater club. I'm not much in the mood."

Lee braced himself for her to add that she really preferred to order room service and eat alone, but instead she asked if she had time to go to her room and freshen up and phone her daughter. "Plenty of time," he replied, saved from having to cajole her, if necessary, to have dinner with him.

Both their rooms were on the third floor of the four-story luxury hotel in downtown Pensacola. Lee's was on the opposite side of the corridor and several doors away from hers. Even that proximity was going to play hell with his sleeping the next couple of nights, he reflected as he entered the room, using the plastic key card.

Her words came to mind, *One night would probably be enough for you. If I could afford to be kind, I guess I'd let you get me out of your system.* Lee knew better. Once he made love to her, he would want her more. The sex would unleash all the powerful feelings he had for her, and afterward he would be in worse shape than he was now. It would be even harder to live with the fact that he couldn't have her.

Sleeping with Rachel wasn't going to change the fact that she would never be crazy about him as she'd been about that bastard Cavanaugh. All the talk about trust was baloney. The bottom line was that Lee didn't measure up to her standards and she didn't care enough about him to gamble on trusting him.

The phone at the Wakefield house was busy. As she hung up, Rachel wondered, as she had frequently in the past, why Candy's parents didn't subscribe to the call-waiting service. Their teenagers kept their phone tied up.

While she was disappointed not to be able to get through and hear her daughter's voice, the extra few minutes were welcome. They would give Rachel time to take a quick shower and change clothes. Lee had told her not to rush, because he had a couple of phone calls to make himself. "Just come and knock on my door when you're ready," he'd said over his shoulder as he'd continued down the corridor to his room.

Thinking about him, Rachel stripped in the dressing area. She caught sight of herself in the mirror as she turned from hanging up her clothes and stopped short. The only man who'd seen her nude like this was Blaine. He'd worshiped her with his eyes and told her she was beautiful with flowery, poetic words. She'd felt alluring and special and complacently happy that she was the one woman in his life.

Of course, she hadn't been. He'd probably told other women they had skin like satin and the figure of a goddess. Was it only her youth and romantic naiveté that had made her gullible?

Could she rely on her instincts now as a more mature woman, as Lee had not very forcefully argued?

Rachel didn't know the answer. What she did know was that it excited her to imagine Lee's walking in now and seeing her. It excited her even more to think of being naked with him. For just a few seconds, she allowed herself to fantasize. Then she took her shower and tried to wash away the ache of dissatisfaction.

At eight-thirty she knocked on Lee's door, wearing the one dress she'd brought—a basic black shift that could be dressed up or down and worn with different accessories. She'd chosen a necklace of ornate cloisonné beads and had draped a black cardigan sweater around her shoulders.

Perhaps a minute passed. Rachel was about to knock again when the door swung open, and Lee stood there barechested, his slacks unbelted. "I'm not quite ready—" He broke off midapology and whistled. "Wow. You look beautiful."

"I decided to change," she explained unnecessarily, gazing at him as admiringly as he was gazing at her. It was twice as unsettling to see him partially undressed after imagining him without his clothes. Her imagination hadn't improved on his physique. His shoulders were broad and his chest hard muscled and furred with dark body hair.

"I decided the same thing," he said. "I was expecting you to take longer, so I jumped into the shower after I made my phone calls. I'll just be a couple of minutes." He turned away, leaving the door open and not inviting her in. Rachel was treated to the sight of his back, which was smooth and tautly powerful.

After he'd disappeared, going, she assumed, into a dressing alcove similar to hers, she leaned against the doorframe, recovering her composure. He returned in less than five minutes, wearing a jacket and tie and looking wellgroomed. Rachel found him more ruggedly appealing, more virile than before, following the awkward incident.

"It must be nice to be a man and not have to be modest," she mused in the elevator as they rode up to the top floor, where the restaurant was located.

"I was modest," he objected. "When you knocked on the door, I didn't have a stitch on."

"Under those circumstances, you were modest then," she admitted.

"Damned right I was. Out of consideration for you, I didn't open the door in a towel." He grinned at her.

She smiled back at him. "That *was* very considerate. Thank you."

The conversation cured the awkwardness, but it didn't do anything to settle Rachel's pulse rate or raise her lowered defenses.

Tonight felt so much like a date, and telling herself that it wasn't didn't help at all. The restaurant was very elegant, with an intimate, quiet atmosphere. Lee had evidently phoned from his room and made reservations, although that wouldn't have been necessary because there were empty tables on a Thursday evening. Their own table seemed utterly private, off to itself in a corner. A small vase held a single rose, and the piano player in the adjacent bar played a dreamy love song.

Rachel picked up the small vase and sniffed the rose, desperate to find some flaw in the whole romantic ambience, but the lack of fragrance didn't bring her feet down to earth with a thud, not with Lee's attentiveness. He couldn't seem to take his eyes off her, and his whole attitude was that no entrée could be quite delicious enough for her, no wine quite perfect for her palate. She felt pampered and special.

They talked about food and restaurants, about Pensacola and Florida, but the conversation ran on two levels, the spoken and the unspoken. Lee told her silently and repeatedly that she was beautiful and that he was profoundly interested in any opinion she held, any prejudice, any preference. Rachel told him that he was the perfect escort and that she found him intelligent and fascinating. Or at least she tried to keep her communication that chaste and cerebral and not broadcast how physically attractive she found him.

Banal comments didn't seem banal. Mundane procedure like Lee's signing his name and room number to the bill when they'd finished eating wasn't mundane tonight. Rachel noted with a visceral pleasure how slender the ballpoint pen seemed in his big hand and how vigorous and masculine his signature was.

They'd already agreed to have a liqueur in the bar in place of dessert and to enjoy the piano music longer. Lee guided her to a small table beyond an open area for dancing. As she noted two couples getting up to dance, Rachel had serious second thoughts about prolonging the evening in a place where the lights were dimmer and the atmosphere even more intimate and romantic than in the restaurant. If Lee asked her to dance, she should decline gracefully, plead tiredness, give some excuse.

He didn't ask her, not through two more numbers. Then the piano player started an old romantic ballad and Rachel said wistfully, "I *love* that song." Lee got to his feet and held out his hand without a word. She stood and let him lead her onto the dance floor. Her only hope was that he would step on her feet, that dancing with him wouldn't be the sheer heaven she expected it to be.

At first he clasped her hand and didn't circle her waist tightly, but he rested his cheek against her temple. They moved together to the music, their slow steps in rhythm. Gradually he drew her closer and Rachel felt her bones melting. Turning her head, she looked up into his face and saw his rapt expression.

"Lee—"

"I knew damned well I'd be a goner if I danced with you," he said, and he kissed her on the mouth, a brief, ardent kiss that burned away any remaining resistance. Releasing her hand, he put both arms around her, and Rachel slipped her arms around his neck in total surrender to the rapture of dancing in his embrace.

Now her only hope was that she'd regain her sanity when they left the bar and took the elevator back down to the third floor, where either her room or his would afford them the privacy to make love.

They stayed on the dance floor until the piano player took a break. Rachel couldn't have ventured a guess on the number of songs they danced to or the span of time by a clock. Time had taken on a different dimension, measured in rapid heartbeats.

"Are you ready to go?" Lee inquired. The possessive timbre in his deep voice gave the question far-reaching implications. She answered that she was. On the way to the elevator, he kept his hand at her waist. There were no other passengers, and before the door had closed, he'd taken her in his arms. They kissed on the ride down, a series of quick, hungry, passionate kisses that left Rachel breathless and giddy.

She'd known that she'd be in trouble if Lee ever stopped fighting his attraction to her, and he was giving in to it tonight. Making love with him was an inevitability unless he pulled back. On her part, there wasn't any stopping the momentum.

At her door he held out his hand for her plastic room card, his other arm around her waist. Rachel gave it to him wordlessly and accompanied him inside her room when he'd unlocked the door.

"Lee, this is wrong," she protested without conviction, only after she'd gone into his arms.

He picked her up and held her tightly against him as he replied, "Nothing ever felt more right to me."

"We'll both be sorry tomorrow." Rachel was hugging him back with her lesser strength, reveling in his power.

"Maybe so, but I can't stop now. I want you too damn much." Desire roughened his voice and a tremor of passion ran through his big body as he spoke.

"I should stop you, but I just can't. Put me down, Lee, and . . . kiss me, touch me. . . ." *Love me.*

He set her on her feet and bent his head to kiss her neck, his hands stroking her back and shaping themselves to her waist and hips and buttocks, not boldly or roughly, but almost with reverence. Rachel moaned at the sweet, wild pleasure of his lips caressing her skin, which was warmed by his breath, while his hands acquainted themselves with her body. She wanted him to know every inch of her. "Shouldn't we be taking off our clothes?" she asked, the picture of him naked to his waist vivid in her mind as she stroked his shoulders and felt the fabric of his jacket.

The urgency in her voice embarrassed her, but once again Lee responded to her direction and straightened up, stripping off his jacket. Rachel moved over to the dresser, unhooked her necklace and laid it down. Then she undressed while he did the same, the two of them watching each other intently in the dim light from the lamp she'd left on when she left the room earlier.

In her bra and panties, she was attacked by self-consciousness. "Remember that I'm thirty-four, not nineteen," she said.

He came over to her, fully naked now and fully aroused.

Rachel raised her hands to his chest and tunneled her fingers into the dark curls of his body hair. "Lee, you're so...virile, so...masculine."

"What I am is crazy about you. You must know that." He bent and kissed her shoulder, his hands unclasping her bra and removing it.

Rachel clasped his head in weak pleasure as he trailed kisses down to her breasts. "Lee, you are prepared to take precautions?"

"Yes." He slipped his hand down inside her panties and cupped her intimately as he answered. She clutched his shoulders and whispered his name helplessly.

He didn't comment on his discovery that she was hot and wet with her woman's desire for him, but it had an immediate effect because he withdrew his hand and picked her up in his arms and carried her to the bed. After he'd laid her down, he made a return trip to his clothing. When he came back to the bed, a packet in his hand, Rachel had removed her panties in readiness for making love with him.

But he evidently wasn't ready. He tossed the packet onto the bedspread and knelt over her, kissing her stomach. His hands stroked her thighs apart as he kissed his way down her body to her thatch of blond pubic hair. He nuzzled his lips in it and then kissed her inner thighs, his breath hot on her sensitive skin, hot on the throbbing cleft of her womanhood. Then he pressed a kiss there, too, ordering with rough tenderness, "Open for me, Rachel."

"Lee, you don't have to— I'm already aroused enough."

"I want to." He used the tip of his tongue to set off rockets of erotic sensation, and Rachel opened her legs wide in a reflex of helpless delight. She lost all embarrassment, lost all control as he made love to her with his tongue, reaching up with his hands to capture her breasts and fondle them. Her climax seemed to last forever as spasms shook her body one after another, and she uttered ecstatic cries of release.

Lee kissed his way back up her lax body and stretched out alongside her, gathering her close in his arms. Rachel marveled how he had sensed that holding her would complete her physical satisfaction. "I guess I didn't know what I was missing when I was married," she mused, her cheek nestled on his chest. "I was rather prim and proper. Shall I—"

"No," he answered, cutting her off.

"I don't mind. I might not be very skillful, though." His aroused manhood formed a large, hard obstruction between their naked bodies. She could feel new desire awakening.

Easing apart from him, she reached down and took him in her hand. Lee sucked in his breath and murmured, "Oh, yes, Rachel..."

She moved her other hand down and fondled him where he was most vulnerable, while she stroked the length of his tumescence, arousing herself while she aroused him more. He soon stopped her, bringing her hands up from his groin and raising up and kissing her. Rachel's breathing quickened along with his as their tongues coupled and they kissed with hot passion. She let her hands rove over his muscular chest and broad shoulders, over his taut back and flat stomach, her touch becoming more urgent in response to his own urgent caresses.

When he tore open the packet and sheathed himself, she held out her arms and drew him on top of her. He was gentle entering her, as though mindful that he was a big man and she hadn't made love in years.

"So deep, so wonderful," Rachel murmured in bliss when their bodies were fully united.

Lee didn't answer as he gazed down at her. She felt a moment's disappointment, but it quickly passed as he stroked inside her, and the bliss sharpened. Rachel moved with him in perfect rhythm to some silent rhapsody of lovemaking. The tempo was slow and intense at first. As it gathered momentum, the intensity grew until the sensations of wild joy, intimate joy, shared joy, were more than she could bear. With her hands, her voice, her body, she urged him to bring them to a crescendo, and he did.

As they reached a climax together, his release and hers jolted them as one body.

He didn't feel heavy on top of her as he lay there for a few moments, lax and obviously spent. Rachel hugged him tenderly, awash in the deepest satisfaction.

"That was incredible for me," she murmured. She loosened her arms at the disturbing realization that making love with Blaine had never been as incredible.

Lee levered himself up and looked at her. "What's wrong?"

Rachel decided to tell him the truth. "It struck me as I spoke just now that sex with Blaine was never as good."

"I'm still inside you, and you're thinking about Cavanaugh?" He sounded injured as well as angry. He pulled free of her and swung off the bed.

"I wasn't 'thinking' about him," she protested.

"It's the second time you've mentioned him," he said over his shoulder in the same tone of voice as he headed toward the bathroom.

"I'm sorry. I didn't mean to be insensitive."

There was no response to her apology. With a sigh, Rachel got out of bed and turned back the covers. She was standing and waiting for her turn to go into the bathroom when Lee came out.

"Are you getting dressed and going away mad?" she asked uncertainly.

"I'm not going. I'm staying and sleeping with you," he replied.

When she returned from the bathroom, he was lying in bed, the sheet up around his waist. Another packet containing a condom was on the bedside table. Rachel turned out the light and slid in under the sheet and into his arms.

"I don't understand why you got so angry," she said. "I was completely focused on you while we were making love."

"There's a whole hell of a lot about me you don't understand." He hugged her tightly. "One thing is that I'm jealous of Cavanaugh."

"Jealous of Blaine? You're ten times the man he was."

Rachel waited for him to say more, but evidently that was as much insight into his reactions as he intended to offer. She was afraid to probe further, afraid of offending him and spoiling the closeness, afraid of forcing a discussion about what she felt for him and he felt for her. Tonight's wonderful lovemaking didn't change anything, and Rachel didn't want to think about that.

She sighed and confided softly, "Tomorrow I'm going to feel guilty, I know, but it feels so good for you to hold me like this." So *right*. So *safe*.

Of course, it wasn't right. He wasn't her husband. And her sense of security rose out of contentment and sexual satisfaction. Lee was the lover of every woman's dreams. He'd undoubtedly held many women in his arms like this after taking them to a plane of ecstasy they'd never reached before. Rachel definitely didn't want to think about that, not tonight, so she closed off that avenue of thought and whispered, "Good night, Lee."

"Good night...Rachel."

He'd spoken with a brusque tenderness that made her heart miss a beat. During the odd hesitation, she'd been afraid that he would call her darling.

Blaine had almost never used her name when speaking to her. He'd called her darling and sweetheart and light of my life. She'd thrilled to the endearments that fell so easily from his lips, never doubting his sincerity, complacent in the belief that he reserved them for her.

If Lee had said darling just now, Rachel would have bought his sincerity hook, line and sinker. The realization was deeply troubling.

"What is it?" Lee asked.

"Nothing that you'd want to hear."

"You were thinking about Cavanaugh again."

"About both of you."

He said nothing for a long while, then, "Do you want me to go?"

"No." Her answer was quick and unhesitating. "I should tell you to, but I want you to stay."

His arms tightened around her and she nuzzled her cheek against his chest, feeling the steady thud of his heartbeat. "We should get some sleep so we'll be fresh for tomorrow," she said. "If we both show up at breakfast with dark circles under our eyes, it will create suspicion."

"Relax and go to sleep then."

"Sleep seems such a waste since we're together like this. Are you sexually exhausted?" She blushed in the darkness. The heat of embarrassment changed to excitement as his body gave her his answer.

Rachel raised her head and slid inches higher to meet his lips in the darkness. She caressed his face and combed her fingers through his hair as they kissed, tongues coupling. "Rachel, I can't get enough of you," he murmured against her lips.

"You make me feel so sexy. You turn me into a wild woman, Lee."

"You are sexy. And classy. And beautiful."

Their more verbal lovemaking, with intimate expressions of pleasure in each other's caresses, loosened her inhibitions further this time. Rachel trailed kisses over his body and caressed every inch of his big, muscular frame. She reduced him to helplessness when she discovered for herself the erotic pleasures of taking the female lead in oral sex.

When he stopped her, he brought her astride him. Rachel sheathed him first with the condom and then with her body. The union was impossibly deep when she'd taken him completely inside her. Lee grasped her hips and held her still a moment, speaking her name in that tone of endearment.

The silent rhapsody played as she set the rhythm, wanting the ride to ecstasy to last forever. But his hands caressed her breasts and hips and thighs. She leaned forward to let him taste her nipples. He delved his fingers through her pubic curls and found her feminine nub of sexual sensations. All the stimulation combined drove her into a frenzy of pleasure.

Her climax was followed in seconds by his. Rachel slumped forward on top of him. He wrapped his arms around her tightly. She lay there completely vulnerable to her emotions, which took form as thoughts when she was capable of thought. *I love his strength, I love my body being joined together with his body. I love... him.*

It was more of an admission than a revelation.

"You'd better let me get up," Lee said after a while. "We don't want to give Mark and Stephanie a half brother or half sister."

"No, I guess we don't." As they carefully separated, Rachel tried not to think about never being pregnant with his baby.

He made a trip to the bathroom and then she did, neither of them turning on a light. Back in bed with him and lying in his close embrace, she asked, "Would you ever want to have another son or a daughter?"

"Sure," he replied. "But it would have to happen in the next several years. I'm pushing forty." Before Rachel could react to that, he asked, "Had you and Cavanaugh decided that Stephanie would be an only child?"

"No, we were planning to have more children. I had just stopped taking birth-control pills, as a matter of fact, when he was shot. Fortunately, I hadn't gotten pregnant." Rachel could feel drowsiness taking hold. "Good night for the second time," she told him, sighing with contentment.

   He kissed the top of her head and bade her a gruff, tender good-night.
   She drifted off to sleep, using his chest for her pillow.

Chapter Ten

Lee woke up at five-thirty and wanted to go back to sleep and continue his dream that he and Rachel were married and she was very pregnant with his child.

But it was only a dream, one that was never likely to come true, so he stayed awake instead and savored the reality of lying there next to her while she slept peacefully on her side facing away from him, her body curled into his.

At six o'clock he pressed a kiss to her shoulder and eased apart from her, got out of bed and dressed quietly, hoping she'd open her eyes and they'd have a few minutes of conversation before he returned to his room in plenty of time to prevent anyone from discovering that he'd been absent from it. Lee frankly didn't care whether the whole world knew they'd spent the night together. However, she would feel completely different.

To his disappointment, Rachel didn't wake up, not even when he stood by the bed, gazing down at her, and touched

a tress of her blond hair, his heart overflowing with tende
emotion and his mind full of the question, *What now?*

Surely last night was some kind of new beginning. The
couldn't go back to the same standoff, not after what they'
shared. Lee knew what he wanted. He wanted her to be h
wife. But he didn't have a hell of a lot of confidence that sh
was going to wake up and want the same thing.

Rachel had requested a wake-up call for seven. She awok
a few minutes before seven and knew instantly that Le
wasn't in bed with her. Turning over, she rested her hand i
the indentation in his pillow and coped with her feelings c
loneliness and abandonment.

He'd awakened and gotten up and left at some time du
ing the night. Possibly he hadn't slept beside her at al
whereas she'd slept as deeply as she had as a child, with n
serious anxieties. Closing her eyes, Rachel let herself recap
ture being held closely in Lee's arms.

The telephone on the bedside table rang shrilly, jarring he
cruelly to the reality of lying alone and nude under a rum
pled sheet. Draping the sheet around her, she sat on the edg
of the bed and answered the wake-up call.

As she hung up, Rachel was struck by the longing to hea
Lee's voice. She could call his room. But what would sh
say? What would her voice give away and what answe
would she make if he asked, "How do you feel this morn
ing?"

As she gazed at the phone, her impulse slowly dying,
rang again. Her heart began to race after her first startle
reaction. The only person who could be calling her this earl
was Lee. "Hello," she said into the phone, suddenly acutel
conscious of the sheet against her nakedness.

"Mom?" Stephanie said uncertainly.

"Yes, darling. You have the right room." Rachel wa
flooded with guilt that her rush of gladness had followed
pang of letdown. She tightened the sheet around her, sham
setting in.

"You sounded funny when you said hello."

"I just woke up. Is everything okay?" A mother's concern quickly came to the forefront of her emotions.

"Everything's fine. I just figured you'd tried to call me last night and couldn't get through."

"I did try to call you as soon as I arrived. That was about eight o'clock. By the time I came back to my room after dinner, it was too late to try again." On the carpet lay a crumpled condom packet. Somewhere there was a second empty packet.

"You went out somewhere for dinner?"

"No, we ate here at a restaurant in the hotel."

"All of you?"

"Mr. Zachary and I. The others had gone to a dinner-theater club."

"It's too bad that you had to miss seeing a play."

"Did you have a nice evening at the Wakefields' house?" Rachel asked, evading making a dishonest response. Any response she could make to Stephanie would be dishonest.

She and her daughter chatted for several more minutes before they said goodbye to each other. After she'd replaced the phone in its cradle, Rachel reached down and picked up the crumpled condom packet.

Except for concealing the truth about Blaine to shield her from its ugliness, Rachel had always been truthful to her daughter. She'd never had anything to hide, and now she did. It wasn't a good feeling to know that she'd behaved in a way she couldn't condone to her fourteen-year-old daughter. Or to her mother and father, for that matter. They wouldn't approve at all.

For the first time Rachel had done something that, if it came to public light, would be harmful to Stephanie, embarrassing to her parents and possibly both embarrassing and harmful professionally to Alice and Mary Lynn. She'd acted irresponsibly and had put at risk those people who cared for her and depended on her.

It put Rachel in the same league with Blaine, where sh
would never have expected to find herself.

Lee called Rachel's room at seven-thirty. He couldn't wa
any longer to hear her voice.

"Hi. How are you?" he asked.

"I'm fine," she replied, not sounding happy. "Stepha
nie called this morning, and I felt ashamed, talking to he
while I was wrapped in a sheet. How are you?"

"I'm okay," Lee said, anything but okay now. Last nigh
obviously hadn't meant to her what it meant to him. "I wa
about to go on down to the restaurant where we'll be hav
ing breakfast." It was located on the ground floor. "I wor
dered if you were up and dressed."

"No, I'm not quite dressed. I'll be down in about twent
minutes."

"I can wait for you."

"There's no need."

None except the need to see her and spend any time h
could with her before the whole group convened at eigh
o'clock for breakfast. It was a need she apparently didn
share. Lee set his jaw against a stab of disappointment tha
was like a knife thrust in his gut.

"I guess there isn't," he said flatly.

Riding down in the elevator, he closed his mind again
recalling all that had happened with Rachel after they'd le
the piano bar. The memory would only increase his hurt an
frustration.

In the restaurant he sat at a table with six place setting
taking a chair at one end. Five minutes later Carl Beatt
showed up and sat on his immediate left. Ten minutes late
James Livingston sauntered in and sat opposite Carl. Th
two men's wives appeared together next and took the place
beside their husbands, leaving the chair at the opposite en
of the table vacant for Rachel, who entered last, lookin
classy and beautiful in one of her career woman's suits. Th
knife twisted in Lee's gut at the sight of her. It twisted mo

when she included him in a smiling glance and generalized greeting, "Good morning. I see I'm wagging the dog's tail this morning."

He wondered if she even noticed that his "Good morning" was missing from the chorus.

"Carl, honey, why don't you let Rachel sit next to Lee?" Louise Beatty suggested to her husband. "You can sit at the end here."

"Don't be silly," Rachel said lightly. "Keep your place, Carl." She sat down, avoiding Lee's gaze.

Not once during breakfast did she exchange a private glance with him or smile at him with any personal warmth. Lee's waffle might have been made of sawdust for all the taste it had. He didn't even bother putting any sugar in his second and third cups of coffee, because they would have tasted bitter as gall anyway.

The two wives had plans for shopping all day, while the three men and Rachel spent their day at Sea Castle Villas, fulfilling the purpose of the trip—to visit a completed and occupied residential development for retired people similar in concept to Plantation Village.

"Louise and I can use your car or ours, Lee," Janet Livingston said agreeably as they were all rising from the table. "It doesn't matter to us."

Both cars were full-size, American-made luxury sedans. Lee's would be equally as comfortable for four adults, so he said, "I'll drive my car."

"Have fun," Janet advised cheerfully, and she and Louise Beatty told their husbands goodbye.

It would have been a moment when Lee and Rachel could have paired up and exchanged a few words just between them, but they weren't standing close to each other. Rachel wasn't even looking in his direction. By this time Lee's sense of rejection was mixed with anger. He wanted to smash his fist into a wall and vent his emotions.

His car was brought to the hotel portico. The other two men and Rachel exited from the lobby just ahead of him.

She didn't hang back and let him escort her. Outside, Livingston and Beatty both leapt to open car doors for her Livingston the front passenger door.

"You can sit up front, James," she said. "Janet mentioned that you tend to get car sickness."

"How humane of you, Rachel," Livingston declared gratefully in his pompous fashion.

"Don't anyone tell my wife I rode in the back seat with Rachel," Beatty wisecracked.

Lee didn't say a word. He tipped the uniformed valet, go behind the wheel and jammed the car into gear.

It was about a twenty-minute drive to their destination The talk centered around Sea Castle Villas. Both Livingston and Beatty directed remarks and questions to Lee, drawing him into the discussion, but Rachel didn't make a single remark to him or ask him any questions, though she carried her part of the four-way conversation.

Lee had gotten control of his emotions, but he must have been more terse than usual because James Livingston glanced at him curiously several times and finally inquired mildly, "To coin a cliché, did you get up on the wrong side of the bed this morning, Zachary?"

"I guess I must have," he answered grimly, managing no to look in the rearview mirror at Rachel.

"My mother always used that old saying," Beatty mused "Which side is the wrong side, anyway?"

"Good question. I have no inkling of the saying's origin Do you, Rachel?" Livingston glanced over his shoulder a her.

"No, I really don't." She changed the subject back to Se Castle Villas.

On their arrival they were met by members of the home owners' committee and one of the developers. Lee made a conscious effort to be more personable and to convey hi sincere appreciation.

He might feel the way he had at seventeen, but he wa thirty-seven and had to order his priorities. The first tim

Rachel had broken his heart, he'd quit a good job and gone off to lick his wounds. Now he couldn't afford such impetuous behavior. His personal life had to take a back seat.

Rachel was his Realtor, here to soak up information and get pointers on doing her part to make Plantation Village a successful venture, just as Livingston and Beatty were here in their professional capacities. Still, Lee was human. The wounded man in him got the upper hand when he finally found himself with the chance to talk to her without an audience.

They'd watched a video in the building that served as a social center and were having a coffee break. Lee had walked outside onto a tiled patio overlooking the swimming pool and was strolling around the beautifully landscaped grounds. He'd stepped under a thatch-roofed cabana when Rachel spoke his name hesitantly from a short distance away.

"Lee?"

He froze for a second in surprise, then turned around. "Yeah, remember me?" he replied cynically. "The guy who slept with you last night?" He'd pitched his voice low, and there wasn't anyone except her close enough to hear him.

Pink color stained her cheeks, and she didn't answer until she'd stepped under the cabana, too. "What time did you get up and leave?"

"Why?" Lee asked. The conversation was long overdue at this point. She could have asked him the same question at seven-thirty on the phone or on the way down to breakfast with him, if she'd let him wait for her.

She sighed. "You're angry."

"Among other things. I wasn't expecting to be given the cold shoulder this morning."

"I'm sorry. I was so conscious of not wanting to confirm any suspicions that the others might have about us."

"Don't worry. I'm having doubts myself about whether last night really happened."

"It happened," she said, looking away, the color in her cheeks rising again. "And your acting hostile toward me for the rest of this trip is only going to make the situation worse than it already is."

"How the hell do you want me to act?" Lee demanded. "Tell me."

"Like my most important client." She clasped his arm lightly. "Please, Lee . . ."

If his life depended on it, Lee couldn't have kept himself from laying his hand over hers and trapping it against his jacket sleeve. "We'd better go back inside and see what's next on the agenda," he said gruffly, squeezing her hand.

Their hosts were his guests for lunch at a Chinese restaurant they recommended. When the whole group loaded into three cars, James Livingston rode with the developer, and Rachel got into the passenger seat beside Lee. At the restaurant she didn't sit next to him, but took a place between the man who was president of the Sea Castle Villas homeowners' committee and a very talkative woman who served as chairperson of social activities. Lee understood that Rachel was leaving the seats near him open to his lunch guests and was playing unofficial hostess. She wasn't avoiding sitting by him.

Several times he exchanged glances with her and she smiled at him. The restored friendliness was like a salve that eased the rawness of his hurt feelings. But a dogged hopefulness also flickered to life, and Lee knew he would stick out his chin again for another knock-down blow. He was like a punch-drunk boxer who couldn't stay out of the ring.

That afternoon the owner of the interior-decorating firm responsible for the basic decor of the homes at Sea Castle Villas and the landscape architect were on hand, as scheduled in advance. Their talks, complete with visual aids, were very informative for Rachel. She was able to absorb much more than she had that morning, when the horrible tension between her and Lee had interfered with her concentration.

On the ride back to the hotel, she once again let James have the front seat. "A very good day from my viewpoint," he declared. "Extremely worthwhile."

Carl Beatty and Rachel added their wholehearted agreement.

"What are your feelings, Lee?" she asked when he didn't speak up.

"I'm glad we came," he answered. His gaze met hers in the mirror, but there was no secret message in his words. "I got some insights."

He shared those insights with typical brevity, and Rachel was impressed, but not surprised, by his astuteness and powers of observation. She reflected that, if only one of them had been able to come, he would have been best served to pick himself.

The other two men shared what they'd gotten out of the day, and Rachel did, too. The discussion took them to the hotel. Crossing the lobby to the elevator, James brought up the subject of dinner plans. "Where are we going to eat tonight? It's Friday, and we would be prudent to make reservations."

"Pick a restaurant and make a reservation," Lee replied. "It doesn't matter to me where we eat."

"The rest of us haven't had dinner here at the hotel," James said. "You both recommended the restaurant where you dined last night rather highly, it seemed to me. Would you be averse to dining there again tonight?"

"I would," Lee said curtly, before Rachel could voice her opposition.

The architect raised his eyebrows, obviously slightly taken aback. "Very well. Then that's not an option."

Carl spoke up, mentioning another restaurant, and James assigned him the job of making a reservation for seventhirty.

In the elevator the architect suggested, "Shall we have a cocktail beforehand up in the piano bar on the fourth floor?"

"Count me out," Lee said.

"Me, too," Rachel said quickly.

Neither of them looked at the other.

James Livingston seemed taken aback again. "Very well. In that case, I suppose we'll meet the two of you in the lobby about twenty past seven."

They all got out on the third floor. Rachel stopped off at her room and the men walked on, Carl and James with parting comments and Lee silent. At breakfast she'd learned the location of the Livingstons' and the Beattys' rooms. They were down another corridor, not at all close to hers and Lee's. Still, there had been the danger that Lee could have been observed by his architect or contractor or one of their wives as he was leaving her room.

Had he made sure he'd left early enough to avoid being seen? Rachel wondered as she unlocked her door. That thought hadn't even occurred to her as an explanation for his absence when she'd woken up this morning. In fact, the fear of discovery hadn't dawned on her until she'd heard Stephanie's voice on the phone.

Last night hadn't *seemed* furtive and clandestine, though it should have.

Rachel's bed was neatly made, the maid having been there during the day. The sheets would have been changed. Tonight Rachel would sleep in the bed alone. She would go home on Saturday and resume the lonely occupation of her bedroom in her home. Yes, *lonely* occupation. Stephanie's all-important presence in Rachel's life didn't fulfill the need for a man.

The need had been there since Blaine's death, but Lee had brought it achingly to life last night, satisfying her completely and making her feel cherished afterward when he held her in his arms. Rachel could get along without the sex, as wonderful as it had been. What she missed much more as an unmarried woman was the closeness, the emotional support, the outpouring of love to a lifetime companion.

Yet did she have the courage to gamble on marriage a second time? Rachel didn't know if she could survive the devastation of broken wedding vows again.

Did Lee even want her as his wife? That was another question she couldn't answer.

Aside from these major uncertainties, there were other serious problems and considerations. Stephanie disliked Lee, as she would probably dislike any man who loomed as a replacement for her father. Lee would have to win her over somehow.

Then there was Mark, who was anything but a model stepbrother. Even if he went away to college next year, he would be home for holidays. Rachel shook her head at the idea of her daughter and Lee's son being thrown together.

The chances were slim to none that marriage between her and Lee would work. And any other intimate relationship was impossible.

Having come to that very disheartening conclusion, Rachel still longed to pick up the telephone and call him now in his room, hear his voice and talk to him. As much as, in a way, she dreaded the evening ahead, she eagerly looked forward to being in his company.

Instead of calling Lee, she called Magnolia Realty and talked to Alice, giving a report on the day from the real-estate angle. Alice updated her on what was going on with clients.

After she'd hung up, Rachel noted the time, remembering that this morning Stephanie had mentioned going to the mall after school with Candy and two other girlfriends. They planned to do some shopping, eat their supper in the food court and then see a movie. Barbara Wakefield, Candy's mom, was transporting them to and from the mall.

So it would be pointless to try to call Stephanie now; she wouldn't be at the Wakefields' house. Rachel pushed aside a vague pang of anxiety, knowing that it rose from separation. Her daughter was fine, probably enjoying herself this very minute.

* * *

"Oh, *no!*" Candy Wakefield groaned. "Would you look who's here in the food court—Heather and Megan. Sitting at a table with Betty Sue Hagen."

"Just ignore them," Stephanie said, as dismayed as her friend was.

"You know that won't do any good," Candy answered, and the two other girls, Lindsey and Patricia, concurred with her.

"Let's come back later," Lindsey urged. "Maybe they'll leave."

"Yes, it's not worth it, putting up with their nastiness," Patricia complained.

"They've already seen us," Stephanie observed. "Look at them smirking at us and pointing. We can't turn around now and let them know they've chased us off. That would please them no end."

"I guess you're right," Candy agreed with a reluctant sigh.

The four girls waved to teenage acquaintances as they approached the food court, studiously ignoring Stephanie's enemies and pretending to be unbothered by their presence. After buying sodas, they sat a table as far away from Megan and Heather as possible, Stephanie with her back to them.

Candy's expression, though, served as a warning. "They're getting up and so is Betty Sue," she murmured. "Maybe they're leaving with her. No, the three of them are just moving closer to us."

"Betty Sue's been hanging around with them at school lately," Patricia offered in an undertone.

"Hi, Candy. And Patricia and Lindsey," Heather Smith called out from behind Stephanie. She added in a voice that was more sing-song and more snide, "Hi, Stephanie. Been dating Mark Zachary lately?"

Candy answered scornfully for her friend. "You know good and well Stephanie's been dating Michael Curtis, Heather."

Heather's sidekick, Megan, piped up sarcastically, "We have better things to do with our time than keep up with who she's dating. Betty Sue was just telling us something very interesting about Stephanie's mom and Mark Zachary's dad. She's gone off to Florida with him, supposedly on a real-estate trip."

"Megan!" Betty Sue protested. "You're gonna get me in trouble! I said not to repeat what I heard Daddy saying to Mama!"

Stephanie's back, already stiff, had straightened into a ramrod. Betty Sue's father was a real-estate agent. Without turning around, Stephanie stated with icy disdain, "Not *supposedly* on a real-estate trip, Megan. It *is* a real-estate trip. Mr. Zachary's architect and his contractor went, too. Betty Sue's father is probably just jealous because my mother is more successful than he is."

"She is *not!*" Betty Sue exclaimed hotly. "Daddy's a million-dollar agent, too!"

"Megan's already let the cat out of the bag, Betty Sue." Heather took over the role of tormentor. "We might as well tell the rest—about how your dad said he didn't have a chance at being Mr. Zachary's real-estate agent because he wasn't a good-looking woman who could go to bed with Mr. Zachary."

"That's a *lie!*" Stephanie practically choked on the words.

"Better watch out, Stephanie," Heather jeered. "Your mother might end up shot, too, like your father."

"Would you look who's coming?" Megan exclaimed. "Mark Zachary!"

"Oh, I think he's seen Stephanie and is about to head in another direction," Heather chortled. "I guess one date did it for him, huh?"

It was all too much for Stephanie. Her mortification was more than she could handle. Pushing back her chair, she burst into tears and ran from the food court, past Mark Zachary, who stopped dead in his tracks.

"Stephanie! What's wrong?" he asked. He had seen her at the table of teenage girls and had experienced some uneasiness about running into her. Had the sight of him caused her to bolt in tears?

Now her friend, Candy, jumped up and followed after her, almost in tears herself. Mark stopped her, putting out his hand. "Say, why was Stephanie crying?"

"Some mean girls said ugly things about her mother and your father."

"About Mrs. Cavanaugh and my dad?"

Candy blushed. "Yes, about them going to Florida and about his picking her for his real-estate agent because she's pretty. I have to go after Stephanie—"

"No, I'll go after her." Somehow, with his dad and her mother both out of town, Stephanie was his responsibility.

Mark took off at a trot. He was starting to think he'd overlooked her when he finally spotted her sitting on a bench near an entrance to the mall, her face buried in her hands and her shoulders shaking with sobs.

"Stephanie! Don't let those girls get your goat," he said with gruff sympathy, dropping down beside her and patting her on the back.

She leapt up from the bench and ran crying toward the glass doors. Mark went after her, catching her outside and bringing her to a standstill by clasping her arms. Sobs racked her body alarmingly.

"Come on, Stephanie," he pleaded. "Don't cry like that. You'll make yourself sick."

His words seemed to have no effect. Aside from being concerned about her, Mark felt highly conspicuous standing there in full sight of people going and coming. An overweight woman waddling by gave him a frowning glance.

He put his arm around Stephanie's shoulder and tried to turn her toward the doors, but she resisted. He heard his own desperation as he urged, "Let's go back inside."

She shook her head hard and sobbed out, "No, I can't face them!"

Mark's car wasn't far from the entrance. He'd lucked out on a parking space. They couldn't just stay there, making a spectacle of themselves, and he was truly worried about her. "Tell you what, why don't we go to my car? Okay?"

To his immense relief, she let him walk her along, his arm around her waist. At his car, he gently helped her into the passenger seat and then circled and got behind the wheel. "How about some music?" He put the key in the ignition and turned it, then switched on the radio. Her weeping quieted gradually, but she kept her face buried in her hands.

"I wish I could die," she whispered.

"No, you don't," Mark chided, squeezing her shoulder. "Things are never that bad."

"Would you take me to my house?"

"To your house? Nobody's home." No way was he taking her there, not in her current mood.

"Please."

Her pitiful plea wrung Mark's heart. Poor kid, she was in a really bad way. He started up the car. "I'm thirsty. I was on my way to get a soda in the mall. You mind if I drive by a fast-food place and get something to drink?" He really wasn't thirsty, but he figured drinking a soda might do her some good.

"No," she answered with a little hiccup.

Mark bought two sodas and handed one to her after he'd stuck in the straw. She took the soda, thanking him politely, and sipped it. "Now would you take me home?"

"I'd rather take you back to the mall."

"Okay," she said dully, with another little hiccup. "I can call a taxi from the pay phone."

"You're not staying at your house while you mom is in Florida, are you?"

"No, I'm staying at Candy's."

"Why don't I take you to her house, then?"

"I'll call Mrs. Wakefield later to come and get me. My eyes are all red and puffy, and I want to be by myself." Again, there was no spark of life in her words, no defiance.

"Let's go for a ride," Mark said, for lack of any other better plan.

"You feel sorry for me."

"Wouldn't you feel sorry for me if I was as down in the dumps as you are right now?"

"Boys don't get down in the dumps."

"Sure they do."

They rode along the beach highway. Maybe if he could get her to talk about what had upset her, she would spring back, Mark reflected. Instead of beating around the bush, he said, "So tell me what happened."

"You seemed to know. I thought Candy must have told you."

"She said that some mean girls had said some stuff about Dad and Mrs. Cavanaugh."

"Two girls who hate me. It was a bunch of lies. They insinuated that Mom and your dad aren't really on a business trip, and they are."

"Sure they are. Dad told me all about the trip."

"Another girl, Betty Sue Hagen, who's friends with these two girls, has a father who's in real estate. She told them she'd heard him complaining to her mother that Mr. Zachary picked Mom for his real-estate agent because she was a good-looking woman who could..." Stephanie faltered.

"I think I can figure out the rest," Mark said. "Who could give him sex. Your mom is definitely pretty, but it's total garbage that Dad would pick her for his real-estate agent based on her looks or on her being a woman he might like to have as his girlfriend. He's got too much riding on Plantation Village. He's not about to risk letting it go down the tubes."

Stephanie sipped her soda. She seemed much more like herself. "You don't think he would like Mom to be his girlfriend, do you?"

"I'd just be guessing," Mark said evasively. "How would you feel about it?"

"Not good," she admitted.

"Why? My dad's a great guy. Don't let his bark scare you. He's as softhearted as they come."

"Are you in favor of him and Mom getting together?"

Mark shrugged. "I'm going away to college next year, and I kinda worry about him being lonely. The same thought must cross your mind about your mom."

"It has," Stephanie said thoughtfully. "But Mom seems happy, and I'm only fourteen." She rolled down her window and let the breeze blow in her face. "Could we drive out into the country?"

"Sure. I guess we could do that. When we get back to town, will you let me take you to Candy's house or to the mall?"

"Probably to the mall."

Mark breathed a sigh of relief that she was no longer insisting on going to her house. He hoped Mrs. Cavanaugh didn't get bent out of shape when she heard Stephanie's version of his taking her for a ride. His dad would understand once the circumstances were explained to him. Mark wasn't worried on that score.

He settled back, taking a highway out of Gulfport. Stephanie turned up the volume of the radio. With the windows rolled down and the wind ripping through the car, they had to talk loud to hear each other.

"How fast are you going?" she inquired with a lilt of excitement.

"I'm going sixty. The speed limit's fifty-five. The cops don't give you a ticket for an extra five miles an hour." He passed along this sage advice with a grin. She seemed a whole generation younger than him. It was hard to believe that he'd been interested in dating her.

"I can't wait until I learn to drive. Next year I can take Drivers Ed."

"You're not going to like some of those gory videos they show you."

They were riding through rural terrain now, with no houses in sight. A souped-up pickup truck with big tires came fast up on Mark's rear. It was crusted with mud, and an arm holding a beer can was stuck out each window. The driver blasted the horn, cruising along right on Mark's bumper.

"What the hell's your problem?" Mark muttered. "Go around me." If Stephanie hadn't been in the car, he'd have stuck his hand out and given the driver the finger.

The pickup roared up beside him and veered into his lane, the horn blaring. Mark turned his wheel and pulled over as far as he dared without going off the pavement. "You crazy redneck!" he shouted, glancing sideways into the grinning, drunken face of the man on the passenger side.

"Have a beer, rich kid!" the man shouted, tossing his can through Mark's open window. The beer landed in his lap and spilled on his clothes, but that was the least of his worries. He couldn't take his hands off the wheel with these lunatics threatening to force him off the highway.

"I'm scared, Mark!" Stephanie cried.

"Just stay cool, Stephanie!"

The pickup veered again, closer. "We want that side of the road!" the man yelled, his head stuck out the window. Mark didn't have any choice but to cut more to the right. His outer wheels spewed gravel. The pickup came closer and nudged him, pushing him farther onto the shoulder. It nudged him a second time, harder, then accelerated and roared ahead, the horn a steady blare.

There was plenty of highway now, but Mark's car was out of control and airborne across a deep ditch. His despairing shout blended with Stephanie's scream of terror. He was vaguely aware of the stench of beer and the wetness of his trousers during the seconds before the car crashed into the trees. Then he wasn't conscious of anything.

Lee hadn't arranged with Rachel for them to go down to the lobby together to meet the others for dinner. By twenty-five past seven, he hadn't rung her room or tapped on her door. Rachel hesitated out in the corridor, as though willing him to emerge. Then she walked down to his room. As she was raising her hand to knock on it, the door opened. She sensed his surprise when he saw her. His gaze ran over her, and she knew he was comparing her appearance tonight with a very different appearance last night. She was wearing the same suit she'd worn today, with a different blouse and accessories.

"Ready?" she said, though he obviously was leaving. Her stomach had tightened in familiar reaction to the first sight of him, when she felt the initial, forceful impact of his masculinity, his personality.

"I've been ready."

"So have I." They'd both been holed up in their rooms, while the others were having a drink in the piano bar. "I didn't dare look at you this afternoon when James was playing social director and came up with the suggestion that we have dinner and drinks here at the hotel," she confided, moving back and giving him room. "That was an awkward moment, wasn't it?"

He stepped out and closed the door. "I didn't find it 'awkward.'"

"You nearly bit off his head, after just claiming to have no preference at all about restaurants."

"That was because the idea of having another meal up there was like a kick in the gut, after last night and then today."

The graphic, honest description of his reaction moved Rachel. Underneath his toughness, he was a sensitive man. "It would have been very painful for me, too." They walked together toward the elevator. "I was glad this morning when

I went down to breakfast that there were other people in the elevator," she recalled. "Otherwise I would have had more trouble trying not to remember the ride down from the fourth floor last night."

"There weren't any other people in it when I went down. I had to count the seams in the paneling," he disclosed cynically, but she knew his cynicism was a cover-up. This morning he'd probably been smarting from her treatment of him on the telephone.

"I started the day out wrong with our phone conversation this morning. I was so focused on my feelings that I didn't show much consideration for yours. I'm sorry."

"Don't worry about it."

They'd arrived at the elevators. He punched the button near one and they stood waiting. "Part of the problem," Rachel said, "is that you hide your feelings so well."

"Do I? To me, I seem like an open book."

The elevator doors slid open following the bell-like *bing* that announced its arrival. Inside were the Livingstons and the Beattys, on their way down to meet Rachel and Lee. She did her best to hide her dismay and smooth over the fact that Lee didn't make any pretense whatever that he was pleased to see them.

"I took the liberty of requesting that the hotel limo transport us to and from the restaurant, Lee," James divulged. "That way we can have a cocktail or two and not fret over the alcohol level in our blood."

"The piano player upstairs is really good, you guys. You should have joined us for a drink." Janet didn't leave a pause for Lee to answer. She obviously assumed that he would be as pleased as her husband was pleased at his attention to details.

Rachel didn't miss Lee's slight headshake and knew he was experiencing her same frustration that they wouldn't have a chance to continue their conversation on the way to the restaurant in his car.

He made it his business to make sure she sat beside him in the limousine, which was parked in readiness under the portico. His attitude had become resigned. He was making the best of things. At the restaurant, where he again took no chance of being separated from her at the table, he put forth an effort to be sociable and not a wet blanket, but it wasn't easy for him. Rachel sensed all that, sensed that he wanted to be with her and her alone.

She wondered if he could see through her and knew that she wanted the same thing. Rising to the occasion in social situations was something that came more naturally to her. She thought about his words, *To me, I seem like an open book.*

How well was he able to read her? Was she more successful than she realized in hiding her feelings for him, though she, too, seemed like an open book to herself?

Rising from the table when the dessert course had finally ended for those who'd ordered dessert—not her or Lee—Rachel chimed in with the unanimous agreement that Carl had made a good choice of restaurants. Her mind was on returning to the hotel and escaping from the others and going somewhere to talk with Lee. But where? Not her room or his. She would suggest the piano bar, she decided in the limousine, seated once more beside him. They could sit in a corner and not dance tonight, just talk.

"Hey, guys, it's only nine-thirty," Janet Livingston said as the limousine pulled away from the curb. "When we get back to the hotel, let's go up to the piano bar and dance off some calories."

"You don't actually think I could get Carl out on a dance floor, do you?" Louise Beatty exclaimed.

Janet made some answer, and the husbands commented in turn, but Rachel wasn't listening. Disgruntled, she looked over at Lee, who had stiffened at mention of the piano bar. He looked at her and uttered a muttered curse, and she knew he'd been on the same wavelength.

Rachel wasn't giving up. There were other places to go ir
Pensacola, but there was no opportunity to say that to him
the merry hubbub among the two couples having ended witl
the adoption of Janet's proposal for continuing the eve
ning.

"Will you two join us?" she asked, not with a lot of ex
pectation.

"Thank you, but I have a slight headache," Rachel lie
politely.

"No, thanks," Lee said, not offering any excuse.

"I'm glad I'm not single," Janet retorted, razzing then
good-naturedly. "Us old married folks seem to have mor
fun."

At the hotel the six of them trooped into an elevator. Or
the third floor, Rachel and Lee said good-night and got off
They both came to a halt when the elevator doors closed
Rachel smiled at him. "Do I have time to go to my roon
and get an aspirin for my imaginary headache before we g
out somewhere away from the pack?"

"Sure. I need to check for messages, anyway."

"I need to do that, too."

He expelled a deep breath and tugged at the knot of hi
tie, loosening it as they walked along the corridor. "Di
dinner really last five or six hours, or was that my imagi
nation?"

"It seemed to last that long. They're nice people, but tc
day was rather intense and socializing takes a lot of energy
I would much rather have had dinner with you."

"I wish you'd said that beforehand."

"Wouldn't it have been awkward to arrange?"

"Not with Janet and Louise along. If we'd come with ju:
Livingston and Beatty, that would be different."

"If we'd come with just them, the four of us woul
probably have traveled together. Last night wouldn't hav
happened."

They'd reached her room. "Are you sorry it hap
pened?" Lee asked hesitantly.

"That's not a simple yes or no question. Can I answer it later?" In a less public place. A couple had emerged from a room not too far away and were headed toward the elevators.

He nodded. "Why don't you knock on my door when you're ready to go?"

"I won't be more than ten minutes."

Holding her key card, Rachel gazed after him. "Lee?" He stopped and turned around when she spoke his name. "I wouldn't mind in the least if you took off the tie."

"Don't tempt me." He grinned ruefully.

Rachel's smile lingered on her lips as she unlocked the door and entered. The message light on the telephone was lit up. Its bright red color seemed more cheerful than alarming with her heart aglow with her love for Lee. Stephanie might have called, or Alice or Mary Lynn with some stupendous news. Unless there was an emergency, Rachel wasn't returning anyone's call—not even Stephanie's—and delaying her date with Lee.

All the obstacles were still there between them, but if he loved her, maybe they could get past those hurdles, one by one. Rachel's thoughts were more on that all-important "if" than on the identity of the person who'd called her as she went over to the phone to dial the front desk.

"You had a call from Barbara Wakefield. Please call her. It's concerning your daughter. It's urgent." The female operator read from a written message she or someone else had taken down. "The number is—"

"Thank you. I know the number," Rachel interrupted, cutting the connection. Her blood had frozen in her veins and fear clutched her with a giant, icy hand as she sank down on the bed. Something was the matter with Stephanie.

"Urgent" didn't mean tragic, she told herself as she punched innumerable numbers, placing the call to the Wakefield residence. *God, don't let the phone be busy.*

It wasn't busy. Barbara picked up immediately. "Rachel I'm so relieved you called. I'm worried out of my mind about Stephanie."

Stephanie was alive. Rachel squeezed her eyes closed, almost fainting with the unspeakable relief in learning that her worst fear hadn't come to pass. "Is she ill, Barbara? Is she hurt? Has there been an accident?"

"She's missing."

"*Missing?* You mean *kidnapped?*" The discussion she'd had with Stephanie about Blaine's murderer being released from prison whirled through Rachel's head.

"She left the shopping center this afternoon—we think with a boy—and she hasn't come home yet. Nor has she called."

"Who was the boy?"

"Mark Zachary."

"Mark Zachary? He took Stephanie off somewhere?"

"Let me tell you as much of the story as I've been able to piece together. Candy and Stephanie were at the mall this afternoon. Lindsey Cook and Patricia Simpson were with them. In the food court they had an unpleasant run-in with three girls in their class. Stephanie got very upset and started crying. She got up and ran into the mall. Apparently Mark was just arriving at the food court. Candy started to go after Stephanie. He stopped her and went after Stephanie himself. After a few minutes, when they didn't return, Candy and Lindsey and Patricia went looking for them, and they'd disappeared."

Rachel felt as though a stone were crushing her chest. "Did you call Mark's house, Barbara?"

"Yes, but there was no answer. I also called the friend he's staying with, Carl. Candy knew his name. Carl didn't know where Mark was. He was worried because Mark hadn't shown up. I started getting frantic and wanted to call the police, but Burt thought I should talk to you first." Burt was Barbara's husband. "He brought up the possibility that Mark's father might be able to shed some light."

Lee could be depended on to offer excuses for Mark's behavior whether he could shed light on it or not, Rachel reflected dully. She promised in a heavy voice, "As soon as I hang up, Barbara, I'll go to Lee Zachary's room and fill him in. I can't tell you how sorry I am that you're being put through this."

"You try not to worry yourself sick, Rachel. Stephanie may walk in the door any minute, safe and sound." Barbara's reassurance was hollow.

After she'd hung up, Rachel sat there on the bed a moment, the combination of anxiety and despair almost more than she could cope with—anxiety was for Stephanie and despair for herself. The obstacles between her and Lee were too great for them to overcome, especially the one Mark posed. It had just grown into a mountain, with Lee on one side with his son and her on the other with her daughter.

Rachel would wait to learn the facts before she assumed that Mark had gone to the mall on the lookout for Stephanie. Whether he had or not, he'd seen his chance and seized it, taken advantage of her vulnerability and youth. Rachel prayed that they both were safe, but she couldn't ever forgive Mark for this. His actions confirmed the disapproval she'd felt since that initial meeting in front of her real-estate office. She'd guessed within five minutes that he was spoiled.

Lee had allowed him to run wild. Mark knew he could pull off stunts like taking Stephanie on a date without her mother's permission and spiriting her away from her friends at the mall, knowing full well that his conduct wouldn't bring any punishment. Someday Mark's self-centeredness and lack of respect for the rules might well end in tragedy, and Lee would wake up to his errors as a father, but it would be too late. The thought made Rachel's heart ache for him, as full as it was of bitter reprisal for his son.

Please, God, don't let this escapade of Mark's end in tragedy.

The distance to Lee's room seemed to have lengthened as Rachel walked down the spacious corridor. The soft lighting had become gloomy now, the quiet ominous. Lee opened the door immediately when she knocked. He hadn't taken the tie off, but had tightened the knot again. His expression was less guarded than Rachel had ever seen it. Her despair grew as she read in his eyes and in his hard features that he'd been eagerly awaiting her return. It was so cruel to feel special at a time like this one, cruel to know that the ending of their relationship would only leave him more cynical than he already was.

His expression quickly changed to sharp concern. "Rachel, what's wrong?"

She tried her best to be factual. "I've just gotten very disturbing news about Stephanie. She disappeared from the mall this afternoon, probably in Mark's company. No one seems to know where they are."

"What do you mean, 'probably in Mark's company'?" He opened the door wider. "You'd better come in and sit down and tell me exactly what's happened." The concern had increased, but his guard was back up. He didn't offer to touch her as she stepped over the threshold of his room.

Rachel sank down in the armchair that was a duplicate of the one in her room, over which Lee had draped his clothes last night. He dropped down on the foot of the bed, loosening his tie with a jerking motion. "Okay, who did you get this news about Stephanie from?"

"Barbara Wakefield, Candy Wakefield's mother. She called while I was at dinner." Rachel related the events of the afternoon as Barbara had reported them. Lee didn't interrupt until she came to the part about Carl's claiming that he had no knowledge of Mark's whereabouts.

"Something's wrong here," Lee said grimly, shaking his head. He stood abruptly, went to the phone and started punching numbers. Rachel surmised that he'd called Carl's house and Carl answered. He questioned Mark's friend, who evidently stuck to his same story. "That's not like Mark at all," Lee said gravely. Carl evidently said quite a bit more. As he listened, Lee glanced at Rachel, and she saw that he had grown haggard during the conversation. "I'll be in touch, Carl, and I'd appreciate it if you would stick by the phone."

He hung up and sat down on the edge of the bed, not taking his hand from the phone. "Why don't you go back to your room? I'm going to make some more phone calls."

"Who're you going to call? Other friends of Mark's?"

"No, I'm going to call the Mississippi state police first and then the Gulfport and Biloxi police."

"What did Carl say that upset you so much, Lee? Don't keep things from me. My daughter is missing!"

"Your daughter *and* my son are missing," he answered soberly. "Carl's mother was expecting Mark to eat supper with them tonight. He wouldn't have just not shown up. Mark's much too considerate a kid." Rachel said nothing, and Lee went on, "Carl drove around Gulfport and Biloxi to the teenagers' hangouts and didn't see any sign of his car."

"He may have taken her to Oceans Springs or in the other direction, to Pass Christian, even to New Orleans. I'm sure he had lots of money in his pocket and probably a credit card...." Reproachfulness had crept into Rachel's voice.

"You've already decided that Mark has taken Stephanie off somewhere, haven't you?" Lee asked harshly. "Your main worry is for her virginity."

"My main worry is for her safety. I don't want to hurt your feelings, Lee, but it frightens me to think of Stephanie riding with Mark in his car. You have to remember that he had a head-on collision right outside my office."

"That *wasn't* his fault."

"By his own admission, he was speeding. It gives me nightmares to imagine how fast he might go on the interstate! I'm sorry, but that's the truth! For Mark's sake, you've got to stop defending him and start disciplining him, Lee."

"I don't have time for us to sit here and point the finger of blame at each other, Rachel, but Stephanie's not the innocent little girl you make her out to be." He picked up the phone again, jerking open the drawer of the bedside table. Taking out a leather-bound address book, he opened it and started punching numbers again.

Sitting tensely in her chair, Rachel soon realized that the number for the Mississippi state police was written on the page he'd turned to. So, it turned out, were the numbers for the Biloxi and Gulfport police. The fact that he didn't have to get those emergency phone numbers from an information operator spoke for itself. He'd probably enlisted the help of policemen before in tracking Mark down.

When he hung up after the third call, she'd been able to tell from his end of the conversation that he wasn't any the wiser about Mark's actions or whereabouts, but at least there hadn't been a traffic accident, yet. Rachel rose to her feet. "I'd better go to my room so I'll be there if Barbara Wakefield calls."

"Pack your clothes," Lee said soberly, rising, too. "I've got to get back to Biloxi and find my kid."

"They're probably okay, Lee."

"I sure hope to God they are because—" He broke off and picked up the phone to call down and order his car to be brought from the garage.

Rachel didn't need him to finish his sentence. Mark meant the world to him, just as Stephanie meant the world to her.

Thirty minutes later, they were on the interstate heading home to Mississippi. Barbara Wakefield had the number of Lee's car phone and so did the various police departments he'd contacted. Before leaving, they'd informed the Livingstons and the Beattys of their departure.

"What did these girls say to Stephanie to get her upset enough that she would run off and leave her friends?" Lee asked, breaking the heavy silence in the car.

Rachel had asked Barbara that question when she called her to let her know she and Lee were coming home. "They insinuated that I'd gone away with you to Florida on the pretense that it was a business trip. Also, that you chose me as your Realtor to get sexual favors. One of the girls is Jim Hagen's daughter," she explained. "Apparently she overheard him running off at the mouth and slurring my character."

"Wait until I get my hands on that dirty..." Lee didn't finish his description. "Is that all?"

"Isn't that enough—to have her mother smeared in public? Girls are more sensitive than boys."

"They also learn at a young age how to manipulate boys," he said cynically.

"Lee, you're not suggesting that Stephanie faked being upset!" Rachel was outraged as well as incredulous. "That she ran off down the mall in tears so that Mark would go after her!"

"I'm just trying to make some sense out of a story that doesn't add up. Why didn't Stephanie's girlfriends go after her and comfort her? Why did they leave that job for Mark?"

"I don't know, but I'm sure there's an answer beside the one you're thinking—that they were in cahoots with Stephanie! Why was Mark at the mall? Did Carl say?"

Lee shot her a narrow, discerning look. "No, he didn't say. But Mark sure as hell wasn't there scouting around for Stephanie."

"How can you be so sure of that?"

"Because I have good communication with my son. The only reason he would have followed after Stephanie was that she acted on his sympathy. He's a softhearted kid."

"You don't admit to any possibility that Mark has been biding his time and saw his chance today and took it?"

"No. None. One date with Stephanie made him realize she's too young and immature for him."

"Then where are they? Why didn't he bring her back to the food court? Why did he take her somewhere in his car?"

Lee shook his head in grim bafflement. "I don't know, but something tells me Mark's explanation and Stephanie's would be different."

"And you'd believe Mark's, of course?"

"Yes, I'd believe Mark's."

They rode in silence after that. At least once a minute, Rachel prayed, *Please, God, let Stephanie and Mark be safe.* She was certain that Lee was offering up the same prayer, with the names of their children reversed.

He took an exit after they'd been on the road an hour and gassed up the car. Rachel offered to drive, but he refused. "Try to get some sleep, why don't you?" he said.

As soon as they'd gotten back on the interstate and traveled only a few miles, the phone rang. "I want to hear, too," she pleaded, clutching his arm when he grabbed it.

"Brace yourself, Rachel," he warned and clicked on the speaker.

A Mississippi state trooper identified himself. "Mr. Zachary, your son and his passenger, a teenage girl who fits the description you gave, are alive and not in critical condition, but they've been in a one-car accident and are hospitalized. I suggest you pull your vehicle safely over to the shoulder of the highway at this time."

"Thank God!" Rachel murmured, and Lee sagged in his seat. He slowed the speed of the car and reset the cruise control, ignoring the advice to pull over.

"Go ahead, Officer," he said.

The trooper described Mark's and Stephanie's injuries first. They both had concussions and multiple lacerations. He had broken ribs, and her left arm was fractured. Considering the condition of Mark's car, the trooper was of the opinion that both teenagers had been lucky.

The car had been spotted in the trees along a rural highway outside of Gulfport about an hour and a half earlier. A man had pulled over on the shoulder to change a flat tire and his flashlight had shone on a portion of a rear fender. Then he'd looked for skid marks and found them. After hurriedly changing the tire, he'd gone to the nearest house and had had the owner notify the state police. Mark and Stephanie had both been conscious, but in shock, trapped in the car. A wrecker had dislodged it, and they'd been rushed to the hospital in an ambulance.

"My poor baby," Rachel whispered, the thought of what her daughter had been through causing her agony.

"Was my son able to explain why he lost control of the car?" Lee asked.

The trooper replied that Mark hadn't been in any condition to be interrogated, but he'd claimed a pickup truck had run him off the highway. An empty beer can had been in the car, and Mark's blood would be tested for alcohol level.

Rachel shook her head at the news that Mark had been drinking. She didn't believe for a moment that he'd been run off the highway. He'd probably been speeding and showing off and simply had lost control of the car. Except for the grace of God, he might have killed himself and Stephanie.

Chapter Eleven

"Where on earth was Mark taking her?" Rachel was voicing her puzzlement to Lee, not expecting him to have an answer. He'd accelerated, bringing the car back up to the speed limit and beyond after the phone call was terminated.

"I don't know that he was 'taking' her anywhere. I think the question would be more fairly worded, 'Where were they going?'" he replied grimly. "Don't build up a case against Mark and turn him into a juvenile delinquent before you learn all the facts. He *wasn't* driving under the influence of alcohol. I'd bet a thousand bucks on that."

"Lee, there was a beer can in the car!"

"I heard the patrolman."

"Are you telling me that you've never known of Mark to drink beer? Hasn't he come home with the scent on his breath?"

"How could I smell beer on his breath when I'm a beer drinker myself?" he countered with a hard, knowing look that said she was thinking he made a poor example for his son.

"You never have more than one or two beers and you're an adult."

"Of course, Mark's drunk a few beers by now. He's had a beer with me a time or two at home when we were watching a football game together. But I don't believe he was drinking a beer and driving. There's some other explanation for the beer can."

Rachel started to hold her tongue, then decided that Lee needed to hear her thoughts. He needed to wake up as a parent, for his sake and Mark's sake and the safety of other girls like Stephanie. "I'm sure Mark will give some other explanation, Lee. Whatever it is, you'll accept it as the truth because you want to."

"I'll accept it as the truth because it'll be the truth. Mark doesn't lie to me," he stated angrily. "I'm violating his confidence in telling you this, but it was Stephanie's idea for him to take her out on the date without your permission. She let him take the heat, and he was too damned honorable to get her in hot water."

"He actually told you that?"

"I pulled it out of him. I smelled a rat."

Rachel shook her head in defeat. She was wasting her breath by trying to open his eyes, but she had to speak up in defense of Stephanie. "Lee, Stephanie would *never* point-blank ask any boy to take her out on a date, any more than I would have at her age. I know my daughter. But let's not be at each other's throats. Thank God Stephanie and Mark have both survived this latest stunt of his, which I'm sure he'll convince you wasn't his fault. I just beg you to help me prevent something like this from ever happening again. Keep Mark away from Stephanie!" she implored.

He looked at her. His voice was weary and bitter as he replied, "I'll go one better than that. Mark and I won't be bothering you or Stephanie."

"It's not a matter of your 'bothering' me," Rachel objected sadly. "Surely you realize that."

"I don't realize anything of the kind." He picked up the phone and handed it to her. "Why don't you call the hospital?"

She got the number from an information operator and put the call through, then clicked on the speaker so that they could both hear and both ask questions of the hospital personnel. Mark and Stephanie had both been sedated and were resting after their injuries had been attended to. As the state trooper had indicated, they weren't in critical condition. To have his report confirmed brought a new wave of thankfulness.

Remembering Barbara Wakefield, Rachel called her next, making this conversation private and giving only the barest details. Barbara declared her intention of going over to the hospital immediately to stay with Stephanie until Rachel got there. "You would do the same if I were out of town and Candy was taken to the hospital," she said when Rachel expressed her deep gratitude.

Lee used the phone when she was finished talking to Barbara and called Mark's friend, Carl. He was as brief and factual as Rachel had been and thanked Carl just as gratefully at one point. Rachel surmised that the teenager was also headed straight to the hospital.

"I'm glad Mark will have someone with him, too," she said when Lee replaced the phone between the seats.

He didn't answer, and she sensed his skepticism about her sincerity. They rode in silence. There didn't seem to be any topic of conversation other than their children lying in the hospital and all the ramifications of how they'd ended up there. Enough had been said already to drive a permanent wedge between Rachel and Lee, although she loved him and thought he might love her.

Stephanie and Mark had been moved to rooms in different wings of the hospital. Before Rachel and Lee parted, to go in separate directions, they carried on a brief discussion in a corridor.

"What about your other piece of luggage?" he asked, handing her her small suitcase, which she'd opted to bring in with her since she planned to stay the rest of the night with Stephanie.

"Could you drop it off at my office when you get the chance?"

He nodded. "You'll need transportation."

"I'll arrange to have my car brought here."

He nodded again and walked away, half turning to say, "I hope Stephanie gets along well."

"I hope Mark does, too."

They might have been in an airport about to take flights to far parts of the world. Rachel's heart ached and tears glazed her eyes as she hurried off after one last look at his back.

"Mom. I dreamed you were here," Stephanie said drowsily.

Rachel caressed her daughter's cheek very gently, marveling again that her face didn't have a scratch or bruise on it, whereas her right arm was bruised and bandaged, as was the visible portion of her left arm not covered by a plaster cast.

"I got here at three o'clock this morning. You woke up a little and said hi to me."

"Was Mrs. Wakefield here?"

"Yes, she rushed right over when she learned you'd been in an accident. How do you feel?"

"I hurt all over. Is Mark okay?" Stephanie asked anxiously.

"He has some broken ribs and a concussion, like you do, and probably lots of cuts and bruises, too. But he'll be fine. You were both very lucky."

"I just knew we were going to be killed, but I buried my face in my arms anyway, just in case we weren't. I didn't

want to be all scarred up. It was so awful, Mom. This big
dirty pickup came up behind us with the horn blowing loud
It pulled up alongside Mark's car and kept pushing us far
ther off the highway. One of the men stuck his head out o
the window and yelled at Mark. He threw a can of beer, an
it landed in Mark's lap and spilled on his clothes."

Rachel's hand had stilled on her daughter's cheek. "S
Mark hadn't been drinking beer?"

"No, he bought us both sodas. I don't think he wa
thirsty. He just said he was because he thought I might stop
crying if he could get me to drink a soda." Stephanie's eye
filled with tears. "I guess I've gotten him in real bad trou
ble this time. He's going to hate me."

"Don't cry, darling." Rachel wanted to cry with he
daughter. Lee's faith in his son regarding the beer can foun
in his car had been justified. There had been an explana
tion, just as there really had been a pickup truck. "Yo
haven't gotten Mark into any trouble with his father, i
that's what's worrying you. Mr. Zachary was certain whe
he heard about the accident that it wasn't Mark's fault."

"It wasn't. Mark wasn't going real fast, although it fel
fast because we had the windows rolled down. He says it'
only safe to go five miles an hour faster than the speed limi
without risking getting a ticket."

"Where were you going?"

"Nowhere. After he bought us the sodas, he wanted t
take me back to the mall or to Candy's house, but
wouldn't let him. I asked him to take me home. I was fee
ing so miserable and couldn't stand facing anyone. He too
me for a ride along the beach instead. I started feeling bet
ter. I asked if we could drive out into the country. He wa
going to bring me to the mall again when we got back. So
you see, everything was my fault." Tears welled up again in
Stephanie's eyes once more and a lump formed in Rachel'
throat.

Lee's son had come to her daughter's rescue. He hadn'
been taking advantage of her at all. Rachel had completel

misjudged Mark's motives, had misread the whole incident.

"It was your idea to leave the mall with Mark?"

"He took me to his car because I ran out of the mall and was crying so hard I couldn't stop. People were staring at us."

"Then, after you'd gotten into his car, he said he was thirsty and took you to buy sodas." Rachel could fill in the gaps for herself by this point. "A minute ago you suggested that you'd gotten Mark into trouble before. You must have been referring to the date you had with him."

Stephanie nodded, wincing at the pain of moving her head. "I let him take all the blame, when I'd sort of pushed him into it."

"I made it very easy for you to let him take the blame because I was so quick to believe the worst of Mark. I owe him and his father a big apology." Rachel patted her daughter's cheek. "Why don't you take a nap now, and we'll talk some more later."

But Stephanie finished pouring out the whole story, backtracking to the scene at the food court that had upset her so much. Rachel gleaned one last detail exonerating Mark—that he'd evidently seen Stephanie and had appeared to be hesitant about encountering her. It had been one humiliation too many for Stephanie when she, along with the other teenagers, realized that Mark wanted to avoid her.

"Now he won't ever want to see me or talk to me," she said despairingly, two big tears rolling down her cheeks. "Mom, you're crying...."

Rachel lifted a tissue from a box and blotted her daughter's cheeks and then her own. "I'm sad, too, because Mark's father is going to feel the same way about me—after the way I reacted to the news that you and Mark had been in an accident." She didn't think Lee would ever forgive her. The worse part was she couldn't blame him.

"You think he'll get another real-estate agent and you'll lose his big listing?"

"No, I don't expect that to happen. Mr. Zachary is too good a businessman. He respects my abilities and talents very much. And he isn't petty." She didn't think Lee would deal that kind of devastating blow to her professionally. As angry and hurt as he was, he wouldn't retaliate. Rachel was sure of that.

Stephanie asked her next question hesitantly. "You like him a lot, don't you?"

"Yes. And also admire him a great deal."

Her daughter absorbed her honest reply without any evidence of surprise. "Mark thinks that his dad would like for you to be his girlfriend."

Not anymore. Rachel didn't dare speak the words aloud for fear of breaking down and sobbing. "If Mark isn't in favor of the idea, I couldn't blame him. I haven't treated him very fairly."

"He wasn't against it. He's afraid his dad will be lonely when he goes to college next year."

"Mark sounds like a sensitive, remarkable young man."

Stephanie's face got a dreamy, faraway expression. "He's the neatest boy in the whole world." Her long eyelashes dropped. "I think I will rest now, Mom...."

"I'll be right here in your room, darling."

Lee was probably with Mark this very minute, perhaps being filled in by his son on the course of events. Rightfully so, he would believe every word.

With her daughter asleep, Rachel might have shed more tears, but tears wouldn't help to relieve her aching regret. She felt even worse, if it was possible, when a florist delivered two bouquets of flowers for Stephanie, one from Mary Lynn and Alice and Cindy and the other from Mark. His card read, "Hang in there. Mark." Lee would have ordered the flowers at his son's request.

When Stephanie woke up again, she was pleased with the flowers, but asked for pain medicine. Rachel buzzed the nursing station, and a nurse soon arrived with a pill. Stephanie dropped off to sleep again when the medication had taken effect. At noon, when her lunch tray was brought, Rachel woke her. She ate some of her food and expressed concern about her appearance, a sign that she was feeling much better.

"I'm probably going to have some visitors," Stephanie said. "I know Candy will come to see me this afternoon."

Rachel gently combed her blond hair, wiped her face with a cool, damp cloth and applied pink lip gloss. Stephanie turned on the TV and stayed awake until midafternoon. Before she dropped off to sleep again, she took another pain pill. Later in the afternoon her doctor, the same pediatrician who'd been in charge of her health care since she was an infant, came by. He read Stephanie's chart and, after spending a few minutes chatting with her, stated confidently that she was on the mend and should be going home the next day.

No sooner had he left than Candy and her mother came to visit. Since Stephanie was in a private room, the observance of visiting hours wasn't strict. As they were leaving, Mary Lynn and Alice arrived. Rachel asked them to keep Stephanie company for an hour while she went home to shower, change clothes and get her car. Barbara Wakefield gladly dropped her off.

Feeling refreshed, but as if her lack of sleep was definitely catching up with her, Rachel returned to the hospital with intentions of sleeping on a cot in Stephanie's room. Even though her daughter would probably get through the night fine, Rachel wanted to be there for emotional support.

The meal carts were being wheeled through the corridors. Rachel had ordered a dinner tray for herself, too. As she came in sight of Stephanie's room, a hospital employee bearing two trays was entering it. Mary Lynn and Alice departed, and Rachel elevated the head of Stephanie's bed, opened her carton of milk for her and helped her get set to feed herself before sitting down to eat.

She'd consumed half her green salad and eaten several bites of mashed potatoes, roast beef and gravy when Mary Lynn stuck her head back in the door.

"Sorry to interrupt, but we ran into Lee Zachary downstairs. He asked if we'd take your garment bag off his hands. Do you need anything from it? If not, we'll drop it off at your house."

Rachel had missed encountering Lee by minutes. The knowledge filled her with dismay and the yearning to see him. Trying to hide both those emotions, she replied, "Would you, please? You know where I hide the spare key."

"Did Mr. Zachary say how Mark was feeling?" Stephanie asked the question before Rachel could.

"Apparently he's chomping at the bit to go home and recuperate there. His doctor is releasing him first thing in the morning. Mark was sending his father home. Zachary looked like he could use a good night's sleep." The last was addressed to Rachel, and Mary Lynn added silently, looking at her with raised eyebrows, *So do you, partner.* She went on to Stephanie, "We told Mr. Zachary that you were tickled over Mark's flowers. He said they'd kept track of your progress today and were glad you were bouncing back fast. But I'll go now. Alice is waiting, and I'm interrupting your dinner." With a wave, she was gone.

Stephanie ate more of her meal, chattering and sounding like her normal self, but Rachel couldn't have swallowed another morsel of food.

Mary Lynn had been paraphrasing Lee: "He asked if we'd take your bag off his hands." He didn't want her luggage in his car, in his safekeeping.

Was there any hope of reinstating herself with him?

Lee felt more like sixty than thirty-seven as he climbed into his car after Rachel's partners had driven off with her piece of luggage. Which one of them was he going to put in charge of handling Plantation Village instead of her? He was too damned tired and sick at heart to even think about it now. To even care.

It was a foregone conclusion that Rachel would ask him to let one of her partners take over for her. He would agree. It wasn't necessary to stipulate that he still expected her to have input, because she would continue to do everything she could to make his real-estate venture a big success. He was certain of that.

Plantation Village would go over big. Lee had few doubts on that score, especially after visiting Sea Castle Villas. He would end up a wealthier man and get into another, bigger venture. But at this moment it all seemed meaningless.

Everything seemed meaningless, except the all-important fact that Mark was alive and not badly injured physically. Nor did he seem to be suffering any serious psychological effects from his frightening brush with death.

For Mark's sake, Lee had to pull himself out of his funk and go on.

In a way, there was a kind of relief in reaching rock bottom, where he'd been headed since the night he and Mark had run into Rachel and Stephanie in the restaurant in Biloxi. He'd known right from the outset that he wasn't going to end up with Rachel.

What he needed tonight was sleep. What he didn't need was to dream about her.

Mark was pacing around his room, impatience written all over him, when Lee arrived the next morning with a change of clothes for him to wear home.

"Where have you been, Dad? I'm ready to get out of this place!"

Lee glanced at his watch. "It's quarter of eight. I thought I'd find you still asleep."

"You've got to be kidding. I don't see how anybody sleeps in a hospital. Every time you drop off, somebody's sticking a thermometer in your mouth and taking your blood pressure." Mark was shucking his bathrobe.

Together they got him into his clothes. His chest was tightly bandaged, and he had numerous bandages on his arms, one on his forehead and another on his right cheek. Both legs sported purple bruises. Lee knelt down to put on his socks and shoes for him. "Boy, this takes me back a few years," he remarked.

"Should do you good to spend a little time on your knees down there, Dad," Mark joked, his irritability gone. "Oh, yeah. Last night after you left, Stephanie phoned to thank me for the flowers."

Lee stopped in the midst of tightening a shoelace. "Her mother must have stepped out of the room," he said flatly.

"No, Mrs. Cavanaugh was there. I heard her talking to a nurse. Anyway, Stephanie sounded real good. She'll probably be getting out today sometime, too. I told her I'd stop by her room and say hi on my way out."

"You shouldn't have told her that, because we're not stopping by Stephanie's room," Lee stated, tying the shoelace with a little jerk. He stood up.

"Come on, Dad, I promised her I'd autograph her cast."

"Mark, Mrs. Cavanaugh doesn't want you within a mile of Stephanie, and neither do I. Stephanie has been nothing but trouble for you."

Mark held up his hands, palms out. "Dad, I don't want you to get mad at me, but there's no reason in the world I shouldn't be friends with Stephanie—not after we've been in a wreck together, among other things. When I see her out somewhere, I'm not going to turn around and go the other way. If Mrs. Cavanaugh doesn't like it, well, that's her problem."

His son was right and had him over a barrel. There wasn't any good reason why Mark should avoid Stephanie if he didn't feel so inclined. There wasn't any reason he shouldn't visit her briefly on his way out of the hospital. "Okay," Lee said, giving in grimly. "You win. We'll go by Stephanie's room, but only long enough for you to sign her cast and say hello and goodbye.''

Lee's objection to the visit wasn't any less strong after he'd conceded, but once he had, the prospect of seeing Rachel unleashed a hunger in him. *You damned fool,* he cursed himself angrily.

Rachel had slept the sleep of exhaustion, but she'd awakened numerous times and didn't feel well rested as she got up at six and dressed in the skirt-and-sweater outfit she'd changed into yesterday afternoon. Combing her hair and applying light makeup, she noted the dark circles under her eyes.

Stephanie's first waking thought was of Mark's promised visit. She was in a hurry to get her breakfast eaten so that she could have her sponge bath and be at her prettiest when he came.

"Darling, you talked to Mark after his father left the hospital," Rachel reminded her, trying again to prepare her for disappointment. "I told you last night that Mr. Zachary won't agree to come by your room. On the way home from Florida, when I was blaming Mark for the accident, I asked his father not to let him come near you, and he gave his word. Mark must not have known about that." Rachel went on, making the same promise she'd made last night. "I'll tell Mr. Zachary the first chance I get that I was wrong and that I'll agree to Mark's taking you out on dates.''

"Mark will talk his dad into coming by here, and you can tell him yourself that he can take me out." Stephanie's certainty that Lee's son would keep his word couldn't be shaken.

Rachel attended to bathing her daughter herself and helped her put on a pale pink sweatshirt, with the left arm lopped off to accommodate the cast, and matching sweatpants. Stephanie was taking aspirin this morning instead of the prescribed painkiller. They would almost surely be going home themselves, perhaps during the morning, too.

After she was dressed, Stephanie sat in a chair. She was on the phone talking to one of her girlfriends when someone knocked on the door, someone who obviously wasn't a doctor or nurse or hospital employee because it was a jaunty *rat-tat-a-tat-tat*. Rachel froze at the window, where she was gazing out, hoping to catch a glimpse of Lee in the parking lot.

"Come in!" Stephanie called. She hastily ended her conversation, saying, "Patricia, I've got to hang up. Mark's here!"

The door opened as Rachel turned around, and Mark entered, wearing dark blue sweats. Lee loomed in the door behind him, tall and somber.

"Hi, Stephanie. Hi, Mrs. Cavanaugh." Mark greeted them with a grin. "Got my wheelchair parked outside. Hospital rules say I can't walk out of here. Isn't that a crock? But anything to get out of this place. How're ya feeling, Stephanie?"

Stephanie's face was flushed with pleasure, her cheeks a deeper pink than her sweatsuit. "I'm feeling much better today."

Rachel stepped forward. "Have a seat on the bed there, Mark," she said in invitation. "I know you don't feel like standing." They seemed to have bypassed greetings. "Come in, Lee. I'll have some more chairs brought in."

"We can't stay long," Mark said. "Just long enough for me to sign Stephanie's cast." But he perched on the edge of the bed, and Lee left the doorway and walked farther into the room. He wore jeans and a shirt open at the neck, with the cuffs turned back on his muscular forearms. Rachel wanted to keep her gaze trained on him.

Stephanie took her eyes off Mark long enough to smile winningly at his father.

"Hi, Mr. Zachary."

"Hello, Stephanie. I hear you're going home today, too." Even devoid of friendliness or warmth, his deep voice was music to Rachel's ears.

Stephanie rattled off a reply and then turned her attention to Mark again.

"Got a pen handy?" he asked.

Rachel spoke to Lee, leaving the teenagers to their conversation as Stephanie gave Mark a pen and held her cast toward him.

"I must have just missed you yesterday afternoon. I left the hospital to go home and change clothes, and had come back just a few minutes before Mary Lynn and Alice saw you downstairs."

"I gave them your bag."

"Mary Lynn came back upstairs and told me. Thank you."

Mark had finished writing on Stephanie's cast. "Guess we'd better be shoving off," he announced, standing up and ending the brief, dissatisfying exchange between Rachel and Lee.

"Mom has something to say to you," Stephanie said. "Don't you, Mom?"

Mark glanced at Rachel warily and went to stand next to his father.

"Actually, I have a big apology to make to Mark." Rachel directed her next words to him. "I made a snap judgment of you, Mark, the day we met in front of my office. You were upset over the damage to your car, and I thought you were rude and sized you up to be a spoiled, irresponsible boy."

He grimaced sheepishly. "I really lost it that day and let some cuss words fly. Dad has taught me better. Honest."

"He's brought you up to be a fine young man. I realize that I was completely wrong about you. Stephanie told me all about what happened at the shopping mall and afterward. I'd jumped to the conclusion that you'd taken advantage of her and put her in danger, and it turns out that you were quite a hero, coming to her rescue and refusing to take her to our house, where no one was home."

"Aw, I'm not any hero," Mark protested, turning red. "It was just common sense that she shouldn't be by herself."

Rachel continued, aware that Lee was gazing at her, his expression hard. "Stephanie also confessed that she'd pushed you into taking her out on a date that Saturday night. Now I know that I had no cause to be as worried as I was. She was safe with you."

"Tell him that he can take me out on dates if he wants to, Mom," Stephanie prompted, growing impatient with Rachel's apology for things past.

"I was just about to tell him," Rachel said.

The embarrassment on Mark's face turned to chagrin. He looked at his father, and some communication passed between them. Lee nodded slightly, as though giving encouragement.

"I'm real flattered, Mrs. Cavanaugh, that you've decided I can be trusted to take Stephanie out, but you were right in the first place. She's kinda young for me. She's a real sweet kid, though. Maybe in a few years." He looked at Stephanie, obviously concerned about her feelings. "Hey, I'll call you in a day or two and check on how you're doing. And I'll see you around, okay?"

Stephanie nodded. Despite her downcast air and tremulous smile, she didn't seem as surprised as Rachel herself was by Mark's response. "Bye, Mark. Thanks for coming by and signing my cast."

"So long, Stephanie. Bye, Mrs. Cavanaugh."

"Goodbye, Mark. Have a speedy recovery," Rachel said.

Lee said to Stephanie with gruff kindness, "You're looking too pretty to have been in an accident. Take it easy, now." He looked at Rachel and spoke her name in terse farewell.

Father and son turned to go. Rachel got control of her voice and managed to say, "Goodbye, Lee."

The phone rang as the door closed behind them, and Stephanie answered it. The caller was Michael Curtis. She brightened instantly.

Rachel escaped to the bathroom and wept in despair.

Lee wasn't going to forgive her.

"So, Dad, what do you think about Mrs. Cavanaugh saying all those things to me?" Mark asked in the car. Lee had pulled around to a hospital exit, and Mark had gotten in. "Pretty big of her to come straight out and own up to being wrong, huh?"

"It doesn't change the fact that she was wrong to begin with."

"If I don't hold a grudge, why should you?"

"When you have a son, you'll understand," Lee replied.

"I was glad you thawed out a little and were nice to Stephanie when we were leaving. For a while there, you were making me out to be a liar. I'd told her your bark is worse than your bite."

Lee looked at his son inquiringly. "When were you discussing me with Stephanie?"

"Friday afternoon, after she'd calmed down and we were riding around. I'd set her mind at ease that there wasn't any truth to what those girls had said. You and Mrs. Cavanaugh *were* on a business trip, and you hadn't picked her for your real-estate broker because you liked her as a woman. Then we got onto the subject of you and Mrs. Cavanaugh getting together. I asked Stephanie how she felt about it and she said, 'Not good.' I put in a positive word for you," Mark summed up.

"Mrs. Cavanaugh and I aren't getting together, so Stephanie doesn't have any worries." Lee's statement had a ring of bitterness.

He pulled out onto the highway. His son questioned gently, "So the trip to Florida was a bust, Dad?"

"It turned out to be a bust."

"Gosh, I feel bad. I guess I really fouled things up for you, crashing my car with Stephanie in it and causing a big fight between you and her mom."

"If things had been right between her mom and me, there wouldn't have been a big fight. Your and Stephanie's accident would have brought us closer together. But that didn't happen. It was better to face up to facts," Lee assured him with bleak conviction. He was through hoping for the impossible. He'd climbed into the ring for the last time and was down for the count.

Mark sighed. "I was kinda hoping..."

"That makes two of us. But your old man's tough."

"Sure, Dad."

Chapter Twelve

"Eileen, I'm Rachel Cavanaugh. We finally meet face-to-face."

"Hi, Rachel." The pleasant, questioning look on the face of Lee's secretary changed into a friendly smile. She stood and came around her desk to shake Rachel's hand. As Rachel had guessed, she was an African-American, probably in her thirties and very attractive and professional. "How's your daughter?"

"She's fine. Today she started back to school." It was Wednesday. "I understand that Mark went to school Monday and didn't miss a day." The information had been channeled through Stephanie. Mark had called to check on her. Rachel hadn't heard from Lee.

"That boy's something else. He's got his father's grit and determination and is just brimming with personality," Eileen said fondly. The phone rang and she quickly returned to her chair and answered it. After she'd hung up, she inquired helpfully, "What can I do for you?"

"I stopped by to see Lee, if he isn't too busy. I saw his car parked outside." Rachel's words held a great deal of truth—she literally wanted to *see* him. A phone call would have served the purpose of clarifying where they stood as client and Realtor.

Eileen's hand hovered over the intercom, then she apparently changed her mind and stood up. "Excuse me a moment. I'll let him know you're here." She disappeared down a hallway and returned in a short time. "You can go into his office. On your right. The door's open."

Rachel's eagerness battled with her sense of dread as she found her way to Lee's office for her first—and perhaps last—visit. The latter emotion got the upper hand as she entered and Lee greeted her, remaining seated behind his desk. "Hello, Rachel." His tone was flat and held no welcome. "Come in and sit down."

"Hello, Lee." She glanced around. "Your office is just what I expected." It was masculine and not at all pretentious.

"Why don't we get down to brass tacks, Rachel. You're not here to inspect my office. Let's cut the preliminary garbage. It doesn't matter a damn to me which one of your partners takes over for you. The three of you decide and let me know." He picked up a pen and tossed it down again impatiently.

Rachel walked over and sat down in a chair facing his desk. She'd thought she was prepared for the inevitable, but she wasn't. "You're that angry that you would let your personal feelings interfere with your business judgment?"

Lee frowned at her words. "Well, that's what you're doing, isn't it? The reason you're here is to ask me to let you take a back seat."

"No, it isn't. I don't want to hand over Plantation Village to Mary Lynn or Alice. I have great confidence in their abilities, but I think I can do a better job."

He stared at her, picking up the pen again and tapping it on the blotter. Dropping it, he stood abruptly and walked to a window, his back to her. "Then we'll leave it as it is."

Rachel waited for him to turn around. When he didn't, she ventured, "I'll need to be in communication with you, Lee. I hope we don't go back to using Eileen as a go-between."

He wheeled around. His expression was hard. "We won't be going back to any phase. Call me when it's important. Leave a message if I'm out of pocket, and I'll get back to you as soon as I can. Was there anything else?"

"I guess not." Her throat was so tight that it hurt to speak. "I won't take up any more of your time." She got to her feet and walked to the door. "Shall I close this or leave it open?"

"Either way."

She glanced over her shoulder. He had his back to her again and was gazing out the window. Fighting tears, she closed the door.

There had been a matter to bring up with him—the agents' open house, which was set for the weekend following this. Rachel was on her way to the printers to pick up the invitations. But she was in no condition to discuss anything with him now, not with her heart breaking wide open.

His decision to keep her in charge of Plantation Village rather than appointing one of her partners wasn't a hopeful sign at all. It meant that being in communication with her might be unpleasant for him, but not unbearable. She'd killed his feelings for her and now had only his regard for her as a Realtor.

Lee sat down at his desk after Rachel had gone and gazed bleakly at the chair she'd occupied. He could handle talking to her on the phone, even meeting with her in person. Today had proved that to him.

His hopes really had died.

The knowledge caused the sense of futility that had been eating at him to well up in an enervating tide.

Rachel passed by Lee's office the next day and dropped off one of the invitations for the open house. His car wasn't there, and she assumed he wasn't, either. She hadn't meant to hand the invitation to him, anyway, but to leave it with Eileen.

"You want him to get back to you?" Eileen asked.

"No, not necessarily." Rachel kept her voice strictly under control and didn't let any wistfulness creep in.

However, he did call her and state his unequivocal satisfaction with the invitation.

"I was very pleased with the way it came out," Rachel admitted. "Will you be there at the open house, Lee?"

"I plan to be," he answered.

"Good. I thought you should be the one to draw the lucky number and pay the cash jackpot to the winner."

He agreed. After inquiring whether the arrangements were going smoothly and being told that they were, he said goodbye and hung up. They hadn't carried on any personal conversation. He hadn't asked about Stephanie, and she hadn't asked about Mark. Still, talking to him briefly and impersonally was better than not talking to him at all.

During the next week Rachel had occasion to call him several times. She even encountered him at Plantation Village when she and Kim Lamberts both went to supervise the placement of furniture in the model home and condo on Friday, the day the furniture was delivered. Kim's flirting didn't get a lot of response from him, but it provoked a lot of jealousy in Rachel.

The decorator would be on hand at the open house on Saturday afternoon. Rachel could guess that she'd be wearing one of her provocative outfits and paying Lee a great deal of attention, while Rachel would be dressed as usual and probably wouldn't say a dozen words to him. The thought stuck in her mind like a thorn.

How would he react if she came on to him like Kim did? It was a silly speculation, because Rachel wasn't extroverted like Kim. She was also completely out of practice in using feminine wiles. Certainly she hadn't used any on Lee up until now. Her problem—and his—had been fighting the strong attraction between them.

Had that attraction died for him?

Rachel had to find the answer to that question. The problem was that when she sent out woman-to-man messages, they would be different from Kim's. Rachel wouldn't merely be signaling *I'm available,* but saying *I'm yours.* What if he stuck by the message he'd been sending her since the trip home from Pensacola, *It's over between us?*

She'd be devastated, but she had to find out whether it was over.

The realization changed Rachel's whole outlook on the open house. A lot more was at stake than selling her real-state colléagues on Plantation Village. She was going for her own jackpot—a future with Lee.

"You look lovely, Rachel!" Alice exclaimed.

"Pretty dress," Mary Lynn remarked, adding her less-effusive approval for Rachel's appearance. "Shows off your figure."

Instead of one of her suits, she'd chosen a winter white sweater dress with a cowl collar. She'd also applied her makeup with care and had fussed with her hair. Next to Kim Lamberts, she would undoubtedly look ladylike, but Rachel had gone for a look that was alluring and feminine and yet still professional. From her partners' reactions, she thought she might have succeeded, but Lee's reaction was the important one.

"You both look very nice, too," she said, complimenting them sincerely, then turned her attention to conferring with the caterers, who'd just arrived.

The three partners were there an hour early. At three o'clock the agents attending the open house would start showing up. Busy with all the last-minute details, Rachel forgot about being dressed any differently than usual.

The weather had cooperated beautifully. It was a crisp, sunshiny fall day. A gaily striped tent had been set up on the site of the future clubhouse, and food and drinks would be served there. A combo had been hired to play music. Rachel and Alice and Mary Lynn would all be busy as hostesses, conducting group tours through the model house and model condo unit. At five o'clock, the drawing would take place.

Lee was going to a lot of expense, and the open house was basically Rachel's project. When he pulled up in his car at ten minutes to three, she was suffering jitters. A different case of nerves took hold as she gathered her courage and went to meet him.

He'd gotten out of his car. He glanced up, saw her and did a double take. "I'm glad you're here," Rachel called gaily. "I could use someone to hold my clammy hand at this point."

Lee didn't come toward her. He seemed rooted to the spot. She reached him finally, suffused with self consciousness by now. "Is that what you wear to open houses?" he asked.

"I decided to go for a different look. Do you like it?"

"I'm a man. Of course I like it. What the hell's going on Rachel?"

She managed to hold his frowning gaze. "I'm coming on to you, Lee. Am I that rusty that you can't tell? I'll have to take some more lessons from Kim."

As though on cue, Kim Lamberts's car pulled up next to his and she climbed out, wearing a short, tight dress that was a brilliant blue color. She greeted them in her outgoing way and complimented first Rachel and then Lee. "Don't you look elegant, Rachel. Lee, you're a real hunk in a coat and tie." She brushed one hand across his lapel as though removing a speck of lint, her bright red nails flashing. Rachel's fingers curled involuntarily, causing her own nails which were painted a delicate shell pink, to cut into her palms.

Another car had driven up, and a married couple in their forties, both agents, emerged and apologized for being early birds. Rachel introduced them to Lee and Kim, and the five of them headed to the tent, Kim managing to walk next to Lee and Rachel seething with jealous annoyance.

Cars began to arrive steadily and a crowd of agents were soon gathered under the tent. Rachel's worries about the event being a success evaporated. She mingled and played hostess and accompanied small groups on tours. She took full advantage of the necessity for introducing people to Lee, and several times touched his arm lightly. There was no opportunity to talk to him, but when she caught his eye, she smiled at him. He never smiled back, but she wouldn't have caught his eye so often if he hadn't been keeping track of her.

Five o'clock came, and it was time for the finale—the draw. Lee was surrounded by a group that included Kim. Rachel went to his side and slipped her arm in his. "The time has come to make some lucky agent a winner," she said lightly. Accompanying him over to a table where a gaudy cardboard replica of a casino held gambling chips with numbers on them, Rachel kept her arm in his.

"What do you want from me?" he asked her in a low, fierce voice.

"It's going to take me at least an hour to answer that. Can we please talk afterward?"

He didn't reply, but she knew his frowning silence was acquiescence.

"Try to smile and look like you're in good humor," she cajoled. "Otherwise people will think you're begrudging the winner his or her jackpot."

Her coaching had some effect and he carried off his role as master of ceremonies and host. She stayed beside him as he made a brief speech and then drew out a chip, the combo striking up appropriate music to heighten the suspense.

There were shrieks of excitement when he read the number, which corresponded to that on one of the invitations.

A woman agent Rachel liked very much came forward and received her jackpot. Fellow agents milled around her. Soon the combo started packing up, and the caterers waited for a signal to start clearing away empty trays. Rachel's only thought was to hurry the exodus.

"Let's go," Lee said grimly in her ear, clasping her arm in a firm grip.

"I can't leave yet," she protested, but he was propelling her out of the tent. Rachel didn't drag her heels; Mary Lynn and Alice could carry on in her absence.

She collected her purse from her car and got into his. There was no discussion of destination until they were driving along the beach highway headed toward Gulfport and Biloxi.

"Stephanie's spending the night with Candy," she volunteered. "We could go to my house and talk. Or your condo. It doesn't matter." She eased off her pumps. "Were you happy with the open house? I certainly was."

"Yes, I was well satisfied," he said shortly.

Rachel sighed. "Can't you forgive me, Lee? Couldn't we pick up where we left off in Pensacola?"

"No, we damned sure *can't* pick up where we left off in Pensacola."

So why were they in the car headed somewhere to talk? Rachel didn't dare ask that question. Nor did she make any other attempts at conversation as he drove them to her house.

In silence she led him to the carport, rather than the front door, and took him through the kitchen and into the family room. "Please sit down. I'm sorry I don't have any beer to offer you. I have—"

He cut her off. "I don't want anything to drink."

Rachel sat down on the sofa and he sat down, too, perching on the edge of a cushion. She drew in a deep breath for courage. "Okay, now for the answer to your question, what do I want from you? I want so much that I hardly know where to begin. I want to talk to you every single day, have breakfast with you in the morning and supper with you at night, go to bed with you and wake up with you, go to church with you on Sundays, celebrate Christmas and Thanksgiving and every other holiday with you." She stopped, giving him a chance to say something. He was gazing at her searchingly, but otherwise not reacting.

"Don't tell me all this unless you really mean it, Rachel. I can't take being shot down for a third time."

"I do mean it, Lee, with all my heart."

"What about that business of not being able to trust a man?"

"I'm still afraid to trust you. I'll be jealous and insecure. You're not even my husband, and I wanted to slap Kim's hand this afternoon when she put it on your jacket."

"You don't have any cause to be jealous of Kim or any other woman. You know I'm crazy about you."

"What does being crazy about me translate into? What's your wish list, Lee?"

He answered somberly, "There's only one item on it. I want you to be my wife."

"Then why don't you ask me?"

"Because if I ask you and you say yes and later back out—"

"I *won't* back out. I love you too much." Rachel moved toward him and he turned to her, his arms opening. She went into them, and he hugged her to him.

"Did I really hear you right?" he said with raw yearning.

"Let me say it again. I love you, Lee. I want more than anything to be Mrs. Lee Zachary." When he didn't speak, she understood that it was because his emotion went too deep for words. Finally she prompted wistfully, "Do you love me?"

He hugged her even tighter. "So much that nothing had much value when I gave up on us."

"I'm so happy," Rachel whispered.

They held each other a long while and then his arms loosened and so did hers, enough so that she could tilt her head back and they could look into each other's faces. Lee's tender expression was one of adoration. "Can we have a short engagement?" she asked. "Just long enough for Stephanie and Mark to adjust to the idea?"

"Very short, if I have anything to do with it. I'm going to buy you a rock," he warned. "It's going to blind any guy who comes within a mile of you."

"You don't need to buy me an engagement ring at all. A simple wedding band is fine." She smiled as she issued her own warning. "I intend to buy the broadest wedding band I can find for you. I want you to wear it all the time, too."

He kissed her on the mouth. "I won't take it off."

Rachel drew his lips to hers again, and as they kissed, the love welling up became heated with passion. Postponing the discussion of the future, they became involved in the moment. She led him to her bedroom, and they made love. During and afterward Lee spoke those most wonderful words in the language, *I love you*. Each time Rachel repeated them, the effect on him was obvious.

Their lovemaking was more satisfying than it had been in Pensacola because they were committed to each other now, committed to a future together. Lee held her closely in his arms as they lay naked under the sheet, talking about random and important topics.

"Stephanie's going to be thrilled to have Mark for a stepbrother," Rachel said. "She idolizes him, and I have a crush on him myself. It won't take her long to realize, as I do, that he's such a special young man partly because he takes after you."

"Mark already feels like a brother toward Stephanie. I have an idea she'll wind him and me around her little finger," Lee predicted gruffly. "She's the spitting image of you at fourteen."

"Family holidays are going to be fun. Also, we'll have to take some trips and visit your sister and mother, and your brother in Texas. Stephanie will have cousins now."

Lee asked with a trace of hesitancy, "How do you think your parents are going to feel about me as a son-in-law?"

"They're going to be deeply pleased. They've never stopped hoping that I'd remarry, this time to a finer man. You are a finer man than Blaine was in every way, Lee. You're honest and compassionate and sensitive and ethical." She rubbed her cheek against his shoulder. "Not to mention that you're the lover of my dreams."

"You're the woman of my dreams, Rachel. I'm having trouble believing that you're mine."

"I'm yours," she assured him happily, and he hugged her tighter for several moments while they both rejoiced in the wonder of mutual love.

"I can reform," he said earnestly.

"Reform?" Rachel wasn't following his train of thought.

"Change myself to suit you better."

"Don't you dare change yourself," she threatened lovingly.

"Oh, come on. I realize my faults. I'm too blunt, I cuss, I drink beer. I'm not a gentleman."

"In the best sense, you're a gentleman. Lee, I love your rough edges along with the rest of you." Rachel made her own thought connection. "I can work on being less prim and proper. I don't have to wear clothes that are so understated."

"You always look beautiful to me. And sexy. I'm going to burst with pride that you're my wife."

Rachel raised up and smiled into his face. He cupped her head with one big, strong, gentle hand and brought her lips to his. The tender kiss deepened and their tongues coupled. Once again the discussion was halted as they delighted in each other. After all, they had a whole future to talk and make love and build a life together.

* * * * *

Silhouette celebrates motherhood in May with...

Debbie Macomber
Jill Marie Landis
Gina Ferris Wilkins

in

Three Mothers & a Cradle

Join three award-winning authors in this beautiful collection you'll treasure forever. The same antique, hand-crafted cradle connects these three heartwarming romances, which celebrate the joys and excitement of motherhood. Makes the perfect gift for yourself or a loved one!

A special celebration of love,

Only from

Silhouette®
™

—where passion lives.

MONTANA Mavericks

Stories that capture living and loving
beneath the Big Sky, where legends live
on...and mystery lingers.

This April, unlock the secrets of the past in

FATHER FOUND
by Laurie Paige

Moriah Gilmore had left Whitehorn years ago, without
a word. But when her father disappeared, Kane Hunter
called her home. Joined in the search, Moriah and
Kane soon rekindle their old passion, and though the
whereabouts of her father remain unknown, Kane comes
closer to discovering Moriah's deep secret—and the child
he'd never known.

Don't miss a minute of the loving as the passion
continues with:

BABY WANTED
by Cathie Linz (May)

MAN WITH A PAST
by Celeste Hamilton (June)

COWBOY COP
by Rachel Lee (July)

Only from **Silhouette®** where passion lives.

A MAN FOR MOM
Gina Ferris Wilkins
(SE #955, May)

Struggling to keep a business afloat plus taking care of the kids left little room for romance in single mother Rachel Evans's life. Then she met Seth Fletcher. And suddenly the handsome lawyer had her thinking about things that were definitely unbusinesslike....

Meet Rachel—a very special woman—and the rest of her family in the first book of THE FAMILY WAY series...beginning in May.

"The perfect Mother's Day gift...for your very special mom!

Silhouette

SPECIAL EDITION ™®

WHAT EVER HAPPENED TO...?

Have you been wondering when much-loved characters will finally get their own stories? Well, have we got a lineup for you! Silhouette Special Edition is proud to present a **Spin-off Spectacular!** Be sure to catch these exciting titles from some of your favorite authors:

Jake's Mountain (March, SE #945) Jake Harris never met anyone as stubborn—or as alluring—as Dr. Maggie Matthews, in Christine Flynn's latest novel, a spin-off to *When Morning Comes* (SE #922).

Rocky Mountain Rancher (April , SE #951) Maddy Henderson must decide if sexy loner Luther Ward really *was* after her ranch, or truly falling for her, in Pamela Toth's tie-in to *The Wedding Knot* (SE #905).

Don't miss these wonderful titles, only for our readers—only from Silhouette Special Edition!

Five unforgettable couples say "I Do"... with a little help from their friends

Always a Bridesmaid!

Always a bridesmaid, never a bride...that's me, Katie Jones—a woman with more taffeta bridesmaid dresses than dates! I'm just one of the continuing characters you'll get to know in ALWAYS A BRIDESMAID!—Silhouette's new across-the-lines series about the lives, loves...and weddings—of five couples here in Clover, South Carolina. Share in all our celebrations! (With so many events to attend, I'm sure to get my own groom!)

In June, **Desire** hosts
THE ENGAGEMENT PARTY by Barbara Boswell

In July, **Romance** holds
THE BRIDAL SHOWER by Elizabeth August

In August, **Intimate Moments** gives
THE BACHELOR PARTY by Paula Detmer Riggs

In September, **Shadows** showcases
THE ABANDONED BRIDE by Jane Toombs

In October, **Special Edition** introduces
FINALLY A BRIDE by Sherryl Woods

Don't miss a single one—wherever Silhouette books are sold.

Silhouette®

AAB-G